PRAISE FOR ROBERT BOYCZUK

"Robert Boyczuk is a supremely talented writer."

—Cory Doctorow

"Boyczuk has a real knack for creepy, *Twilight Zone*-style atmospherics. The scary stuff is often made more threatening by being kept just out of sight, concealed in shadows or half hidden behind a window. [His] stories all have a twist — a turn of the screw — that breathes new life into some of the old forms and results in fiction as clever as it is entertaining."

—Alex Good, *Quill & Quire*

"Page-turning thrills aplenty . . . Boyczuk's [*Nexus*] borrows from sources as diverse as Tolkien, Star Wars, and Alan Moore, and integrates the miscellany admirably into a fast-paced plot. The dystopian human dynamics, on the other hand, are the stuff of an epic nihilistic hangover."

—*Publishers Weekly*

"Boyczuk builds up his hauntings and often gruesome metaphors and imagery from the base of his stories' human relationships, which imbues his fiction with an uncanniness that mimics the feeling of being trapped in a maze-like dream. Readers need not worry, however. The horror here is very real. Boyczuk just wants you to have a little fun finding it."

—*Rue Morgue Magazine*

"In [*Nexus: Ascension*], the writing is vivid, the characters . . . interact in a believable and thrilling way, and there is enough tension to make us suddenly start turning the pages hurriedly. . . . [Boyczuk is] a writer to watch."

—*The New York Review of Science Fiction*

"As Thomas makes his way through the world [in *The Book of Thomas*], his backstory is gradually revealed, adding richness and somberness to a dark novel that is reminiscent of Walter M. Miller Jr.'s classic *A Canticle for Leibowitz*."

—*Library Journal*

ALSO BY ROBERT BOYCZUK

Horror Story and Other Horror Stories

Nexus: Ascension

The Book of Thomas

ROBERT BOYCZUK

The Book
of David

CZP

ChiZine Publications

FIRST EDITION

The Book of David © 2015 by Robert Boyczuk
Cover artwork © 2015 by Erik Mohr
Cover and interior design © 2015 by Samantha Beiko

Distributed in Canada by
Publishers Group Canada
76 Stafford Street, Unit 300
Toronto, Ontario, M6J 2S1
Toll Free: 800-747-8147
e-mail: info@pgcbooks.ca

Distributed in the U.S. by
Consortium Book Sales & Distribution
34 Thirteenth Avenue, NE, Suite 101
Minneapolis, MN 55413
Phone: (612) 746-2600
e-mail: sales.orders@cbsd.com

Library and Archives Canada Cataloguing in Publication
Data Available Upon Request

Shelfie

A **free** eBook edition is available
with the purchase of this print book.

CLEARLY PRINT YOUR NAME ABOVE IN UPPER CASE

Instructions to claim your free eBook edition:
1. Download the Shelfie app for Android or iOS
2. Write your name in **UPPER CASE** above
3. Use the Shelfie app to submit a photo
4. Download your eBook to any device

CHIZINE PUBLICATIONS
Toronto, Canada
www.chizinepub.com
info@chizinepub.com

Edited by Brett Savory
Proofread by Elisabeth Nielsen

Canada Council   Conseil des arts
for the Arts   du Canada

We acknowledge the support of the Canada Council for the Arts which last year invested $20.1 million in writing and publishing throughout Canada.

ONTARIO ARTS COUNCIL
CONSEIL DES ARTS DE L'ONTARIO

an Ontario government agency
un organisme du gouvernement de l'Ontario

Published with the generous assistance of the Ontario Arts Council.

Printed in Canada

Heaven.

the waters above.

Lower Heaven.

the Sphere of Peter

the Sphere of Andrew

the Sphere of John

the Sphere of James

the Sphere of Philip

the Sphere of Bartholomew

the Sphere of Matthew

the Sphere of Thomas

the Sphere of James the Less

The Book of David

To Karen, without whom I wouldn't have a wife.

MEPHISTOPHELES: So. Now, Faustus, ask me what thou wilt.

FAUSTUS: First, I will question thee about hell.
Tell me, where is the place men call hell?

MEPHISTOPHELES: Under the heavens.

FAUSTUS: Aye. So are all things else. But whereabouts?

MEPHISTOPHELES: Within the bowels of these elements,
Where we are tortured and remain forever.
Hell hath no limits, nor is circumscribed
In one self place, for where we are is hell,
And where hell is must we ever be.
And, to conclude, when all the world dissolves,
And every creature shall be purified,
All places shall be hell that is not heaven.

—Christopher Marlowe, *Dr. Faustus*

Foreword

Any editor worth his salt must consider his readers, particularly when asked to edit works that have already been published in numerous editions and by various (and sometimes questionable) publishers. So, having been given the daunting task of taking disparate versions of essentially the same story and cobbling together a *definitive* edition—whatever you might imagine *definitive* to be—I began by considering the audience for *The Book of David*, and its predecessor, *The Book of Thomas, Volume One: Heaven*. Three kinds of readers immediately came to mind: the first would take everything on the page literally, swallowing whole the miraculous as readily as the mundane; the second would believe some events true, while others completely figurative and symbolic, believing the books an account not of the journey of one boy, but of several boys (some real, some fanciful), stitching together a comprehensible narrative from what otherwise would be chaotic and meaningless (as real life often is); the third kind of reader would not be so concerned with the veracity of the events, but rather view the books as a thinly veiled and despicable piece of propaganda, in essence a self-interested justification of the violence and upheaval visited upon the Catholic Church and the Spheres of Creation.

In doing an honest edit, I realized I would satisfy none of the three. Nevertheless, I have endeavoured to be as fastidious as possible in choosing what to include and what to leave out—in effect, separating the wheat from the chaff.

The general setting, of course, is not in question, for it is not the fanciful worlds about which Thomas (or David) reads in his books, it is the world we live in, the Spheres of the Apostles as God created them, one nested within another, from Heaven above to Hell below. Nor could anyone deny the veracity of the troubles that Thomas/David would have endured—drought, famine, plague, war—for, even if ameliorated, these are our woes still, and ones we are not likely to see an end of anytime soon.

Thus, I could find no fault with the setting, save perhaps for some detail of Lower Heaven which (for reasons that become obvious by the end of the second volume) could never be verified by the living.

What of the details, then?

Some would argue little can be taken at face value in these books. That, for example, despite David's/Thomas's professing an eidetic memory, inconsistencies can be found in detail he reports, particularly where he refers to events of the earlier volume. That the confusion between the interchangeable names, Thomas/David, and the discrepancy between the titles of the first book, *The Book of Thomas, Volume 1: Heaven* (presupposing a second volume), and the second book, *The Book of David* (with no allusion to a previous volume) suggests multiple authors and stories rather than a single voice and vision.

Perhaps.

But having been an editor for too many years, I know details like these, even so far as the differing titles, are not as important as they might seem, for in books the devil is in the detail—or, more precisely, in the fingers of the would-be editor who is wont to make small alterations to a story (including their titles) pleasing to his own sensibilities, rather than staying true to what was originally on the page. How I've been tempted to do the same myself! Nevertheless, I have tried to be true to my intent of self-effacement, collecting as many editions of these two books as I could find in lieu of having the long lost originals at hand (if there ever were ones to have) so that I might perform a comparative analysis, winnowing out the essential text and identifying (and removing) spurious additions. To further verify the veracity of the texts, I poured over such related records as exist in the Vatican Archives and Library, having been granted unprecedented (although not complete) access for this project. Finally, I spent a great deal of time interviewing those still alive who bore witness to some of the events described in these books (and was both surprised and happy to find that even after this many years, I found few inconsistencies between their accounts and what was in the books).

In broad strokes, then, here is what I know to be true:

○ with all the Spheres suffering drought and its attendant troubles, the Church looked, with envy, towards the plenty of Lower Heaven, the Pope ordering built a tower (commonly called the *Babel Tower*) that His army might breach Lower Heaven;

○ three indentured boys, all orphans, were brought to the Vatican by a man reputed to be a former member of the *Cent Suisse* that they might audition for the *Capella Sistina*—that is, to sing for the *archicantor* of the Sistine Chapel Choir;

○ during the audition, the *archicantor*, Cardinal Adolpho, a prominent advocate for the war on Lower Heaven, was assassinated;

It's not much, you might say, given the scope of David's/Thomas's story. But these simple facts are no less a sturdy scaffold for the story than the scaffolds used to construct the Babel Tower. Though it is true a very different *looking* building might emerge from the same scaffolding, the essential dimensions of the building (its height and volume and general shape) would be very much the same. Extending this analogy to these two works, I can say that if certain things did not happen exactly as described, then the essential dimensions of the events were nonetheless the same.

To be clear, here is what I found impossible to verify, but what I believe to be true (and so included in the books):

○ of the two boys brought to the Vatican, one was the eponymous David/Thomas and the other a girl, masquerading as boy, whose name was Ali;

○ after the assassination of Cardinal Adolpho, Pope Pius's daughter effected their escape;

○ that, being summoned to Lower Heaven by the Angels, this boy and girl made their way to the Babel Tower, and with the aid of a slave named Sam, climbed the Tower and slipped into Lower Heaven ahead of the Papal army;

○ in Lower Heaven, the Angels made a behest of the boy, that he journey to the lowest Sphere and beyond to Hell, that he might staunch the flow of God's tears and so save the all the Spheres of the World;

○ concomitant with the Church's invasion of Lower Heaven, Thomas/David and Ali escaped to the Holy Lands in the Sphere below.

If you choose to quibble over whether or not these events occurred exactly as they are related in the text, I would not gainsay you, for you could well be right. But if you try to convince me that minor discrepancies should be reason to repudiate the essential dimensions of these books, I would ask you this simple question: No matter how differently the Babel Tower might be described in a dozen different editions, does it not always lead to the same place?

—*Monsignor B. Savory, Officina libraria editoria Vaticana*

A Warning to Readers of this Work

All books are lies. So Father Norman—the aged, myopic pastor of my childhood—was fond of proclaiming from his pulpit. He told us the impulse to create a text came from a misguided and vain attempt to be God-like ourselves. To write a book was to covet the power of God, an attempt to usurp control of the world He had created. Writing, of which the worst kind were histories and made-up stories, was, therefore, a sin without peer—akin to the one that had both deposed the highest of all Angels and exiled us from Eden.

I was young enough that these admonitions made little impression. If anything, Father Norman bored me with his repetition of the obvious: any written work was, at best, a distortion of the one true Book, *The Bible*. God had given us this Gift, His story, our story, complete and perfect. What more could we desire?

But I now know men *are* creatures of desire, many of whom lust most keenly for that which they are told they cannot have. Did the Church not realize this before they banned books?

Once, during a sermon on the evils of heretical texts, Father Norman's eyes, which normally swept over every man, woman, and child with equal measure of accusation, lingered just a moment longer than necessary on my father—and his expression seemed to soften.

Had he known about my father's hidden books?

When the charges were read out, Father Norman did not stand as an accuser, though. Old enough to know a time before books had been proscribed, I like to think that maybe, just maybe, Father Norman had caught my father's eye from his pulpit to say, *I remember, and have my own secrets to keep.*

So, what would Father Norman, or even my father, have made of this book?

I do not believe I have sinned in writing this book. But I would grant that Father Norman was right, and that this book, perforce, contains lies—inasmuch as it cannot possibly capture all of the details of, and perspectives through which, reality is apprehended.

Yet, I stand by the essential truth of it.

Certainly I cannot know all that has happened and never will. Only God can. Nor am I able, in relating the events contained within this volume, to possibly inhabit the perspective of all those who bore witness to these events. Of necessity, this is a subjective account. Were Kite or Ignatius or Meussin to have told their stories, they would have been very different. But I like to think that all three works would carry the same thread of truth. Indeed, in my wanderings of the lower Spheres, I have chanced upon raucous markets where many different versions of *The Bible* are openly sold, each of which has its own collection of contradictory Epistles and Psalms and Gospels, each told in its own way, and each of which proclaims itself, by dint of divine and infallible authority, to be the one true Book of God.

How could this be?

The only answer I can see is that truth of a book has nothing to do with the details of its story.

Perhaps it is a blessing that a story may be written and rewritten a thousand times. Perhaps with each telling we creep closer to the truth, approach the *meaning* of the parable in the same way calculus tells us a function approaches its limit through infinitely smaller and smaller steps.

Or perhaps the obverse is true, and we wander hopelessly further and further away from the truth.

I would like to read the books of Kite and Ignatius and Meussin. And of the brigand into whose neck I plunged my dirk. I often wonder, what would their books have been like?

So, is this book a lie?

This I will leave you to judge:

A Vision in the Wilderness

Sleep eluding me, I stumbled out of the gloom of the arroyo and into the oven of day. I struggled up the hump of the escarpment, dirt and pebbles and clouds of parched dust cascading down the slope in my wake. Sun-off would be soon, and I'd thought to take this chance to survey the wilderness before we must be on the move again in the marginally cooler night. I knew I was dehydrated, and I knew expending the energy on the climb was, at best, a vain hope. But what choice did I have? We'd been two days in the desert, and if we didn't find water before next sun-on, we might not live through the day.

The climb was short, but taxed me to the limit, made doubly difficult with my broken arm bound to my chest. I had to struggle up the last few metres on one good hand and both knees, small cruel stones pressing into my palm, and it occurred to me that, had I but borne a Cross, I might have been part of an absurd passion play.

Reaching the summit, I struggled to my feet.

The landscape unrolled as far as the eye could see, blasted and lifeless, an arid desert of terraces and crumbling escarpments. All had been scoured by the cyclical work of seasonal rains as they flowed through twisting wadis—only these were no longer wadis, for it seemed unlikely that there had been a rainy season to fill them in some years. A few kilometres behind us, a sheer cliff thrust thirty or more metres from the ground, cut here and there with deep channels where water once ran. The previous night we'd wound along the upper edge of that cliff for several hours, until we'd found a ravine deep enough to allow us to descend. We cautiously picked our way down the canyon wall to the dried river bed, then followed that past the foot of the cliff. Here was an endless series of rises on either side of wadis too numerous to count. We'd dragged ourselves over the backs of dozens of these low hills, checking one dried riverbed after another, hoping for even a dirty trickle, and then just for the remains of a sere plant, anything to indicate water that had flowed here once might still. Our efforts were for naught. We'd decided to rest, and the next sun-off follow a wadi to where it emptied into a lake. Or, more likely, what was left of a lake. I squinted at the horizon, in the general direction the wadis seemed to run, hoping to catch sight of the glimmer of a distant bowl. Nothing. Nothing but more of what we'd seen for the last two days. I looked back to where Ali slept beneath the tattered remains of the Angel's wings, but saw just the undifferentiated black of shadow.

I thought not having the claustrophobic walls flanking me might lift my spirits, but it was no better up here than in the arroyo—the same breathless, oppressive heat coddled me. I licked my cracked lips and tried to swallow, a dry grating that brought no relief; instead, I began to cough. I felt fingers of bile creep up my throat, then doubled over and retched. But nothing came up.

After a time, the nausea subsided, and I straightened.

Still, I was having trouble focusing, my thoughts muddled. I became aware my eyes were closed, and felt myself swaying dangerously.

I suppose I passed out, for I found myself prone, cheek on scorched earth, drawing wheezing breaths filled with dust and grains of sand. *It would be so easy*, I thought, *to lay here, just lay here and fall asleep.*

You're better than that, boy, Ignatius's voice chided me.

I shook my head feebly, even though I knew his admonishment had been dredged up from the recesses of my memory. Still, I felt slighted at his imagined words. With an effort of will, I forced my eyes open.

Atop the rise adjacent to mine, perhaps ten metres away, a small, elderly man floated above the ground.

Our descent from the sun had taken place at night, the land below cloaked in darkness. As soon as I had recovered my wits, I realized that we must be sailing over wilderness, for there were no fires to be seen, no light of the sort one would expect from a city, town, or village. Nor could I descry the regular shapes of anything man-made, of fields or buildings or fortifications. Whatever was below was deserted. I knew the Angels had carried me far away from the Church's breach of Heaven, but how far I had no idea. Nor did the landscape seem to correspond to any of the places I had memorized when peering through the Eye of God. I studied the terrain as best I could in the dark, but saw no distinguishing features. The land was anonymous. Wasted, rolling hills slashed impenetrable ravines. In the distance was a vast plain, utterly featureless, as flat as the surface of an immense black mirror. We drifted down, a dark-winged bird of the night, and when we were close enough I could see all was bereft of even tree and shrub. Then what had seemed a slow and graceful fall abruptly became the breakneck rush of ground towards us.

"The Judean Wilderness," Ali whispered in my ear, as if reading my thoughts.

We dropped like a rock into the chasm of a canyon, the tip of our right wing catching the slope, cartwheeling us into the darkness of the Holy Lands.

The man was garbed in a deacon's cope that hung to his ankles. But he was not a man. For had he been flesh and blood, I would not have been able to see the light shining through him, diffuse enough to wash out detail, but translucent enough to make out the peaks behind him. Nor would the soles of his sandals have rested on nothing but air, for he floated fully half a metre above the ground. The apparition blinked behind crooked spectacles, which he incongruously adjusted, and looked past me, as if I wasn't there, scanning the land, searching intently for something. I tried to speak, but only the smallest croak emerged. So I raised my hand and waved.

This seemed to catch his attention. His head stilled, and he looked—not exactly in my direction, but somewhere a few paces off to my right, as if at someone standing nearby. I waved again, and he nodded this time and waved in return, his gaze never wavering. *Perhaps*, I thought, *he has a disease of the eyes*. I'd known such men, who seemed to look past you when they addressed you. Yet he was not a man. Why, I wondered, would a supernatural being suffer such a pedestrian malady?

The spectre gestured in a direction almost perpendicular to the one in which we had been travelling. His lips moved, but no sound emerged. Then he trembled. Or, more precisely, his *aspect* trembled, in the same way a reflection in a pond ripples when a light breeze disturbs its surface.

"Who are you?" I rasped, my words barely audible. "What would you have me do?"

But he was gone—or maybe had never been there at all.

Ali methodically gathered up the tattered remains of the Angel's wings, rolling the fabric around the broken struts, carefully tying the bundle with one of the leather straps which had once secured us, slinging the whole thing over her shoulder. Our only possession of value. Unless you counted the old leather purse slung round Ali's neck. Once, that purse had been Ignatius's, but after his death, Kite had emptied its contents into his palm and discarded it—and Ali had claimed it. Rather than tie it around her waist as Ignatius had, she'd shortened the leather thong and hung it from her neck. Somehow, she'd managed to collect a few tarnished brass deacons to weigh it down. I'd never asked her how she'd come by them.

"I saw him."

Ali looked at me squarely at last. Her eyes were puffy and red-rimmed, her lips cracked. After the first day we'd both stopped sweating, and the usual dusky sheen of her skin had fled, leaving her face blotched like old parchment. She slouched, and limped like an old woman, for she'd twisted her ankle badly upon landing. Yet, for all that, she was beautiful. "A hallucination," she said, her voice as raspy and cracked as mine.

I shook my head, and it dizzied me.

"What then?"

I feared what I wanted to say would sound preposterous. "A vision." I had expected Ali to snort, or make a derisive comment, but she did neither. Perhaps she didn't have the energy. "He wanted us to go that way," I said, pointing, as the apparition had, towards the tallest peak in a range of low-slung mountains.

Ali looked at the slope, and I could see her imagining the endless travails beyond it. "It will take us five times as long to travel half the distance. We will perish."

"I did not say I wanted to go in that direction, just that I think *he* wanted us to go in that direction."

Ali looked at me for a moment, appraisingly. No doubt her mind, like mine, was turning ever more slowly. "Not a vision, then," she said, as if sounding it out to herself. "A temptation. You fear what you saw was not an Angel, but a demon."

I said nothing because she had the truth of it. She always did.

"So what would you have us do?"

"Climb this slope, at least."

"Why?"

"Your eyes are better than mine. When we reach the summit, you can look for the Red Sea. If you sight it, then we continue the way we were going." I had not looked at the Holy Lands through God's eye, for I had not believed we'd be journeying anywhere near them. But at *San Savio*, old Brother Martin had drawn a shaky rendering of the Holy Lands as part of a lesson, and despite his wildly inaccurate map, I'd realized the immense plain I'd seen during our descent must be the Red Sea. Whether or not it contained water was moot, for the salinity of the Red Sea meant we couldn't drink from it; however, Ali's notion had been to follow a wadi to its mouth, and from there to travel along the shore, searching for a fresh water stream that might still feed the sea.

"If not?"

"Then we strike out in the other direction."

"We'll find no fresh water streams at the sea," Ali said, making a weak kick at the dry bed of the wadi in which we stood, wincing for her trouble. "Might as well do as your *demon* bids." With that, she turned to limp up the slope.

I seized her shoulder, surprising myself as much as her. It may have been the fatigue, but she allowed herself to be turned around. "But what if it *was* a demon?"

"There are no demons—save for those we carry with us." She looked at me, at my hand resting on her shoulder. She could have easily struck it off. "I don't believe in God, because I do not want to believe in the devil."

When I was younger, two years before the Church took everything, I'd attended a fire-and-brimstone sermon from a visiting Bishop. He told us that *intentions* damned us every bit as much as actions, that Satan lurked in every questionable thought and deed. That he was in us, in every one of us. Until that time I had not given much thought to Satan, nor believed I was in any way important to him, but that zealous Bishop convinced me I was, and that Satan waited around every dark corner, hoping to steal my soul. Satan became real for me that day, tarnished my childish optimism about the world. For the first time it seemed to me that the triumph of good was not inevitable; rather it was problematic, hard-earned, and unlikely. This notion cultivated a dread in me (that I haven't wholly lost to this day), and that dread blossomed into a near panic, dogging my thoughts incessantly. I was damned and there was nothing I could do. I obsessed over this to such a degree that I don't think I slept more than an hour or two for the next three nights. On the fourth day, my overwrought mind hit on something: if such terrible evil could exist (as it surely must, for did we not see it all the time in the actions of men, and elucidated from every pulpit in the Sphere?), then so too must its opposite, a benevolent, forgiving God. If Satan existed, then so did God. Simple as that. And I could breathe again. I drew great comfort from this notion, this naive proof of God's existence. Only now, turned on its head, here was the same reasoning from Ali. Only hers was a denial of Satan rather than an acceptance of God. To Ali, the loss of Heaven went hand in hand with losing the terrors of Hell. Wasn't that a reasonable bargain? The notion was appealing—especially for someone destined for Hell, as I now believed myself to be. For all that, I couldn't so easily repudiate my own belief as she had. Despite my sins, didn't I still have a chance for redemption? Isn't that what Christ had preached? Yet, her logic left me uneasy, for her reasoning seemed somehow more concise, and if I've learned anything, it's that the simpler an explanation, the more likely it is to be the correct one. "If not a demon or an Angel," I said, "why follow a hallucination?"

"Angels spoke to me who weren't there, a levitating palanquin carried you halfway across Heaven, and I peered through the Eye of God." She spoke slowly, slurring her words slightly. "I didn't think any of these miraculous then and I don't now. Just because we don't understand something doesn't make it miraculous."

"Faith requires—"

"—only doubt, *Thomas*." Her use of my assumed name stung me, as she probably intended. "If there is no doubt, then it is certainty." She looked at me as if saddened at my ignorance. "Any man who tells you he is certain about something he's been told to believe in, well, he's a fool or a liar or both." Ali laid her hand on her belly, and my heart skipped a beat at the tableau we struck—me with my hand on her shoulder, she with hers over our unborn child. A family. "I only believe in what I can touch."

Foolishly, I let my hand drop towards where hers rested. She recoiled, snapping out of her lethargy and slapping my hand away—

and this cut me deeper than any blade could. I looked at her in desperation, hoping that she had done so through force of habit rather than revulsion, but her face, as usual, was an impassive mask.

Mine, on the other hand, must have gone through contortions.

Perhaps that's why her tone changed abruptly, became conciliatory. Or at least less hostile. "You said you thought your vision real," she said, "and I believe you." Astonishingly, she took the hand she had just slapped away and awkwardly placed it atop the one on her belly. If she stiffened at what must have been unnatural to her, it was only a small thing. "I need you, David," she said, the exhaustion in her voice plain. "We both do."

At first I didn't credit what I heard. Ali was staking her future on me? On a belief that I might save her? That I might save *them*? I looked at her then, locked eyes, and saw no lie there. Dizzy with thirst and hunger, I felt a sudden elation. Redemption, it seemed, was possible.

Ali let my hand fall, then turned and limped slowly and painfully up the slope, following her absurd belief in me.

Before she'd climbed a metre, though, my elation evaporated, and I experienced the pangs of the greatest fear I have ever known, a fear that has dogged me since that moment and for all my life. One known intimately to husbands and wives, parents and children, and perhaps to God and his believers, too: the dread that we are fated to disappoint the ones we love.

The Temptation

Throughout the night we dragged ourselves up and down the backs of the hills that divided the wadis, pausing every hour or so for a brief rest that seemed to do nothing to allay my fatigue. As soon as we were in motion again, my heart resumed hammering, and the headache that had dogged me for the last day increased so much in intensity that it became impossible to think straight. Within steps my breath returned to wheezing gasps. Half conscious, I shambled insensibly in Ali's wake as she limped ahead. We didn't speak—nor do I believe we could have had we wanted. What I recall of that night is the endless scrambling up and down, and a dull realization that at some point the hills, which at first had risen ten metres or so between riverbeds, had flattened and widened into dun-coloured hummocks, looking like nothing so much as the backs of armadillos, now rising at their summit no more than the height of a tall man.

I stumbled after Ali, watching the shuffle of my own feet, glancing less and less frequently to make sure we still made a line for the peak to which the apparition had pointed.

The next thing I remember clearly is sun-on.

In the Holy Lands, dawn does not creep up on you in the way it does elsewhere in the Spheres. The shadows of night recede imperceptibly until, all at once, you blink and realize you can see the indistinct grey outlines of things in the middle-distance—none of which was visible a moment before. Within minutes the suns brighten painfully, flattening and washing out the landscape, and you find yourself thrust into the harsh glare of day, the heat beating down on you as intensely as if it were already noon. I don't know why this is so, but it is, and though there is no knowing the mind of God in these matters, I would say that He must have his reasons.

We didn't stop to sleep at sun-on. No words passed between us on the matter, but none was needed, for we both knew, day or not, we must now walk until we could walk no more.

I closed my eyes for what seemed like a moment—and stumbled. What little breath I had left was knocked from me as my weight fell upon my broken arm; jagged bolts of pain blinded me. I emitted a thin whine, the sort of sound a fox in a trap might make as it lay dying.

For several ragged breaths I lay there.

Then I blew out the grit in my mouth, levered myself up on my good arm, and looked ahead. Ali was nowhere to be seen. Had she outdistanced me by so much she was no longer in sight? Or had she fallen behind? I turned my head to look back and the world swam. When things settled into a slow see-sawing, I saw her sitting cross-legged behind me, facing the way we had come, hands folded in her lap. The bundle of Angel's wings she'd been carrying lay discarded several metres behind her.

I tripped over her, I thought, *and she didn't even notice.*

Crawling back to her, I could see her eyes were closed; but she breathed, albeit shallowly. I reached around her and gingerly lifted her pant leg; her ankle was discoloured and swollen to twice its normal size. What pain she endured I cannot imagine, and that she had made it this far was a miracle. I let her pant leg drop, then hesitantly put a hand on her knee, hoping to elicit a reaction, hoping she'd swat it away—or even open her eyes—but there wasn't a flicker, no indication that she felt anything. Although I had prayed for a time when she wouldn't flinch from my touch, I had never thought it would come this way, insensible as she was to anything but her own death.

I pulled myself into a sitting position, placing my back against hers, mostly because I didn't think I could sit up for long any other way. I heard her sigh, and felt her relax into me so that we supported one another. I briefly toyed with the idea of trying to encourage her to move, but gave it up quickly. She was past encouragement. *And if she is*, I thought, *so am I.* I sat there, drawing what small comfort I could from the contact of our bodies, while we waited to die.

I cannot guess how long we sat thus, for I drifted through memory and dream.

The sound of her voice, small and cracked, barely audible, called me back: "Wr . . . wrong way."

"No," I managed to croak. "It was our only course."

I felt a weak shake of her head. "He . . . he pointed." Ali half-lifted her arm and made a feeble attempt at pointing. Her arm fell as if weighted, and she sagged.

"Ali?"

No answer.

She's delirious, I thought, *as am I.*

For a time, my thoughts drifted listlessly—yet something niggled at the back of my mind, drawing me back into this moment. As best I could, I tried to gather my wits.

He pointed. Ali spoke of my vision—what else could it be?

Wrong way? I'd thought she'd been trying to take responsibility for bringing us here. But that wasn't it, not the way she'd said it. I craned my neck; behind us were the drag lines our feet had left in the dirt and dust of the wilderness. I could see our path receding across hump after hump, could clearly see how we veered away from the straight line we'd been trying to carve, away from the peak to which the apparition had pointed. We'd swung back towards the cliff, and now we sat, back to back, no more than a hundred metres distant from the face of the escarpment.

A deviation of no consequence.

Why should she care?

I stared at our tracks and the gears of my mind laboured.

In the day we'd travelled, the peak had grown minimally. Even with a full water-skin, I was now certain we had no hope of attaining it. If the apparition meant to help us, why would he point us to a destination we could never hope to reach?

He pointed.

I'd shared my vision in detail with her. What had she seen that I'd missed? I reimagined the moment exactly as I'd experienced it, him looking off to my right as if he saw me there instead of where I lay. Like the pins of a lock, something in my mind *snick*ed into place. I replayed the scene, this time reorienting the apparition as he would have appeared had he been looking directly at me—and understood what Ali had already realized: he had been pointing not to the peak, but to a prominence on the cliff face.

Turning my head, I found we sat opposite that prominence. I'd noticed nothing special before, but exhaustion and pain had half-blinded me. So I blinked back the haze that dogged the edges of my vision, not expecting to see anything remarkable. Only I did. In the past there must have been a waterfall here, for there was a deep notch cut in the top of the cliff, and directly below it the smooth, concave outline of a dried up pool. To its left were the remains of a monumental tree that was many years dead, the tips of its uppermost branches still scratching the heights of the cliff. And beneath the tree something so unexpected it took me a moment to comprehend: six people standing in a circle around its trunk.

I blinked and blinked again. They didn't disappear.

I had believed myself past feeling hope or excitement, past caring about anything, but I must have tapped one last tiny reserve, for an urgency unlike I have ever felt before flooded me. I was being offered a last chance to save us. Without thinking, I rolled off Ali and onto my knees; I caught her with my good arm as she sagged, and laid her down as gently as possible. A clump of her hair stuck to the back of my hand. All of the tension had gone out of her face and, for the first time since I'd known her, she looked at peace. This terrified me.

"Wait," I said. Or tried to, only an incomprehensible croak emerged.

Then, on one hand and knees, like a supplicant, I crawled towards those figures. Vicious stones tore my pants, and my knees and palm were soon shredded and bleeding. Though I had no voice to call, I had assumed they would notice my movement straight off; but none turned in my direction. The effort required was so all consuming that it wasn't until I was finally within a few metres of the figures that I realized they were not men. They were statues. Smooth, cold, dead, and faceless. Shapes of men, not men. Perhaps not even that, for three had barbed tails. Had I been able, I think I might have laughed.

I let myself collapse to the ground. Only my cheek slapped against something hard and angular. I winced, pain and surprise startling me enough to lift my head.

A plaque, half buried in sand, bearing an inscription: THE FIRST TEMPTATION. And I understood what those six statues depicted: Jesus and the Devil, each pair representing one of the three Temptations of Christ in the wilderness.

What happened next astonished me so much that my deprivations were washed from my mind: on the two nearest figures the featureless ovals that were their faces swirled, then sprang to life, translucent in the way the deacon had been, but distinct, too; and the flat, smooth surface of the Devil's body blossomed with red scales, the lump that was his hand becoming a fell claw wrapped around a large stone, while Christ now wore a simple white robe, and what I'd taken to be a twisted band of cloth on our Saviour's head had grown spines to become His Crown of Thorns.

Satan spoke in a voice that chilled my blood: *If you be the Son of God, say to this stone that it be made bread.*

And our Saviour replied: *It is written that Man lives not by bread alone, but by every word of God.*

I gaped. And then again when the Devil hissed, a red tongue like a snake's flicking out, the obscene sound crawling along my spine. He cast away his stone, but before it hit the ground it faded from sight. I gaped again, but not because of the stone, but because Christ's eyes now rested on me, his face writ with Fatherly concern. To me he said, *Whoever drinks of the water that I will give him shall never thirst; but the water that I will give him will become in him a well of water springing up to eternal life.*

A moment before His hand had been an indistinct lump, like the devil's—but now it held a small pitcher, and from its mouth the barest trickle of water fell to collect in a small stone bowl fixed at His feet.

Unlike the spectral mist that swirled across the stone figures, the trickle was real. I heard it patter against the side of the bowl. I launched myself at Christ's feet, embraced them as I pushed my face deep into the bowl, felt the dribble on the back of my head. It had an odd taste, sweet and salty at the same time, with a metallic bite. For all that, it was the best drink I had ever tasted. I lapped it up, licking the bowl like a dog might.

Then I levered myself up on my good arm.

The statues were smooth, stone shapes again, their features fled. The trickle had stopped. Then, only then, did I think of Ali.

I cursed my selfishness.

I thought the water would revitalize me, and I attempted to gain my feet, not sure what I was going to do, but determined to do something; yet I found myself in a heap on the ground. My stomach convulsed. A tingling ran through all my extremities and, despite the great heat, I shivered uncontrollably. There was a hollow, rhythmic drumming on the ground. *Me*, I realized, *it's me making those sounds.* Distantly, I sensed my limbs flailing, and the back of my head beating repeatedly on the hard-packed earth, and I heard the foul, unctuous voice of Satan: *If you be the Son of God, say to this stone that it be made bread.* This time, the Devil's words reverberated inside my skull, thumped in my chest like a malevolent heart—though my ears heard nothing. The world wobbled around me; I was a spinning dervish at its centre. My eyes were dazzled, as if by a brilliant light, so all things became vague blurs amidst the effulgence. A great shadow rose before me, and with it I heard the beat of monstrous, leathery wings. I felt the air buffet me as Satan's fetid stink curled into my nostrils.

Until this moment, I had never been under the influence of opiates or other drugs that warp the senses. However, it has been my shame to have been so, willingly and otherwise, since. I now know that what I witnessed that day was another vision, precipitated by that strange water. In that moment, however, I believed Satan hovered before me, leering in anticipation.

I screamed.

Fear impelled me to my feet. I threw my arm across my eyes against that ghastly brilliance and spun away. I ran towards Ali—or where I guessed her to be, for coruscations still beguiled my vision. I heard Satan's churlish laugh. *Too late*, the Prince of Darkness said. *She is dead.* A new fear seized me, and I found myself no longer fleeing Satan, but rather staggering desperately towards the heap I believed to be Ali.

When she swam into focus, she lay on her back exactly as I left her—save for her eyes, which were now open and lifeless.

The grief that rent my soul was indescribable. I collapsed atop her, hugging her corpse, and wept.

This, God has done to you. Satan alighted and knelt, a great wing unfurling over us, as if to protect and console me. *There is nothing left for you.* My broken arm was no longer splinted, and in that hand I clutched a gleaming, golden knife. I knew it to be the one which Abraham had thought to use on Isaac. *Rest now*, the great tempter said. *There is no longer a soul here for you to save.*

I lifted the blade, placed its tip against my throat, felt blood well against its metal point.

What is it, my son?

My other hand lay on Ali's abdomen; through the tips of my fingers I felt the faintest of stirrings.

Why do you hesitate? Do you not wish to be with her again?

"Forgive me," I said, and plunged the blade into Ali's belly, once, twice, thrice, making an incision the shape of a capital *I*. Through the flaps of flesh I thrust my hand and pulled out a small object that fit easily into my palm. It writhed in its placental fluids; a twisted umbilical, sheathed in blood, wrapped around my wrist.

The consoling wing snapped back, and torrents of dust rose, scouring my face. I cupped my hands to shelter my child.

You will lose her forever!

I cut the umbilical, no larger than a piece of baling twine, and let the knife drop. Then, with my small finger, gently, ever so gently, I wiped Ali's fluids from its tiny face, and with my fingernail cleaned out its mouth. It cried, a sound barely perceptible, both heartbreaking and joyous.

Satan recoiled, enraged, and I steeled myself for his blow.

Be gone. A sweet, high voice this time, untroubled and innocent. The impeccant voice of our child. *Get thee hence.*

I did not see or hear Satan's flight, only felt its consequence, as if a great pall had been lifted from my soul.

I lay back against Ali, feeling the comforting warmth of her body, of her fluids. I held out our child so she might see. "Is he not beautiful?" In my dream I knew it to be a boy.

When Ali didn't answer, I pulled the homunculus back, and looked upon him and smiled. I fancied my son smiled back. Then a shiver wracked his tiny frame.

The world is cold.

"Yes."

Careful not to jostle him, I slipped one hand under the leather thong around Ali's neck and lifted away her purse. I emptied the miserable brass coins it still contained onto the desert, then eased my son into it. I cradled him against my chest; I imagined the beat of my heart would have been like a distant drum to him.

"Sleep," I whispered to both of them.

And you. His words were a balm. *Gather your strength that you might live.*

And so I slept.

The Anchorite's Den

Beneath me, a bed of sand, fine-grained and cool; above, a scalloped stone ceiling. And to either side—hewn into the rough, limestone walls—a row of niches, each containing a single, yellowing skull.

A crypt.

But it was not dark, merely gloomy, and the air, though pent up, was not stale as one would expect in a tomb, only desiccated. I was in a cave in the wilderness.

Then, all at once, a cascade of memories crashed upon me like a dark wave.

My son.

I attempted to push myself up—and collapsed, gasping, blinded by tears. Stupidly, I'd tried to use my broken arm.

My arm was healed. I held the knife. I remembered this as clearly as I remembered everything that had happened: the Temptations of Christ, the Gift of Water, Ali's death, my temptation—and the birth of my son.

A fever dream.

I rolled onto my stomach and managed my knees. The wracking nausea I'd expected was only a mild disorientation. I had a thirst and a hunger, but nowhere near as acute as before. My body still ached, but not so badly. Perhaps the Gift of Water had done me some good after all. So, hand on the lip of one of the niches, I pulled myself to my feet. A brief bout of vertigo made me wobble, but when it passed I found myself still standing.

I was in a shallow cave, narrow enough that a large man might touch both sides with outstretched arms. At the far end two iron spikes had been fixed in opposite walls, and between these hung the tattered remains of a hammock. Against the side wall were two pieces of roughly constructed furniture: a three-legged stool and a rickety table composed of sticks bound together with strips of disintegrating leather. Resting on the table was a cracked wooden bowl; a dusty *Bible*, the gilt letters on its calf-skin cover all but rubbed off; and a curled cat-tail whip with knotted cords, the sort used by the Flagellants in rituals of self-mortification. The entrance to the cave was opposite, a low-slung arch, no higher than my waist, through which midday light scratched at the sandy floor.

A hermit's cave.

I'd no idea how I came to be here—the only visible disturbance in the sand were my own footprints. I hadn't been dragged here or carried, but found my way here under my own volition. I dredged the recesses of my memory, but found not even a hazy recollection. For the first time in my life, I felt betrayed by my power of recall. The notion unnerved—so much so that I had to put a hand on the wall to steady myself, forcing one, two, three deep breaths, trying hard not to let my mind race with the implications. Then it passed. Or at least I managed to suppress it, if only for the moment.

Hobbling to the entrance-way, I noticed vertical scratches above the arch, as if someone had recently taken a stone and scored the limestone. I knelt—and winced as scabs on my knees cracked and blood oozed anew. Girding myself against the pain, I rolled beneath the low arch, scraping my head against stone for my troubles.

Fresh from the gloom, I was dazzled by full sun-on. I groped blindly, found the rock face outside the cave, and pulled myself up.

Directly in front of me was the broad trunk of the dead tree; behind it, the three stone Temptations of Christ. Both obscured the mouth of the anchorite's cave. Shuffling past them, I moved to a vantage where I should have been able to see Ali, and spotted the dark bundle she'd made of the broken Angel's wings. Not far from it was a less distinct mound in the same dun colours as the desert.

I skirted the Temptations, hobbling past the place where I'd suffered my seizure—the frenetic actions of my body still clearly imprinted on the soil. Much to my dismay, however, the mound, which I'd expected to resolve itself into Ali's familiar form still remained an anonymous heap of earth. I hurried forward. And when I was but a few metres from the mound, I could see what had been hidden by the mound itself: a small Cross.

I fell to my knees at the foot of Ali's grave.

Though memory still failed me, I knew I was alone. There was no one else. I had dug the grave, heaped the scorched soil of the wilderness upon her, found sticks for the makeshift cross—for, once again, mine were the only footprints. Nor did the footprints, or the places where I must have scraped up soil, look fresh. Their edges were softened, windblown, as if days old. Looking back, I was disquieted to see the path I'd followed had been tamped down by numerous passages.

Yet I had no memory of doing any of these things.

I sat next to the grave, pulled my knees up, and clasped them with my good arm. It occurred to me that I ought to offer a prayer for Ali, and for my son. But I was paralyzed by a terrifying emptiness—no, not emptiness, but an *emptying*, as if all that was me, that made up who I am, poured out of me, leaving a pointless shell.

She is with God.

I said these words to comfort myself, the same words I'd so often heard Priests offer to the grieving. They sounded stupid and banal, and I could find no solace in them. Instead, I felt anger suffuse me. An outrage such as I'd never felt before. Anger at the Church and its machinations; at the fatalism of the Angels; at Kite and Ignatius and Meussin and all their stupid, futile plans; at Ali for her inscrutability; and most of all at myself for having miserably failed everyone who had trusted me. In short, I railed at the stupidity and manifest ignorance of men—and equally at He who had made us thus. In all that had happened, I could see no design, certainly not the loving hand I'd been schooled to expect. Although years of inculcation pressed me to pray for them, I could not bring myself to do so.

Instead I bowed my head in grief and shame, and dug my heels into the hard earth, pushing back and forth as if trying to grind down the very world—but my feet were already in ruts that could be worn no lower.

I thought and felt all this and much more that I shall not—cannot—share, for it would be impossible to convey in graceless and unwieldy words all that Ali was, and all that she meant to me. All I will say is that I raged for a good time, and after wept in the same measure.

In the end, when the storm had passed, I wondered, while moving my heels in the smooth, worn tracks in the earth, why this all seemed so familiar.

I Am Alone

Sitting on the small stool in the hermit's cave, I held the wooden bowl, tipping it first one way then another, watching the Gift of Water swirl within. Though I thirsted mightily, I did not drink. Instead, I put the bowl down, and pulled out the small leather pouch from beneath my shirt.

Yahweh then said to Moses, 'Put these words in writing, for they are the terms of the covenant which I have made with you and with Israel.' He stayed there with Yahweh for forty days and forty nights. . . .

I'd had thirty-nine visions, and woken from each as I had from my first, the sun of another new day limning the mouth of the cave, not knowing how I got there, panicked and desperate to find Ali. In my grief I had never realized I had the pouch around my neck, leastways not until I sat next to Ali's grave, digging my heels into ruts I'd worn. I *remembered*. Not as a proper memory, of which I could claim none since I'd found the Temptations of Christ, but as one of thirty-nine visions. They were there, in my memory, as if they'd always been there. All I had to do was touch that small leather purse that hung about my neck, and I remembered each and every one of the thirty-nine intimately, could recount each surreal moment in detail. The devil was in them, Jesus, too. As were many other people I had known, and some I had not yet met but would. Most were alive, but a few spoke from death. The scenes were manifold, their meaning beyond my understanding. The only commonality was my son, who comforted me in every vision.

The flood lasted forty days. . . . Every living thing on the face of the Spheres was wiped out, people, animals, creeping things, and birds; they were wiped off the Spheres and only Noah was left, and those with him in the ark.

Often my son spoke in my visions. Not in words, but thoughts, with the guilelessness and honesty only a child could claim. The naiveté, too. Always he was alive in that purse, turning restlessly, anxious, I suppose, to be about his business in the world. Always we talked, and he asked me endless questions about my life that I tried to answer honestly. He told me about himself, too, about the man he would someday be. Perhaps one day I will write another book to relate all we spoke of, and all I experienced in my visions, but I suspect this volume would have little interest, or import, to anyone save me.

In my waking life the pouch weighed less than nothing. Once (or thirty-nine times), I'd undone the string around its mouth and looked inside at the desiccated skin and bones.

And at once the Spirit drove Jesus into the desert and He remained there for forty days, and was put to the test by Satan.

Three plaques, one in front of each Temptation of Christ. Pressure upon any of the plaques and the scene played out. All ended the same, with our Saviour proffering the Gift of Water.

I raised the purse to my lips and kissed it. Nothing stirred. Not in this dreary, waking life.

So I lifted the bowl to my lips, knowing the Gift of Water would bring yet another vision, would bring my son back to life, just as it brought forgetfulness of all else.

Thirty-nine scratches in the limestone above the entrance to the cave suggested so.

It wanted only the fortieth.

I drank deeply.

Gift of Water

A shadow where there had been none before.

I froze, on all fours, under the low-slung entrance to the hermit's cave. In my panic, I construed this to be the silhouette of a baleful Satan. Then the shadow broke apart, and a portion swung towards me, its contours rearranging abruptly, resolving into a figure far less menacing. In the semi-light I blinked, and blinked again, and even before my eyes finished adjusting I recognized this small, stooped man with crooked spectacles perched on the end of his nose. Just as in my vision, he wore a deacon's cope that hung to his ankles. But this time he didn't float: his feet were planted firmly in the sand. And he was substantial now, as solid as the rock walls flanking him. I'd not seen him when I'd made my pilgrimage to Ali's grave. Perhaps in my grief, I had missed him, but that seemed near impossible, for as distracted as I was, all around was desolate, with no place for a man to hide; I judged it unlikely he could have made his way to the cave without drawing my attention.

I lifted myself, grains of sand trickling from knees and palms, and it occurred to me that I might still be experiencing a vision. That I had only been tricked into believing myself back in the mundane world, just as a dreamer dreams he is awake. Such had happened more than once during my visions, though never in this cave, nor with him. And always—no matter what—my son had been alive. I gently fingered the pouch slung around my neck; nothing stirred.

"Your forty days of fasting and prayer is complete." His voice was lilting, almost effeminate. In his hand he held the cracked, wooden bowl, brimming with the Gift of Water. He proffered it: "Drink."

Ali was dead, and around my neck I bore the remains of my son. In this world these things would never change. I looked at the bowl. I was parched, dizzy with thirst, but even more with a longing to lose myself in another vision. Yet I didn't take the bowl. Not right away. "I saw you. You tried to tell us that this place would save us." An accusation, as much as anything.

The small man stood against the far wall of the cave, his face fixed with a mix of perplexity and sadness.

"*Answer me!*" My anger surprised me; I thought myself no longer capable of such a depth of feeling.

"You did not ask a question." His countenance remained unchanged, and I wondered if he were feeble-minded.

"Why? Why did you bring us here?" I took a step toward him; he didn't recoil or flinch, though I was slightly taller, and he looked like the sort of man who'd never been in a fight. I balled my fists. "Why would you bring us here to die?"

"You are not dead."

"Ali is. And my—" I could not bring myself to say it. "Why did you direct us to the Temptations of Christ?"

"The Archangel Zeracheil bid this other do so." Incredibly, he smiled.

I'd heard enough. I wished nothing more than to remove myself from the company of this absurd little man, from the reach of the Angels, and return to the place where my son still lived.

I grabbed the bowl, put it to my lips and drank greedily, liquid filling my mouth and sluicing over my cheeks. I revelled in the sensation, waiting to be cast into the throes of yet another vision. Waiting for my son to live.

Nothing.

I stood in the hermit's cave, an empty wooden bowl in my hand, cheeks and shoulders damp, that strange little man standing before me, blinking behind his spectacles. The water, I realized, had none of the odd, metallic tang. I dropped the bowl and scrambled from the cave. Staggering over to the first Temptation, I pressed my foot against the plaque that actuated the scene.

The statues remained lifeless. No scene played out. No water trickled into the carved bowl at the feet of our Saviour. I turned and stared at the insignificant mound that marked Ali's grave—and the harsh light of the world seemed to clamp down around me, to nail me forever to this forlorn place.

"Your forty days of fasting and prayer is complete." The small man stood just outside the cave. "Now you must staunch the flow of God's Blood."

I fell to the ground and wept.

After a time, I felt a hand on my shoulder.

The little man helped me to my feet. I had thought him unremarkable: soft, past middle-aged, the sort of elder cleric one sees in every Parish, counting down his remaining days on the beads of a rosary. But when he'd helped me up, I felt the strength in his grip, and the effortlessness of the way he lifted me, and knew, despite his appearance, there was nothing soft about him—and likely never had been. If anyone was weak, it was me, my legs with scarcely the strength to bear my weight. He guided me to the back of the cave, while I hobbled at his side like a much older man. He sat me with my back against stone and handed me the wooden bowl again. Lifting a large gourd I hadn't noticed before, he tipped it over the bowl. When the bowl was half full, he put the gourd down and drew from within his robes a stoppered vial containing an amber liquid. Using a calibrated pipette, he drew a small amount of the liquid, and held it up before me.

"The *entheogens* will bring the visions you crave." His voice was soft and cloying. "God does not wish you pain. But life is pain as much as it is joy, one allowing us to cherish the other. This," he nodded at the glass pipette, "may blunt your pain. Perhaps even bring a kind of happiness. But it is only temporary, and its effects will diminish over time, and soon what joy you may derive from it will turn to ash. Remember this." He let three drops fall into the bowl. "Now drink."

I think it probable the little man watered down the drug. Or that it wasn't exactly the same kind of drug as in the Gift of Water. For when I woke from my visions this time I had not forgotten him, nor the few words we had exchanged. I had to fight to bring these memories back, but they were in my head. As if the drug had buried, rather than eradicated, them. And, by the same degree, my recollection of my vision was harder to recall, though it, too, was there. For a time, my son had lived again.

My son stirred listlessly. "I am tired," he complained, and I could hear the irritation in his voice. "I am weak, father. Why am I so weak?"

"You are unwell?"

He paused, then said, "No. Not unwell. I'm drawn thin. I am less substantial. Do you not feel the same?"

I lied and told him no. I found myself trying to explain about Ali and the small man and the water and the entheogens, but my justifications sound half-baked and confusing, and I was not certain if they were real or not.

"But why do I feel this way?" he asked with the innocence of a child.

"Because," I said, "this is the only way I may be with you."

"Then," he said, his sweet voice resolute, "it will be enough,"

In that moment I loved him more than I ever had, and it broke my heart.

When I woke, the little man stood over me, his eyes swimming behind thick lenses, appraising me. In his hand he held the pipette again, thumb over one end, trapping the precious amber fluid within. A tiny drop wobbled on the end, threatening to fall.

"First," he said, "you must eat." He pointed at the rickety table. Displacing *The Bible* and cat-tail was a wooden trencher, bearing all manner of fruit, and a tankard filled to the brim with what looked like milk. I felt no hunger—save for that amber liquid. I'm sure he saw it in my eyes.

"Once you eat, you may drink the water."

I rose on uncertain legs, wondering again how strong he might be; my mind turned over as best it could, playing out different scenarios, but none seemed to end satisfactorily, where I had managed to wrest that pipette from him without spilling its contents.

"You are weak," he said, as if reading my thoughts. "Understand the water sustains. But does not satisfy. Your metabolism must be brought back to normal in increments. Eat slowly. Begin with goat's milk. Then fruits that bear the most juice. Stop before you are full. Understand that gastrointestinal disturbance is normal. Diarrhoea, vomiting, and the like. Less often, hypophosphatemia and other complications." He said these things as if he were reciting from a list. "Once you have eaten, and kept food down, I will give you the Gift. Do you understand?"

I considered for a moment, my eyes never leaving the pipette, briefly weighing my alternatives. There were few. I nodded slowly.

"That is good."

I tottered over to the table, chose the jar of milk as he'd advised, but, perhaps to spite him, downed it at one go. A moment later I was on my knees, vomiting it up. I retched until my throat burned with bile, and threads of milk dripped from my nostrils. Through teared-up eyes, I saw the small man kneel next to me. The pipette had vanished.

"Slowly," he said. "Remember?" His words were not angry or reproving. Rather, they seemed to come from an infinite reservoir of patience.

A fit of coughing took me again, and when it subsided I felt his hand on my back. His touch was cool and steady and calming, as I supposed it was meant to be, and I wondered if his gesture was a rote response rather than a genuine expression of sympathy.

"Remember?"

I nodded in answer to his question and his lips crooked into a beatific smile, as if this was the best news he'd ever received.

"That is good." He stood. "This other will fetch more goat's milk."

So saying, he turned and strode deeper into the cave. Where the wall had been, there was now ragged darkness—part of the larger shadow from which he'd first emerged. I hadn't paid it much mind in my overwrought state. Without breaking stride he walked into the nothingness and was swallowed.

If I'd the energy, I would have gaped.

A moment later, he re-emerged, bearing a stoppered gourd, from which he poured a few fingers of milk into the empty jar. He handed it to me where I sat on the floor. Though its odour made my stomach clench, I drank it, but cautiously this time, only small sips, and managed to keep it down.

"That is good. Now grapes."

The taste of the goat's milk had made me nauseous, and I'd no desire for anything else; yet my stomach growled, complaining of its emptiness. My body hungered. So I fought past my aversion and ate three grapes and part of a date before I felt my gorge rising again.

"That is good."

Over the course of the next few hours, and under his patient urging, I ate until the pipette reappeared.

On the day after I broke my fast, he said, "To restore metabolic equilibrium, you must exercise before you drink the water. Can you walk?"

I assented, though I still felt wobbly.

"That is good."

I went to my hands and knees so that I might crawl out of the cave.

"No." He nodded to the shadows at the back of the cave. "Cooler."

He helped me to my feet, and as he did I brushed against him, hoping to detect within the folds of his cope where he kept the vial of amber liquid. Taking my elbow, he guided me to the darkness.

It was hard to make out any detail; the opening through which we passed had no recognizable boundary, and appeared as if it had always been part of the cave. Within a few steps we were in impenetrable blackness. I felt the sand under my feet give way to a flat surface. In the pitch dark I couldn't make out anything. Disoriented, I believed the surface beneath me canted, and I lost my balance and stumbled. The small man steadied me.

"I'm sorry," I said. "I can't see anything."

"Yes."

He pulled gently on my arm to urge me forward as if he'd not heard my complaint.

"I'm likely to trip, or fall into a hole, or dash my skull on a wall."

"Yes."

"But—"

Light cut my words short, dazzling me; I shielded my eyes until the dancing afterimages faded.

"Can you see?"

The small man held a stick above his head, and on its tip an unnatural, white light burnt. This would have taken me aback more than it did, had I not already seen a light burn with a similar kind of radiance—when the Archangel Zeracheil had held aloft his lamp.

I nodded.

"That is good."

We stood in a tunnel. Only this wasn't like the sewer through which Sam had guided us to the Babel tower. This was larger, perhaps four metres at its base, and two at the apex of its arch. And it differed in another, more significant way: instead of being built of brick, its walls were carved and impossibly smooth, its floor impossibly level. There were no joints, not a one, and the tunnel was a geometrically precise semi-circle that receded as far as that eerie light would allow me to see.

I knew what this place was. Or was pretty certain I did. Beneath the surface of the Holy Lands ran an intricate network of tunnels and shafts, no different than the ones Ali had used to effect our escape from Heaven. Before now I'd only seen these tunnels as a series of coloured lines when I'd used God's Eye. Walking through the reality of them, however, was considerably different.

"To restore metabolic equilibrium, you must exercise," he said. "Can you walk?"

I've said before that I am good at reading people. I say this not as a boast but a fact. Yet I couldn't read this odd, little man. I wondered at his penchant for repetitive phrases with exactly the same wording, at the strange way he took my questions, reminiscent of the difficulty I had with the Angels. "I can walk," I said.

"That is good." He tugged on my arm gently.

So, in that bubble of unnatural light, I hobbled beneath the Holy Lands, the darkness receding before us—and closing at our backs.

For a time we moved in silence, the tunnel uniform in every respect; then the little man turned back. This time, as we approached the cave, I saw what had been cloaked in the darkness before: a small handcart pushed against the side wall, its crossbar resting on the floor just where the sand gave out. In its box were three more stoppered gourds, along with several cloth-wrapped packages tied with string. I guessed them to be his provender.

The short excursion had exhausted me; the moment we entered the cave I sank to the floor. Back against the wall, I pulled my knees up and propped my head on them. How had I become so weak?

Your forty days of fasting and prayer is complete.

Forty days. My muscles ached and my head throbbed.

I sensed his presence and lifted my head. The little man stood before me; in one hand he held a bowl of milk, in the other the pipette. If I wanted to return to my son, I would have to do as he bid.

Yet in that moment I also made a vow to myself: I would bide my time—until my strength returned. And then everything would change.

The next three days we walked the tunnel and I ate more. Each day I felt marginally better. And each day I returned to my son.

When, on the evening of the seventh day, he proffered the pipette, I had thought to wave it away. I reasoned that this gesture might serve as a way of disarming him, of making him less vigilant, so that I might more easily overpower him. (Had I known him then as I do now, I'd have realized he was immune to such manipulations.) But my body betrayed me: the thought of refusing the Gift caused my stomach to cramp and my hands to shake.

So I took the water and lost myself in another vision.

When I woke the next morning, I felt feverish. My head spun and my stomach churned. My clothes were soaked through. Violent dreams had haunted my sleep, and although the details had fled, I was left with an overwhelming sense of dread.

The small man offered up the pipette, but I waved it away. "Tonight," I croaked, balling my fists. "I can make it to tonight."

He shrugged, and let the amber liquid back into the vial, stoppered it, and slipped both back inside his robe. Then he laid out a trencher for me. "Eat. You will feel better."

So I did, and he was right.

After he'd cleaned up the remains of my meal, the little man replaced the worn *Bible*, cat-tail, and wooden bowl on the makeshift table and restrung the hammock. Then he bid me follow him into the tunnel. He pulled the stick from his robe, pressed on the bottom to light it, and handed it to me. Without a word, he clambered behind the crossbar of his cart and lifted. The wheels creaked as he turned it one hundred and eighty degrees, then pulled it down the tunnel at a slow, steady pace. Within a few seconds, he'd faded from sight, the ghostly *creak creak creak* of the cart's wheels the only sign he still existed.

Behind me, a great sigh and gust of air, as if from a melancholy giant; I spun around. The opening had disappeared, the tunnel now ending in a smooth arch and flat wall. The only sign the hermit's cave had ever been there was the scattering of sand we'd dragged across its threshold. With nowhere for the sound to go, the creak of the wheels was louder, the echoes buffeting me.

Nowhere to go, I followed.

The Catharsist

For three days (or what felt to be three days) we trudged through darkness, the man pulling the cart, showing little sign of fatigue. Showing little sign of anything. I wondered at the strange way he took my questions, reminding me of nothing so much as the difficulty I had conversing with the Angels. And at his illeism and penchant for repetitive phrases with exactly the same wording. Always he wore the same slightly bemused, slightly melancholy expression, and his disposition was unnaturally even, for he never seemed to anger or grow impatient. I came to the conclusion that he didn't experience the peaks and valleys of existence as do most men, and I wondered if, perhaps, he was capable of feeling at all. Perhaps what little emotion he displayed was merely an aping.

We passed numerous branching tunnels and, less frequently, shafts with ladders that led up or down. From time to time he would turn one way or the other at a juncture. We stopped only when my convalescing body required rest or food, or when a febrile chill would take me, and my teeth would chatter and my hands shake. At these times he would stop and prepare the Gift of Water.

The little man's actions were always deliberate, the ritual always the same. After taking the light from me and placing it in a bracket on the side of the cart, he would set out a bowl in the cart's box and half fill it with water from a gourd. Pulling his cape back with his right hand, he revealed many pockets within, and from the one farthest back on the top row drew out the vial and pipette. He placed them next to the bowl, always in the same orientation, always equidistant. Unstoppering the vial, he inserted the pipette and drew a precise amount of the amber liquid. Carefully he transferred this to the bowl, flicking the top of the pipette with his thumb to clear the vestiges. After returning the pipette to its place and replacing the stopper in the vial, he'd lift the bowl with both hands, and give it three small swirls. Then he'd turn and, because my hands shook so violently, raise it to my lips—as if it were a chalice, as if this were a celebration of the Eucharist—and tip the bowl so that I might drink.

Later (hours, days?) I would wake. Always, he would be waiting for me to resume our journey.

During this time, I watched the contents of the vial slowly diminish. I lived now only for my visions, only for the company of my son—and for the contents of that vial. My waking life had become a dream. I tried not to think what I would do when the Gift of Water ran out. . . .

I spoke with my son. Told him of my first home, of the persecution of my father and my stay at the orphanage at *San Savio*. I told him of Ignatius and Kite and Meussin. Of Rome and my ascension to Heaven. And my fall. Most of all, I spoke to him of his mother, of the hard life she had borne. I told him how quick-witted she had been, how resolute and steadfast. Of her sinuous grace, the litheness of her parry and riposte that bested me and Lark in our sparring, how she was a confluence of beauty and strength and will that made my heart sing. And I told him, too, how I failed her—but in my shame I couldn't bring myself to relate the particulars. *To shield him*, I said to myself, *from the brutality of the world. From my brutality.* And I almost believed it.

To the little man I said nothing of my visions or anything else for that matter. I never initiated conversation, never asked him who he was or where we were going. It was enough that we were in motion, that each day we walked farther and I felt better—that each day the vial came out. For the most part, my headaches had stopped, and much of the fog had lifted from my mind. My muscles ached, but in a way that made me yearn to tax them even more. Even my arm had almost mended. Despite the passing fever I experienced at the end of each march, I felt stronger than at any time since Ali and I had alighted in the Holy Lands. Strong enough, I believed, that soon I might confront him. As I trudged, I imagined the scene over and over, played out hundreds of variations. Many ended in violence. So I recalled, lesson by lesson, all Kite had taught us. *Know your enemy*, Kite had said, *but take care not to know him too well. Do not ask what gives him joy or throws him into despair. Stop your ears when he wishes to tell you the bursting pride he felt at his daughter's confirmation, or the love that scorched his heart on the night he first bedded his wife, or the kindness he showed a lost child. Hear nothing that might make you hesitate, even for the single beat of a hummingbird's wing, when the time comes to kill him.*

This advice was easy enough to follow, for I wanted to know nothing more about this man than what I had already observed: he was shorter, but outweighed me and moved with a fluidity and strength that belied his soft appearance and age. Still, I believed I could overcome him. But if I had to, could I kill him? Another of Kite's maxims echoed in my mind: *If you wish to do a man harm, do not use half measures. Strike once and truly so you won't have to strike again.*

I tried to steel myself to this possibility. I knew his death would be another black stain on my soul. Was it a price I was willing to pay? I reconciled myself to the idea that I would know soon enough. Thankfully, however, I convinced myself I couldn't act yet. Not here, in the lightless tunnels. *When we emerge from this damnable darkness,* I repeated over and over, like a mantra, *I will confront him.*

A promise to my son—and a reprieve for me, from a mortal sin I did not want to commit.

I had the shakes.

Shivering, I clasped my arms around myself, trying to ignore the tightening knots in my stomach, the perspiration running down the small of my back, watching raptly as the man prepared the Gift of Water. This time, however, when he offered me the bowl, I summoned my resolve.

"Not enough."

Other than blinking, the man's expression remained impassive.

I was concerned about how little remained in the vial, but a more immediate problem now preoccupied me: my last few visions had lacked their former clarity and sharpness, as if I moved through a cloying haze, and now it had become a struggle to find my son. But I didn't tell the little man this; nor had I told him anything of my visions. I pointed to the pipette. "The calibrations etched on the side. I've watched, and each time you reduce the amount you give me. You mean to wean me off the Gift of Water, don't you?"

"Yes."

"I need more," I said.

"You will ameliorate the symptoms of withdrawal if you continue the reduction. The symptoms of your withdrawal will peak shortly, then diminish until you are asymptomatic."

"Outside the orphanage at *San Savio*," I said, "there are leaf eaters, gaunt men who live in the shadows and wrestle with their hallucinations. Men who shake like I now shake. They forget their hunger and pain, forget about everything except their craving for leaf. Sometimes they ask the Priests for help, hoping to repair their broken lives, and the Priests make them get down on their knees and pray to God for the strength to chew less and less each day—until their faith sets them free. But if any succeeded, I never saw it."

"You cannot fail," the little man said. "The world has an abundance of *ket*. But once the *entheogen* is gone, there will be no more."

I'd steeled myself for this as I'd watched the liquid in the vial dwindle; less than half now remained. Even so, his statement shook me more than I thought it would. "You . . . you've done this before. Brought people back from the Temptations. Haven't you?"

"Many times," he said. "But not often. This other is a Catharsist, created by God for this vocation."

I struggled to find words, to frame my argument. "You control the Gift of Water at the Temptations, don't you?"

"Yes."

"Can you make more *entheogens*?"

"If God bade this other do so."

"And what if I bid you do so?"

"You are not God."

"You said Zeracheil commands you. Is it through his agency God speaks to you?"

"Yes."

"Did Zeracheil ask you to aid me?"

"Yes."

"In what way?"

"To provide what succour I might. To aid you in your journey as I might."

Something occurred to me, then, that should have occurred to me before. "Then why leave me to fast for forty days?"

"God created me to attend to the anchorites, to watch them during their forty days of fasting and prayer. During this time, this other is prohibited from interceding, save in altering the water that sustains so that it may be more salutary. This other cannot do otherwise."

Like all good clerics, the little man had been following the injunctions that had been handed down, and as literally as possible, no matter that they made no sense. "God asked you to help me. And to help me, you must make more *entheogens*."

The Catharsist blinked behind his glasses, but said nothing.

So I tried a different tack. "Do you believe that God speaks to men through visions?"

"Yes."

"Just as he bid you to aid me, he has bid me take the Gift of Water from you and administer it myself."

He stood there blinking, the bowl still held out to me. I wondered that his arms weren't getting tired.

"Will you give me the *entheogens*?"

"The glass vial is frangible, and your body has suffered mild seizures."

"You didn't answer my question. Would you give me the vial?"

"Those who crave the water are controlled by their craving," he said. "You would do yourself harm. Too much of the Gift and you would be lost in your vision."

Not enough, I thought, *and I will lose my son*. "I ask you again, give me the vial."

"This other cannot. This other is a Catharsist, created by God for this vocation."

A sharp cramp caused me to shudder.

The Catharsist took a step towards me, still holding out the bowl. "Drink."

"No," I said, waving him away, though the scent of the Gift of Water wafted into my nostrils, the contents of that bowl filling my awareness, trying to crowd out everything else. It became nearly impossible to keep my thoughts ordered; though I knew myself to be in the waking world, the tunnel already seemed to be taking on the surreal aspect of a vision: behind the Catharsist, restive shadows churned, and I felt an unnatural chill. I stumbled back another step and shook my head to clear it. There was one thing I wanted to ask yet, a question that wouldn't let itself be pushed out of mind. "You . . . you control the water. Which means you were at the Temptations the whole time—and did nothing to help us. You could have saved Ali." I own that it was a small and ignoble thing, trying to portion out the blame for her death, and I suppose I did in the hopes of assuaging my guilt.

He blinked, but didn't answer. Just as he never answered anything except a direct question. The shadows behind him seemed to share my agitation now.

"Why didn't you save Ali?"

"This other actuated the water when you arrived, as God instructed. But from afar. As my image was projected from afar through the agency of the teleidelon. This other did not arrive at the anchorite's cave until several days after. If she did not drink, it was God's will."

He might as well have said that if Ali didn't drink, it was no one's fault but mine: had I not drunk from the water first, had I taken them to her instead, she might have lived. So the fault was mine and mine alone.

Perhaps he saw the expression of self-loathing on my face, for he said, "It is possible the Gift of Water would have not saved her. As it is possible it would have killed her. The excited state brought on by the water would have released excessive serotonin, stressed her heart and lungs and circulatory system—and those of your son. In her weakened state, it is possible both would have succumbed."

"*Possible*," I said, knowing the Catharsist always chose his words carefully, "not probable." The shadows at his back now roiled.

"This other cannot say. Nor can this other say if she was dead before you drank. This other can only say all that has happened was God's will."

"Tell Ali," I said to him. "Tell my son."

"They are dead," he said.

But he was wrong. I could feel my son's presence now—more than I could the Catharsist's. My son *was* here. The shadows turned in on themselves, thickened, my son straining to come into this existence.

I lunged at the little man.

Easily side-stepping my clumsy charge, he left me to grasp at air—and crash headlong into the back of his cart. I doubled over the back rail and loosed the contents of my stomach into the box. When my retching had subsided, I heard the *click* of the bowl as he placed it on the ground, and I had no doubt that not a single drop of the Gift of Water had been spilt. Inhumanly strong hands pried me from the cart—but gently—and propelled me away. I staggered backwards and watched him as he bent over the box, shifting the jostled contents, searching. It took him a moment to understand what I'd done. He straightened and turned slowly, blinking behind those thick spectacles. I guessed him to have quick reflexes, yet even so he moved faster than I thought possible. But he was too late: I'd already pulled the stopper from the vial and downed its contents in a single swallow.

Gog and Magog

Naked, I stood in the valley of Hamongog, a chiaroscuro desert, the sand as white as snow, the rocks as black as pitch, and I knew I must walk or die. Above me, in a firmament too large to comprehend, a single fulgent sun, too radiant to bear. I walked, and the world rippled beneath my feet, threatening to come undone with each step. Thousands upon thousands of different realities had been woven into the land, overlaying one another, each infinitesimally different, each tilted at a minute angle to the one adjacent, shivering apart at my every step, then collapsing back to this moment. It was a calculus of possible worlds, an infinite number of divergent realities, all real and all illusory. I prayed that God might let me summon my strength and fold them into the singular moments that constituted the sum of my choices, that constituted my life.

There was only one land, and beneath it I saw the dry bones of many men, broken and scattered throughout the open valley. But they came together, bone for bone, and I knew they waited to be cloaked in sinew and flesh, waited for the spirit to be breathed into them. Fearful, I ran, and again the world splintered under the soles of my feet. . . .

I'm afraid, *my son said*. Why am I afraid?

In the cave where we hid, there was no light. We sat in darkness, in silence, waiting for the horns of war to be sounded.

Go to the created man, *said my son*. He will save you.

In the valley of dry bones two great companies assembled, carrying with them all the machinery of war, covering all the land like a cloud.

An army on each slope, a dried riverbed between.

A mighty army to one side arrayed in red and gold, a wall of formations, each with the same count of men, each a square layered with infantry, pikemen, and archers. Behind them, rows of cavalry. Each man in a silver cuirass. All the formations flew the same banner: two keys, one gold and one silver, crossed on a field of red, threaded through by a thick gold cord, above which floated a silver tiara capped with a gold crown. The Pope's insignia.

Against them stood a rabble. Men both ragged and in fine vestments, bearing all manner of arms and armour—some with tools and farm implements that might serve as weapons, some with only slings and stones. What banners they held varied widely in colour and insignia—a few rivalled the magnificence of the Pope's, but most were hastily contrived: two crooked sticks and twine formed into a wooden cross; epithets chalked on bedsheets; stained clothing bearing crude sketches of animals and beasts; and of men and women copulating. I could see no order, no purpose, no leader. Yet for the chaos in the mob, their front rank stood as one, shoulder to shoulder, forming a line as straight as those of the troops opposite, every man's sword against his brother.

At the head of a long dead river, separating two mighty armies in the valley of dry bones, I stood, alone—no, not alone. I clutched my son's tiny hand in mine. A horn sounded. Then another, and the armies collided, the clash of their weapons deafening us, their cries of vengeance and pain piercing us like arrows.

In Heaven above, God wept for his children, while his Angels burnt and fell to earth.

For seven years armies clashed. And the dead were devoured by ravenous birds of every sort, and the beasts of the field.

In the confusion and alarm, nowhere could I find my son.

I was carried from the field to a place of healing, though I couldn't have said whose. If the men bore uniforms or insignias, they were shredded and bloodied and beyond recognition.

I saw myself upon two blood-soaked planks on sawhorses, amidst the cacophony of the dying and the entreaties of the dead, all begging forgiveness or screaming vengeance or muttering prayers of self-condolence. My face was white, vacant, lifeless. No one attended me. The freshly wounded surged around me, and I wondered why they had not removed my body, made room for the next.

I lay on the table looking up through unblinking eyes at the little man, bent over my corpse, hands busy with instruments I could not see. I cried out for him to save me, but my lips did not move, nor did any sound emerge; yet he paused in his work and crooked his head to one side, as if to hear me better. And when he did this I saw the skin above his ear was translucent, and behind it spun miniature gold and silver mechanisms: tiny armatures, gears and flywheels; minute pistons, pulleys, and driving belts. Then the created man straightened, hundreds of small rods and levers folding his face into an expression of fear and concern.

Father, *he said to me,* what have you done?

My Son is Lost

I had a headache so piercing my eyes watered. I blinked away the tears.

I was in an empty room, without doors or windows, and whose walls and ceiling were improbably smooth and an undifferentiated white. I suppose they might have been made of plaster, but if so, the plasterer had surpassing skills, for the room was a perfect cube, its surfaces containing none of the irregularities or blemishes one would expect. In this sea of alabaster, I lay under crisp sheets on a mattress that was strangely buoyant. The bed wasn't stuffed with straw, as ours had been at *San Savio*, nor with feathers, as had been the mattress in Meussin's cell; rather, it conformed to my body, cradling me in a shallow of coolness. The sensation would have been pleasant had I not been pinioned by leather cuffs around ankles and wrists, as well as restraints across my forehead and chest.

The moment had none of the surreal quality of the visions induced by the Gift of Water, nor did it seem like a dream—the pounding in my head attested to that. And I was hungry. Parched, too. But my discomfort was short-lived, for no sooner had I thought these things than an unnatural calmness suffused me, my headache receded, and the room receded, all light obliterated as consciousness quietly slipped away.

The next time I swam into the waking world (or dreamed I did), the created man sat on the edge of my bed, one of my hands clasped between his. His fingers were cool and inanimate, yet the angles of his face, always composed and imperturbable, had inexplicably softened, and he looked at me in the way a father might look upon a child in his sick bed.

Is this a true memory or one concocted by my agitated imagination?

Though I had ample opportunity later to ask the created man, I never did. I preferred then, as I still do now, to believe it happened, rather than to chance that it did not.

For days, I drifted in and out of understanding. Sometimes the created man was there, sometimes not. A few times he spoke, about what, though, I can't recall. Never again did I wake to find my hand in his. This left me sad in a way that I did not understand.

During this time, I had a recurring dream. In this dream, I would sense the presence of my son behind me. But upon turning, there would be nothing there, save a hint of his presence: a door swinging shut; bushes on the verge of a forest shaking as if a boy had just pushed through them; the sound of sandals slapping on the cobbles around a street corner. Yet, I knew it was him, knew he wished me to follow. Always, I crossed that threshold, bulled through those branches, ran heedlessly around that corner. Only to find a darkened corridor at whose end stood open a door, giving onto a featureless, white room in which the created man stood, beckoning.

Later, I heard a voice: "Are you in possession of your faculties?"

I couldn't raise my head, because the strap across my forehead prevented even the smallest movement, but I recognized the Catharsist's voice. Foolishly, I tried to nod; bolts of pain momentarily blurred my vision. When I could see again, I managed to croak out, "Yes."

The created man moved into the periphery of my vision and looked down upon me from the same angle and with the same apprehension as he had in my vision; but this time, as he bent over to peer in my eyes, I could see no gears through his temple. He looked at my lips, then lifted one of my hands and examined the nails. After closing his fingers around my wrist to take my pulse, he seemed satisfied at the results of his examination, and loosed the straps that crossed my forehead and chest, then undid the cuffs binding my wrists and ankles.

"You suffered violent seizures and muscle spasms," he said, "and would have done yourself great harm."

I moved my shoulders, arms and legs, testing them, and, indeed, found I was bruised and sore, as if still tender from a battering.

"Do you wish to sit up?"

I nodded.

He gestured, and the room seemed to cant; but it wasn't the room, I realized. Rather, it was the mattress, its top half levering me up from the waist, so that now I sat with my back on an incline, and could better see my surroundings. Only there wasn't much to see. The bed sat to one side of the room; the other half had no furnishings. Opposite the foot of the bed was what looked to be a privy, seemingly made of the same material as the rest of the room, as if it had been extruded whole from the wall. Stranger than that, however, was that I could find no source of illumination; the light was simply all around us, throwing no shadows. None of this, however, bothered me overmuch—after Heaven, the miraculous had become almost mundane—until the Catharsist pulled away the top sheet. Two pale strands, each about the same diameter as the pipette, snaked from beneath the bed, one piercing my forearm, the other inserted in my urethra. Immediately, I thought of the guinea worms that had plagued some of the boys at the orphanage one summer, and how, once the worm emerged, the infected would have to wrap the still-living worm around a stick, turning the stick carefully, so as not to break the creature, drawing it out over hours or days or weeks. Instinctively, I tried to wrench the strand in my left arm out, but it held firm, my flesh gripping it tightly, as if it had always been part of me.

"If you can feed and relieve yourself, the catheters are no longer necessary."

"I . . . I can."

The Catharsist gestured again, and I suppressed my revulsion as the worms retracted from my flesh and fell away to the side of the bed, limp. Where the one had penetrated my arm, only a red blemish remained, in the centre of which was a tiny dot of blood. I wiped it away with my thumb. In doing so, I noticed the red chafe marks on my chest. "My son," I said, my fingers resting on that mark. "What have you done with him?"

Opening his voluminous cape, the created man drew Ali's pouch from an inner pocket and handed it to me. I cupped it in one hand, gently stroking it with the other, trying to draw comfort from it, hoping that, in its touch, I might once again divine the spirit of my son. But I felt nothing. Nothing but a cracked, leather bag, distended here and there by small, brittle bones and lumps of tendon and dried skin. Without the Gift of Water, my son was lost to me.

I suppose in that moment I should have felt grief, or anger at the Catharsist for refusing to make more *entheogens*, but I felt nothing save a great weariness.

"Are you unwell?"

"No," I lied. "Tired."

"Before the catheters were withdrawn, the apothecary administered a sedative. You will sleep shortly."

"Perchance to dream," I muttered, quoting a passage from one of the books I'd read in Rome. *For in this sleep of death what dreams may come. . . .*

The little man stared at me, his brow furrowed—an expression I'd not seen him wear before. "What bothers you?" I asked, in hope of finding what would satisfy him, so that he might leave me in peace.

"Two things," he answered. "When this other said you would be *lost* in your vision, this other intended it to mean that you might fall into a coma or die. This other believes that you did not understand my meaning and only hoped to remain in your vision. Is this true?"

I wasn't sure I could answer his question honestly; I'd come to realize every important decision I'd made arose from more than one motive, even if I wasn't fully aware of them all at the time. "Yes, I wished to stay in my vision. But there are other reasons, too, and they are muddled and contradictory to me, as they must be to you. If you're asking because you're afraid I intended to harm myself, and may still intend to do so, I cannot provide any assurance. All I can tell you is how I feel at this moment."

"You will not attempt to harm yourself?"

"At the moment, no," I answered honestly, if for no other reason than my limbs seemed too heavy at the moment to do much of anything.

"Then," he said, the look of concern on his face washing away, "it will be enough."

It will be enough. The same words my son had used.

"You must sleep now."

The bed descended until I was prone again, clutching the pouch to my chest like a talisman. Walking over to the wall, the created man placed his palm in the centre, and the outline of a door, imperceptible before, materialized. The door swung out, revealing a darkened room beyond.

"Wait." I managed to lift my head, but barely. "Two things. You said two things."

The Catharsist turned. "Four days ago, when you took the *entheogens*, you went into convulsions. When this other brought you here to heal, your heart stopped."

I suppose I should have thanked him for reviving me, but I felt little gratitude. Instead, I said, "You are concerned my mind might have been damaged." My words were slurred, and it had become a struggle to keep my eyes open.

"No," he said, his manner changed all at once, his voice softening. My head fell back to the mattress, and my eyes fluttered shut. As I crossed the threshold between this world and that of dreams, his last words trickled through to me: "*I am bothered because you died, father.*"

The Catharsist's Soul

I woke to a world of wretchedness. Without the analgesic effect of the drugs, the symptoms of my withdrawal manifested themselves ruthlessly: the sharp edges of my headache had returned; I felt nauseous; every joint ached; flushed one moment, chilled the next, I was wracked by uncontrollable tremors; and a fire seemed to dance on my skin. Had there been anything in my stomach, I'd have vomited it up. I remember thinking, *Too miserable to be dead*.

After a time, I managed, despite my infirmities, to lever myself up. The white room spun momentarily, then settled.

I was alone. But the Catharsist's words still rang in my head: *I am bothered because you died, father*.

Had the Catharsist really called me father?

Perhaps he'd said something entirely different, or nothing at all. Perhaps these words had been dredged from my imagination before the drug had dragged me into sleep.

Hope drove me to sit up. In this I am no different than other men, just as injudiciously optimistic, just as self-deluding, no matter how precarious, no matter the weight of evidence to the contrary. *Hope in reality is the worst of all evils because it prolongs the torments of man*. So I had read in one of Meussin's books. But, if we choose to live, what else can we do but hope?

I swung my legs over the side of the bed; my feet didn't quite reach the floor. Gritting my teeth, I hopped off—then clutched the side of the bed until the room steadied. A moment later I walked on wobbly legs to the privy and relieved myself.

Beside the toilet there was a niche on the wall I hadn't noticed before—or, perhaps, that hadn't been there before. I discovered putting a hand inside caused cool water to trickle from above and disappear into a hollow below; cupping my hands, I drank a bit, then splashed some on my face, taken aback at how refreshing it felt. Having finished my ablution, I shuffled over to where the door had been, and ran my hand along the wall. Only I felt not even a hairline gap, and with my eye only centimetres distant, could detect no seam. There were no other furnishings in the room, so I returned to the bed and, grunting, hoisted myself back up and sat down to wait, shoulders slumped, legs dangling over the side, ignoring, as best I could, the complaints of my body.

For a time, I lost myself in my thoughts.

I didn't hear the created man enter the room, but he stood before me, bearing a trencher that held the same sort of food he'd brought to the hermit's cave, as well as a fresh heel of dark bread and spiced strips of meat, probably lamb. Behind him, the door was open. He placed the tray on the bed, the smell causing my stomach to wrench.

"Eat," he said. "If you are to do God's work, you must regain your strength."

"I will eat," I said, "but not for God. I will do so for truthful answers to my questions."

"This other is always truthful. This other was created to serve God and cannot lie."

"So a liar would say. Swear to the Lord your God. That shouldn't be hard if you are a devout servant of the Lord, as you claim."

"Ask what you wish," he said without hesitation. "This other swears to and by the Lord God to answer your questions completely and truthfully."

"Thank you," I said, nodding—then blinking back the sudden bolt of pain that shot through my skull. I tried to collect myself, at least enough to speak. "Before . . . before you left me, you told me two things bothered you. When I asked you about the second, you gave me a strange answer. At first I thought I'd imagined your response, that it was a trick of the drug you'd given me. Only now I'm not so sure. Did you say, '*I am bothered because you died, father*'?"

"This other does not recall saying this."

"Not recalling," I said, "doesn't mean that you didn't say the words. Is it possible you said this?"

"The words are true. Your heart stopped. You no longer breathed.

You were dead. This other bore witness."

A spasm momentarily seized me; when it passed, I continued. "Yet you don't remember saying those words?"

"This other's perception was interrupted when this other left you to rest."

"You lost consciousness?"

"Perception was lost. Motor function continued, though not under this other's control. There was a limited awareness of movement, a sense of another will working this body." He paused, as if considering. "Perhaps it was then that this other spoke the words that puzzle you."

My poor, beleaguered mind made an effort to sort out his words. "Are you saying you were possessed?"

"This other was not aware and so could not say."

"Has this happened before?"

"Once."

"When?" I leaned forward, anticipation of his answer sweeping aside all my afflictions.

"After you died," he said. "When perception returned, you were alive."

Maybe, I thought, my heart beating faster, *I am not so foolish to hope*. "I can see you aren't like other men. You seem to be able to see in the pitch dark, and you have unlikely agility, stamina, and strength. What's more, you seem to be aware of these differences, for you always refer to yourself as *this other*. Never *I* or *me*." I watched him carefully but, as usual, he evinced no reaction. "Are you not a man?"

"This other is a Catharsist. This other was created by God to do God's will."

"Were you born of woman?"

"Not of woman."

"Then of what?"

"This other was gestated in an analogous manner, but not in a human womb."

I thought of my vision, of the gold and silver gears I'd seen in his head. In Meussin's books I'd read of such things, automatons made to look like men. And I recalled how the Catharsist had called me father then, too. "Are you a machine?"

"No more or less than you," he said, appearing not in the least perturbed by my question. "If you were to look inside a man you would find the mechanics of the heart and lungs and digestive system. If you were to magnify the tissues, bones, and organs, you would find molecular machines which dictate the rhythms of life. This other has analogous workings. But not all, since this other does not draw breath or require sustenance—at least not in the way of men. Similarly, this other does not feel hunger or pain. But, in the way of men, this other can think and reason and communicate."

"And feel?"

He shrugged. "This other has considered this question, but concluded it is not possible to know what it means for a man to feel joy or sorrow—or any other emotion—no more than a man can know what it means for this other to feel. Perhaps this is true between two men, too."

"You said you were created to serve God. And you can reason and perhaps even feel. As the Angels can. Are you a kind of Angel?"

"No. They are spirit, though they may take on flesh. They abide in Heaven. This other is a created man, flesh of the earthly realm, born without free will and so without a soul."

Without a soul—and hence without a chance for redemption. A devout servant of God, helping holy men to find the solace in this life and prepare for the next, yet with no chance of Heaven's reward. I knew now why he called himself *other*; he was fundamentally different from us, and from the Angels, who'd already attained paradise. I didn't think it possible that I might feel pity for him, but in this moment I did. *How*, I wondered, *could God create a creature with no chance of salvation?* "You said you were *created* without a soul. Do you have one now?"

He looked at me, and blinked behind those thick spectacles. "Perhaps."

"The thing that possessed you—you believe it to be a soul?"

"When this other lost perception, this body still functioned, controlled by thoughts that were not this other's. This other could sense the shape of these thoughts, their intention, but not the specific objects at which they were directed. And this other now has memories, too, from times and places this other has never been. And memories of sensations this other has never experienced. If such memories are bound up in a soul, then a soul now resides within this other."

"At this moment, do you sense this other presence?"

He pursed his lips and cocked his head, as if listening for a whisper. "Yes, but it is faint."

"What memories do you have?"

"Many."

"Of me?"

"Yes. Of you, of us, in a cave."

"You said *us*, not *this other*. Why?"

"Because that is the memory."

"Was this the hermit's cave?"

"No. Another place. Perhaps not a real place."

"What were we doing in the cave?"

"Hiding."

"I saw my son in my visions," I told him. "In my last vision, we were hiding in a cave, and he told me to go to you, to seek your help."

"A son who was not born?"

My heart skipped a beat. "Yes." Then I asked the only important question: "Have you stolen my son's soul?"

"This other is incapable of theft."

"But you believe you possess a soul, one that is not yours?"

"This other cannot say what a soul is or how it might feel—or to whom it might have belonged. But if you tell this other what your son was like, this other might be able to determine more about the presence."

So I told him as best I could. Then I shared with him many of the details of my last vision: the disintegrating world; the cave where my son and I hid; the clash of great armies in the valley of dry bones; the field hospital where I lay dead; and, he, the created man, trying vainly to save me.

"Yes," he said, when I'd finished. "Some of this is familiar. Some this other remembers, though these are not this other's memories. These might have come from your son."

I tried to temper my elation—he could be lying, of course. Just as Ignatius and Kite and Ali had all lied to me, if not directly, then by withholding the truth, so that I might do the Angels' bidding. Maybe this was another of their deceptions. But I'd anticipated this. "When I told you of my vision of the battle, I left out one important thing we saw. Can you tell me this thing?"

The created man stepped back and the door closed behind him, sealing us into perfect night.

I was taken aback. "What are you doing?"

"Answering your question."

A ball of light blazed to life in the other half of the room, dazzling me. I gasped, staring at what was both familiar and shocking: the Spheres of the world, just as I'd witnessed them through the Eye of God. The created man placed his hands on the insubstantial surface, and rotated the reflection of the world, then enlarged it, and we dove beneath Lower Heaven and into Peter's Sphere. Unlike the image I saw through God's Eye, here it was sun-off and hard to make out detail—except for the unmistakable outline of the Babel Tower. The device I'd used in Lower Heaven had shown only a static map, one of the world from long before the tower existed. Even more startling was that, as the created man drew us closer to the tower, I saw movement: tiny, ant-like men crawling up the tower's ramp.

"Why are you showing me this?"

"To answer your question completely and truthfully." He pointed to the apex of the tower, to the bridge Ali and I had crossed into Heaven. There, a pinprick of yellow light flickered to life. Breaking free of the bridge, it wobbled downwards. The light must have been a flame, for the rush of air kindled it, and the spark grew until it blossomed into the shape of a fiery bird, its wings extended and swathed in flame. For a few heartbeats, the thing spiralled downward in a controlled flight, at once beautiful and terrifying. Then it collapsed into itself, became a compact fireball that plummeted at a sickening speed, striking the earth, exploding in a fountain of sparks. There it burned for several minutes, dying at last to scant yellow flames.

As it had in my vision.

"The Angels burn," said the created man reverently, and I doubted him no more.

The Teleidelon

As the created man (as I had now come to think of him) had honoured his promise, so I honoured mine: I ate. I did so without relish, though I should have been ravenous, chewing absentmindedly on the first solid food I'd had in days, thinking on what the created man had shown me.

"Will you walk?"

His words jarred me from my reverie. "Walk?"

"You have finished eating."

I looked down, surprised to find nothing but scraps on the trencher.

"If you are to do God's work," the created man said, "you must regain your strength."

I bit back an acerbic comment, and felt better for doing so, for he'd done nothing to deserve it. I let him help me out of bed and, together, we hobbled to the door. The food must have done me good, for, surprisingly, my aches and pain had receded and my mind seemed clearer, and the world sharper, than it had since I'd awoken.

"In Heaven," I said, nodding to the part of the room where the image of the world had been, "I used such a device to memorize parts of the Spheres. But it showed only one map, from long before the tower was built." I thought about the men I'd seen ascending the tower's ramp. "Nor did it show people or motion."

"This other cannot speak of the *teleidelon* you used in Lower Heaven," the created man said, "but it may be that the Angels have forgotten its secrets, or some of its parts have become corrupted beyond repair. However, when it is working as it should, the *teleidelon* may be used many different ways: to witness what is happening in the world, or what has happened; to project one's image onto the world; to ascertain the nature of a problem that lies between the Spheres when the world ails, or within a single man who has taken ill—just as this other used it on you."

"And you use the *teleidelon* to speak with the Angels?"

"Until recently, albeit in a limited way, since theirs no longer projects."

"You don't use it now?"

"No, not for forty-two days."

The duration of my fast. "Why not?"

"Heaven has fallen."

This news shook me more than I thought it would. "What you showed me—the tower, the burning Angels—is this happening right now?"

"It is a memory from two days ago."

"Why?" I asked, fearing I already knew the answer. "Why are the Angels burning?"

"The Church seeks knowledge. The Angels refuse to speak."

"Knowledge of what?"

"Of many things," the created man said. "Of you."

I felt sickened.

"Will you walk?"

My own discomfort seemed a small thing, next to the suffering inflicted on the Angels of Heaven. I acquiesced.

We crossed the threshold of the white room; immediately, a yellow glow emanated from the floor outside. As we moved, the light moved with us, illuminating row after row of shelves crammed with strange and unfamiliar objects and containers, the ceiling so high it was lost in the gloom. Our footsteps echoed, betraying the immensity of the space. Shortly, we came to a wall that gradually curved towards us on either side. Turning left, we followed it, passing openings at regular intervals that gave onto tunnels, much like those we had travelled from the hermit's cave.

"We're walking the interior circumference of a circular storehouse," I said, "with the white room in its centre."

"Yes," replied the created man. "It is approximately six hundred and twenty eight metres per circuit, and approximately one hundred metres to the centre from the wall. For today, one circuit will suffice."

The walk was more taxing than I had anticipated—the rush of energy I'd felt earlier had completely evaporated. Now, less than halfway around (or so I guessed), a sheen of perspiration coated me, and my heart tripped as if I'd just finished a sprint. I insisted we pause so that I could catch my breath. When we walked again, it was at a much slower pace. Save for the noise of my ragged breathing, we moved in silence. But as we approached what I judged to be the end of our circuit, I could no longer hold my tongue. "Can you . . . can you feel my son?"

"Yes."

"Right now?"

"Yes."

"What do you feel?"

"At times, nothing. At other times, a presence, its disposition and desires."

"How often?"

"More as the days pass. And in different ways. Two days ago this other began having thoughts—then realized they were not this other's thoughts; they were your son's."

I was scared of how he might answer my next question: "Do you not fear being . . . displaced?" It was the gentlest word I could find.

"This other believes your son would not do that."

"Then you would not try to displace him?"

"This other has no immortal soul to lose, and only fears losing your son's. This other would carry the soul of your son—if you are willing, and until a more suitable vessel is found."

I had not considered how this soulless creature might desire a soul, might covet it, even if for a short time. I was taken aback by the humility of his offer, and shamed by my selfishness. As gently as I could, I said, "Of course."

The created man looked at me; for a brief instant something flickered across his face. Something that reminded me of my son. Then it was gone and his features fell back into their imperturbable cast. "Thank you," he said, without inflection. Yet for all that, his gratitude seemed far more genuine than most thanks I've been offered in my life.

I asked no more about my son that day. I was tired and light-headed. And I was scared to press the created man, to catch him in a lie. I preferred, as do most men, to live another day in ignorance rather than risk discovering an unwelcome truth.

How long I slept, I couldn't have said (though I'd have guessed it was a long time). When I woke, the created man was still there. My head swam, and I felt disoriented, a feeling that dogged me all that day and for several thereafter.

We fell into a routine. Morning, noon, and night, he'd bring me a meal, and after each I'd feel better, if only briefly; for a short time, my hands shook less and my headaches receded—and the world brightened perceptibly. Yet these moments were evanescent, and after each meal when we walked—he supporting me as he had the first day—we had to pause frequently when nausea or spasms incapacitated me. During this time I seemed to fade in and out of the conscious moment, often stumbling into a fog of memories and dreams. Reality seemed to be clipped and disjointed. In my moments of clarity, I tried to ask questions, which he answered readily enough, but his answers were often lost on me. And, from time to time when I was able, I watched for signs of my son, although I never saw anything other than a flicker pass over the created man's face—and even then, I wasn't sure whether I'd really seen something other than the phantasms of my fevered state.

Bit by bit, lucidity returned.

Three days passed before I had the presence of mind to ask the created man about himself, and discovered that, if he was to be believed, he was old. Old as the world. "Although this other walked the Spheres before there were men," he told me, "this other is not immortal."

What I had called God's Eye, the created man named a *teleidelon*. He told me it was even older than he, among the first things God created, before He created the world.

When I asked him if he'd used it to appear to me, to direct us to the Temptations, he acknowledged he had. "Why did you appear only once? If the Angels directed you to do so, why didn't you give us more help in finding our way?"

"To see great distances, the *teleidelon* relies on eyes that are scattered throughout the Spheres. As in ageing men, these eyes sometimes go blind, and then only the past may be seen, as a blind man might take solace in his memories. To project is even more difficult. It requires working eyes in complementary positions as well as great reserves of power. And its accuracy and efficacy suffers proportionally to the square of the distance over which it projects. Even so, this other tried to send you a projection on seventeen occasions, when sufficient power had been gathered to do so. Had you but looked in the right direction any of those times, you might have seen this other."

I asked him if I might use the *teleidelon* to prepare for God's work, as I had in Heaven. I explained I had not viewed the Holy Lands or its environs since I did not believe we would travel this way; and that the *teleidelon* I'd used before showed the way things had been in the past—centuries at least, by my reckoning. So this would give me the opportunity to see how things had changed, and what might lay ahead.

He agreed, as I knew he would agree to anything that suggested I intended to fulfil God's will. Only I hadn't made any such decision— and I had other uses in mind for the *teleidelon*. But to maintain this pretence, I began by using it to explore my immediate surroundings the next day.

Viewed from above, the catacombs of the created man looked like a demented spiderweb, its centre at the end of the Dead Sea near Masada. The white room was at the very heart of this network; outside the room was the immense, circular storehouse, its shelves cluttered with enigmatic objects and oddly shaped containers, most of which were completely alien to me. Tunnels, identical to those we used to find our way here, radiated crookedly from the storehouse hub, random cross-passages connecting these tunnels, all leading to secluded places where hermits might find the solitude for their spiritual contemplations. This convoluted web ran under the holy lands in all directions—in places up to a hundred kilometres. I zoomed in and out, memorizing the complex of passages, finding it unnerving when the white room was in view, and my movements were mirrored by the tiny figure in the display.

If I can see myself, I thought, *I should be able to observe the created man's movements*. However, this proved to be impossible for a simple reason I should have anticipated: the light, which radiated from the floor and walls and ceiling wherever I went, never rose for the created man; when he left me, he walked in darkness, and whatever mysterious errands he might be running went unobserved.

On the fifth day of my rehabilitation, as we entered the white room after we'd returned from our evening walk, the created man said, "You wish to see inside this other."

How he'd anticipated me, I cannot say. Perhaps he had observed me through the agency of another of God's Eyes, trying, and failing, to look inside myself. But I deemed it unlikely that there was another *teleidelon* in such proximity—if, in fact, there were more than two working *teleidelon*s in all the Spheres. More likely he'd read it in my face and demeanour; as poor as I am at lying, I am even worse at masking my desires. "You said the *teleidelon* might be used to look inside a man, and you implied you used it to look inside me. I assume it could look inside you as well."

"Yes," he said, "But it requires the subject to be within an array of sensors that can penetrate the flesh."

"And where is this array?"

"Surrounding the bed."

I hauled myself up and lay on my back. "Show me."

He invoked the *teleidelon*, and dove down through the spheres until the view penetrated the ceiling above us—and there we were, the created man and I. But while he was a solid thing with an opaque surface of flesh, I was a grotesque, flayed creature: through translucent layers of skin and fat I saw ropes of red muscle stretched across bone, interwoven with glistening, fibrous cords of tendon; skeins of branching arteries and veins ran everywhere without a seeming plan; curiously shaped organs, of salmon and olive and grey, nested amidst snaking, bulbous intestines; and a bone-white cage of ribs harboured lungs and heart. I watched, rapt, as that asymmetric knot of muscle beat on obliviously—and thought it far too thin a thread on which to hang a life.

Then the created man moved over to the bed; I made room and he lay next to me.

Where my body was a random, unruly tangle, in him I saw only order, symmetry, and balance. Some of his organs seemed roughly analogous to mine, but regularly shaped, and fit together like a puzzle in the most efficient manner possible; and the veins and arteries and nerves that fed them ran true, while mine were a chaotic snarl, crossing over one another or tracing inexplicably long routes,. Yet for all that, I could see just as easily that he wasn't a machine, at least not like any machine I had ever seen, for life coursed within him as it moved in me, and to a detectable rhythm, though slower than my heartbeat. That he was a living being, I had no doubt, for it was as if God had taken a man, and redesigned him the way he ought to be, perfect and harmonious. Yet—

Yet I was the one with a soul, the one who had been chosen. Why, I wondered, had God created a perfect being without a soul?

"Have you seen what you wished?"

I examined the created man closely, even though I had no idea what I searched for, or where it might be found, just a belief that I would recognize it as soon as I apprehended it. Yet nowhere could I see anything that might be taken for a soul—in either of us.

Three Gifts

The following morning as I broke my fast, the created man left the white room, returning a few minutes later holding a black cane and a copy of *The Bible*, the latter of which he handed me.

The Good Book seemed unremarkable, no different than hundreds of other Bibles I'd seen: black leather with faded gilt letters on its cover and spine, its edges worn from much use. I opened it. On the title page was an elaborate woodcut, at whose centre was the figure of a heart containing the words *The Holy Bible, Scriptures Contained in the Old and New Testaments, Imprinted at Rome, Officina Libraria Editoria Vaticana*; surrounding this was a square of twelve frames, four per side, each of which depicted one of the twelve Apostles of the Spheres. In the small space above the upper row of frames, I was startled to see an inscription in a crabbed hand: *To David, as my father gave me the Good Book, now I give you the one true book.*

"My father—"

"No," the created man said, "The words are so that others would think it yours."

And not take it from me, I thought, *for what man would steal the Holy Book given by a father to his son?*

The created man bid me place my hand on the page. I did so, and the woodcut vanished and was replaced by small lines of text; I jerked my hand back in surprise, glimpsing only for a moment the first sentence: *This is my favourite book in all the world, though I have never read it.* The woodcut blossomed again.

"That . . . that wasn't *The Bible*," I said stupidly.

"It is *The One Book*."

I touched the edge of the paper again, and the proscribed text reappeared—then disappeared as soon as I lifted my finger. I stared at the page, astonished. *A book hidden within a book.* "When we left Rome, Meussin gave me a book, a work of fiction, wrapped in the skin of a *Bible*. I lost it crossing a river."

"This is *The One Book*," the created man said, "containing the text of all books."

"All books?"

"Millions."

I thought this preposterous, though wanted badly to believe. I looked at the humble volume. Not a book within a book, but an unimaginably immense library, the largest library in all the Spheres. Concealed within *The Bible*. "The Church's interdiction . . ."

"*The One Book* knows your touch—and no other's. And should another happen to look at what you are reading, they will not see what you see on the page."

"And what do you see?"

He shrugged. "A blank page. They are all blank to me."

Oddly, I felt a pang of pity for him. "If this book contains millions of books, where are the others?"

"Think about a list of all books within *The One Book*."

I did so, and the page faded, replaced by a list of what appeared to be titles, followed by the names of what I took to be their authors.

"You may also think of a type of book, its author, or even something that happens within a book, and *The One Book* will present you with a different list."

I thought about how *The One Book* contained all the books the Church had banned. The words on the page faded, and a new list appeared. Curiously, the first line was only a number, and the second was comprised of a word I didn't know followed by a number. Beneath those, however, were what appeared to be titles.

"If you think of one of the books listed, or of any specific book contained within *The One Book*, it will show you the work."

I stared at the second title; after a heartbeat, the list faded and was replaced by a story which began with the words, *Brother Francis Gerard of Utah might never have discovered the blessed documents, had it not been for the pilgrim with girded loins who appeared during that young novice's Lenten fast in the desert.* I scanned the text quickly, then turned the page, and the next, and several more after, noting that sentences not finished on one page continued on the next. *The One Book* had become the book I'd chosen from the list. "These works are banned," I said, lifting my hand from the page, watching the words melt away, to be replaced by verses from Genesis, Chapter 2: *Then Yahweh God gave the man this command, 'You are free to eat of all the trees in the garden. But of the tree of the knowledge of good and evil you are not to eat; for, the day you eat of that, you are doomed to die.'* "You would defy an ecclesiastical decree?"

"The decrees of men do not apply to the works of God, of which this is one. Nor," added the created man, "do the interdictions of the Church apply to created men, who are not men, and are not servants of the Church, but are servants only to God. In giving you this gift, this other defies no law. By accepting this gift, it is you who will stand in violation."

I touched the page again, and the prohibited words reappeared. I thought of the first words I had seen in *The One Book*, and they reappeared: *This is my favourite book in all the world, though I have never read it.*

"If you wish to obey the interdiction, this other will return *The One Book* to its place in the storehouse. But if you keep this gift, it will help pass the time as we journey to do God's will."

I was unable to take my eyes off that sentence. Had the created man selected this sentence on purpose, to remind me I had made my choice long ago, back in Meussin's prison cell, when I'd taken my first book off her shelf? Or had the book chosen it for me? "Let us call it what it is—a bribe—and I will keep it." I looked at the created man. "Thank you."

The created man nodded. Then he proffered a second gift, the black cane he'd been holding. It looked well-used, having a ferrule of tarnished brass, and a large, smooth knob on the top the size of a chicken egg, to which a worn leather wrist-strap had been attached. "So that you may support yourself," he said, "even if this other is not there." I laid *The Bible* on the bed and grasped the cane; it was surprisingly top-heavy, and I almost lost my grip as it twisted in my hand. "It may also be employed as a weapon, like a cudgel," the created man said as I righted it. "The knob has been hollowed out and molten lead poured in to give it extra striking weight."

The third item he gave me that day was concealed in the second. Grasping the cane exactly as the created man directed me—one hand mid-shaft and the other over top the handle—I gave a small twist and the upper part of the cane separated from the rest, revealing that the shaft, too, had been hollowed. Within was a long, narrow flask filled with amber liquid. I put the head of the cane on the bed and carefully extracted the flask from the channel. "The Gift of Water," I said, a tremor in my voice.

He acknowledged it was so.

"Why?"

"No man can discontinue the use of *entheogens* without enduring debilitating side-effects, some so severe they might permanently break a man's spirit or mind. Withdrawal must be gradual."

"But I've felt no—" Then I stopped myself. "You've been infusing my food and drink."

"A single drop in each meal."

When my appetite had returned, I'd thought it the consequence of the food; after each meal I'd felt the world brighten and my mind spark faster—and, in equal measure, my pain and sorrow ebb. "You mean to keep me dependent, but at a manageable level."

"You are already dependent. This other is helping you manage your addiction so we may travel. The dose may be reduced in time and as your recovery warrants."

We? This was the first time the created man had indicated he'd be accompanying me. But I'd presumed as much, for he knew I'd follow the vessel carrying my son's soul, to Heaven or to Hell, or wherever else it might go. "And what if I choose to take no more?"

The created man merely looked at me, but did not essay a response. Had he been a normal man, I suspect he might have laughed, for my hands trembled and drops of perspiration had sprung up on my forehead. I struggled to refrain from unstoppering the flask and downing its contents right then. I shoved the vial back into the cane and pushed the head on so that I wouldn't have to look at it. "The . . . the journey, it will take some time."

"A drop with each meal and the contents of the vial will last for two hundred days."

I am shamed to admit that, in that moment, I wanted nothing more than to ask him what would happen after the *entheogens* ran out. But I fought back that impulse. "You would trust me with this?"

"Were this other to hold it, you would spend your time contriving ways of taking it from me," he said. "You must learn to control your appetite for the *entheogens*, that you may freely do God's will. This other believes you have the strength to do so."

"And if I disappoint?"

"Taking larger doses might induce a state where you would see your son. Or might not. This other cannot say. But the deleterious effects of the *entheogens* are cumulative."

"You mean I would make myself sick again."

"The symptoms would be more acute, and without the apothecary, this other would have no means of ameliorating them. So if you didn't do your body or mind irreparable harm, your withdrawal would be debilitating and likely fatal. And though your soul will live on, it will do so in Heaven or Hell or purgatory, while your son's soul continues to abide within this other on this worldly plane."

I felt a spike of anger. "You would keep me from my son!"

"No." I didn't think it possible, but the created man looked as if my words had hurt him. "You would keep him from yourself for the taste of the Water."

"I did it to be with my son." But my words sounded weak, while his carried the sting of truth: my craving for the Gift of Water had become inseparable from my desire to be with my son.

"This other would never purposefully cause you pain." The created man placed a hand on my shoulder; in that moment, it felt like a dead thing. "And this other would do whatever possible to reunite you with your son—once God's will be done."

God's will be done.

How often had I heard that solemn refrain uttered by a cleric? How often had *I* said those words myself as a child on bended knee, believing them as only a child can, with all my heart? Yet, the Church was composed of men, and it was men who were corrupt and fallible, not the God they served. Thus reasoning, I had been able to hold to my faith in God, but, perforce, lost that in his servants. I even doubted the Angels, whose motives no sane man could fathom. Was it possible to believe again that God spoke to me through one of his servants? The created man seemed guileless. And, truth be told, I wished more than anything to have faith in him—how else could I accept that he harboured the soul of my son? "You said you could sense the shape of my son's thoughts."

"Yes."

"What does he wish for me?"

"That you do God's will."

"And until I do, you mean to hold his soul hostage."

The created man gently withdrew his hand. "This other does not have free will, and did not choose to bear the soul of your son. His soul was given to this other by God."

"So it is God who is extorting me, and you are merely doing your duty."

My words were uncharitable, and I thought their impiety would shock the created man. Instead, he replied, "As should you. How can God extort what you already owe Him?"

I recognized in his answer an uncomfortably familiar idea, one which had been inculcated in me, and all the other souls who'd been taught to fear damnation: in every prayer we offer, in every deacon we tithe, in every kindness and small sacrifice we make, we are already striking a bargain with God, hoping these small gestures will weigh in our favour on the day we are judged.

God's will be done.

It would be easy to have faith in the created man, for I'd begun to think him essentially good (if such a term could be applied to a created person), and I'd no doubt *he* believed all he said. Just as I thought most of the clerics holding forth from their pulpits were well-intentioned, too. But intentions, as I had learned, do not make a thing true, and, not for the first time, I wondered at those who claimed to know the mind of God—a claim so outrageous and immodest, it beggars belief. Yet the Church proclaims it loudly and incessantly, and condemns all others who would do the same. And we accept it without compunction. Why? Perhaps precisely because it is promulgated through unrelenting repetition. Or perhaps we fear the price (as they tell us) of not believing: eternal damnation. Either would suffice, I suppose. But what I think is most important here (and what the Church seems to know well) is that when we are young, our minds are like empty vessels waiting to be filled, and what is poured in them first and most often leaves scant room for anything else.

God's will be done.

I still had faith in God. But I had little faith in men. Most especially those who would proclaim they know what is true. Even so, I believed what the created man told me, at least insofar as my son was concerned. In the end, I suppose that all we can do is choose those in whom we place our trust—and let God do what He will.

We Set Out

Hell lay in only one direction, so we planned our descent accordingly.

From my observations in the *teleidelon*, I'd learned the Sphere of Peter had only four working Assumptions through which we might achieve the next Sphere down, the closest being the one through which we'd ascended to Rome. Between it and us lay at least a hundred kilometres of wilderness, followed by the even longer expanse of the Mediterranean Sea. Of the other Assumptions, the nearest was four times the distance, through even more vexing terrain, with no sizable bodies of water over which we could let the wind drive us. Loathe as I was to return to Rome (the city of Kite's death and Meussin's penitence), it was clear that choosing any of the other Assumptions would add months to a leg of our journey that might otherwise take no more than two weeks. So I bit back my reluctance and girded myself to the inevitable. The only comfort I drew was that this route would take us out of the Sphere of Saint Peter as quickly as possible.

I was for setting out immediately and taking the most direct route—across the Wilderness of Judea and over its mountains to the city of Ascalonia on the Mediterranean, where we might secure passage to Rome.

The created man was of a different mind.

Instead, he suggested we travel parallel the Mediterranean coast by taking the tunnels to the Dead Sea, and from there along the shore to the River Jordan, following its meandering course to the Sea of Galilee. Old roads ringed the Galilee, and would take us to Tiberias, once a sizable city but now uninhabited. From there, broad thoroughfares ran to the Mediterranean coast and the ancient harbour at Akko.

Although this was a considerably longer journey, he believed that it would prove quicker, given the regularity of the tunnels and the more hospitable byways along the shores of the two seas and the river valley; he also said it would allow him to bring his cart, which would have been impossible otherwise. And there would be an additional benefit: when the Church discovered where Ali and I had alighted (a discovery he believed inevitable), our trail would mysteriously end at the hermit's cave. "It has been over a hundred years since this other last ministered to a hermit, and it is possible that the existence of the tunnels has faded from the memory of men. If the Church seeks you, the caves will hide our progress, at least as far as the Dead Sea."

Perhaps, I thought. But the Church, in my limited experience, rarely forgot anything. Nevertheless, I acquiesced, for the most important thing, it seemed to me, was to get back to Rome as expeditiously as we could, which is what his plan promised.

The light faded as soon as we passed from warehouse to tunnel; immediately, a new light blazed to life atop the stick the created man carried. He handed the stick to me.

I trudged in silence behind the created man's cart—now loaded with provender, cooking utensils, and sundry other gear—the creak of the cart's wheels and the *tick* of my cane echoing hollowly in the tunnels. A day and a half, the created man told me, to reach the egress for the Dead Sea.

For every ten minutes we walked, he would allow five for me to collect myself. When I was too fatigued to carry on, he bid me sit in the cart, which he then pulled without apparent effort. I couldn't help but notice our pace quickened.

During the times in which I rested in the cart, I would hold the light over the pages of *The One Book*. I learned that when I wished to see a list of all books within *The One Book*, the order of the items in that list sometimes changed, works sometimes moving up and down, or being replaced entirely by a new work. The only constant was that whatever book I was reading was always at the top of the list. Leastways until I finished it, at which point it vanished (or, more likely, was relegated to a position towards the end of the list, though I had no way of verifying that given the size of the list). I soon came to realize that I delighted most in those works nearer the top of the list. I suppose *The One Book* anticipated my preferences, and organized the works accordingly.

Brother Francis Gerard of Utah might never have discovered the blessed documents, had it not been for the pilgrim with girded loins who appeared during that young novice's Lenten fast in the desert.

So began the second story I read in *The One Book*, a fiction about a world devastated by an unimaginable war, where rampaging mobs destroyed whatever books they could find, while an order of monks tried, at their peril, to preserve this knowledge. I suppose the essential truth of this work was that there are those who would risk their lives that ideas not be lost. Was this why the created man had given me *The One Book*, so that I might read (remembering perfectly everything I read, and so preserving) these stories? To this day, I do not know, and I regret that I had not thought to ask him.

We paused, from time to time, that I might eat.

When we first did so, my hand shook as I lifted the Gift of Water from the cane. Foolish pride had made me think I might forgo the tinctures; but by the time we halted, a piercing headache had beset me and I was seized by intermittent tremors. I felt wrung out and battered, as though I had just suffered a thorough beating. The created man took the flask from my hand and tipped a drop into the cup of water he'd poured, then handed the flask back to me. Softly, he said, "This other waited too long and begs your forgiveness."

The next time we stopped to eat, I managed the *entheogens* myself. My hand shook, but not as badly as before, and I didn't spill anything, or let drip too much of the precious liquid into the cup. As I lifted the cup to my lips, the created man nodded and raised one hand, his thumb bent across his palm, as if in benediction. I am not sure why he did this, or why he did so each time thereafter, but it became part of our ritual.

At some point, the motion of the cart lulled me to sleep, and when I woke all was still and dark. I groped for the light, which came alive at my touch. We had come to a place where the tunnel broadened to four times its usual size. I clambered out of the back of the cart, disoriented momentarily by how the echoes had changed.

"Take care," the created man said as I made my way to the front of the cart. Ahead, the tunnel floor split around a trench three metres wide and running another ten metres, where it ended abruptly at a wall. Rising from the bottom of the trench to the ceiling was a set of double doors. Bidding me wait, the created man bore right and, peering down, walked a dozen or so paces before he stopped and stared. I held out the light and squinted, but could see nothing.

Without warning, the created man hopped from the edge; I heard his sandals slap ground. Holding my light down, I saw a small wan globe that I took to be the top of his sparsely haired pate. The trench was no more than three metres deep.

"What is it?" I called, trying to keep my voice even. "Where are we?"

His head bobbed and, to my astonishment, I watched as the created man leapt from the darkness like an apparition, his deacon's cope fluttering behind him, landing nimbly on the lip of the trench, looking not the least put out by his inhuman leap.

"We are at the end of the tunnel," he said, "though the sea is not."

"The sea?"

"There is a small vessel at the bottom of this slip, and its use would have saved us two days."

I peered into the gloom. "You said nothing of a boat earlier."

"It has been one hundred and thirty-seven years since this other was here. This other did not know if this vessel would still be here, or if it would be capable of sailing." He looked at me. "In dealing with men, this other has learned it is best not to plant the seed of hope when it is unlikely to germinate."

I walked over to where he stood and held out the light. I could just make out a craft of sorts—it appeared to be a flat-bottomed skiff, perhaps four metres in length and two across its beam, oars and a mast pole rolled with canvas laying aft to fore. A design I hadn't seen before, reminiscent of much older boats. "What's wrong with it?"

"Nothing," he said. "But there is no water in the slip. This means the sea has receded more than this other feared, and the egress would now be a hundred metres or more from the water's edge. The vessel is landlocked."

"So if it were in water, it would sail?"

"Yes," he said. "This boat was not made by men. The materials may look like wood and canvas, but they are far more durable."

"You are stronger than any man I have ever seen. Can you not carry it to the water?"

"This other can lift several times what most men can, but this is still not enough."

"Is the slip hidden from the outside, like the egress to the hermit's cave?"

"Yes."

"Closed, might it keep water out?"

"There is a channel at the bottom that is always open."

"If I go down there, will I be able to get back up?"

"This other can help you."

Any other man would have asked me why I wanted to do this, but I knew the created man wouldn't. I walked the length of the boat, from stern to bow, then sat on the edge of the slip, legs dangling over the sheer side. I tossed the light down, rolled onto my stomach and let myself down until my arms were at their full extent. I let go. Although I'd braced for it, the impact still jarred my knees and made my back teeth clack together, and had the wall not been in front to steady myself, I'd have tumbled to the ground. As I picked up the light, the created man landed next to me like a cat.

A few paces away was the end of the channel. A two-door gate ran the height of the slip. At its bottom, however, a semi-circular opening, a few hand spans high at its apex, had been carved where the doors met. I went down on hands and knees to have a closer look.

Over my shoulder, I asked the created man, "Is it day outside?"

"Sun-off is two hours away."

I stood. "I can't see any light, so the channel must be blocked. Can you open the gate? If you can, then perhaps the water level will be sufficient."

The created man blinked; then, in a fluid motion, he crouched and sprang upwards to the lip of the channel. Without a backwards glance he walked from sight. Before I could draw a breath, however, he reappeared, his face hovering over me only long enough to say, "It would be best if you wait in the vessel," then vanishing again.

I tossed the light into the boat and scrambled over the bow just before I heard a laboured creak. Retrieving the light, I turned in time to see the gates open a few millimetres, then seize. Sand spilled from the opening, and thin, dry dust swirled around me. Another creak and the gap widened again; more debris fell, and dirty water trickled from the base of the gate and started puddling. A heartbeat later, something gave way and, from a height of half a metre, water sluiced out, shouldering the gates aside. A hot, moist breeze tickled my face, tasting of salt. In less than a minute the water had risen to the draft of the boat, and I felt the keel scrape across the bottom; then the boat lifted free and jostled so vigorously against the sides of the slip I had to grab hold of the gunwale to brace myself.

When the boat finally gentled, I leaned over the bow; the gates had opened to reveal a cave at whose end burned light as dazzling as a sun—though I suspect my mind exaggerated its brilliance after the perpetual gloom of the tunnels. Small swells radiated outward from the bow and I stared, rapt, as a distorted reflection of that light alternately broke into shards and re-knit across the undulating surface. For only a moment, it felt as if a shadow had lifted from my soul.

Night Sea Journey

With all the miscellany transferred from the cart, the skiff drafted lower, and when we used the oars to push it through the cave, the keel scraped bottom, then stuck. The created man vaulted from the boat and splashed into knee-deep water; placing both hands on the stern gunwale, he rocked the boat until it came free, then pushed the vessel forward, slogging through water.

As the bow of the skiff slipped into the brightness at the end of the cave, I felt suddenly exposed and vulnerable; it unnerved me. "Stop," I gasped, and he somehow managed to arrest the forward momentum of the boat—a remarkable feat of strength. "Might . . . might it not be best to wait until dark?"

"It is unlikely we will encounter anyone before we make the coast," the created man said, pulling himself effortlessly back into the skiff. The floor of the cave had angled away as he'd pushed, and he was soaked to the waist now, but the skiff moved freely. Water ran from his sandals and collected in the centre of the boat. "With the drought, much of the Holy Land became uninhabitable, save for a narrow strip along the Mediterranean coast. From time to time pilgrims still come inland, but they rarely go as far as the ruins of Jerusalem, and none, save the mad, have chanced the Dead Sea or the Wilderness of Judea for many years."

Having said that, he sat himself in the stern and placed his hand on the tiller; immediately, the boat lurched forward, propelling us into the naked light.

In the catacombs of the created man, I hadn't felt claustrophobic; but now, emerging from its perpetual darkness, a suffocating panic seized me. The sweltering air bore me down, drowning me, and I drew one fragile breath after another, staring at the mass of the firmament hanging precariously above. In that instant I saw the Spheres of the world in a way I had not before, the cumulative weight of the sins of my own Sphere and those above, so great, so inexorable, that I could do nothing but be dragged down along with every other soul to Hell.

In Heaven, when I had burst from the Waters Above, I had assumed the expanse I had seen, with its brilliant array of souls, was the last Sphere. But even then that hadn't felt quite right, and now I wondered if what I'd witnessed was just another Sphere, one whose limits were indiscernible to human eyes, which was contained in yet another Sphere, an infinite regress of Spheres within Spheres, like a calculus that approached the perfection of God; and below all this, our poor, corrupt world, a distorted reflection of what lay above. I could not say this was so; but in equal measure, I could not say it wasn't. And were this to be the way of things, I would not rejoice, I would despair at the pointlessness of seeking that unattainable perfection.

Here, in the furnace of the dying day, I helped the created man raise the mast, not because he required my strength, but because the long mast was an awkward thing, even for a creature with his strength. He unfurled the sheet, and it distended as if bellied by a phantom wind I couldn't feel. Despite the sail, the skiff moved no faster, gliding across the eerie calm of the water at the same speed, and I realized the sail was mere pretence. I slumped to my seat, heat rippling the air around me, distorting the worn, rounded hills surrounding the black mirror that was the Dead Sea. We floated higher and more lightly than I would have thought, and everywhere the shore was rimed with salt.

Even after sun-off, it is never wholly dark, though it had seemed so to me as a child. When the suns fade, into the rest of the firmament creeps a soft glow. Perhaps the firmament glows always, and it is only that we don't see it when it is washed out by the brighter light of the suns. Or perhaps the firmament absorbs the light of the suns and re-emits a diminished memory of it throughout the night. In either case, it is a different kind of light, for all colour is stripped from the world, and all we have are black and grey.

On my left, perhaps half a kilometre away, standing knee-deep in the water near the shore, was a man.

Or what I took to be a man. Unkempt, in tattered sackcloth with wild hair and a beard to his waist. Like a hermit. At such a distance and in the fading light, it would have been impossible to see these details. But our minds, I have learned, do not easily abide empty spaces, and are more likely to ascribe features to these blanks than to accept their absence. Thinking back, perhaps I conjured these things.

Leaning on the gunwale, I stared. If it was a man, he stood still as rock. When a thread of sweat trickled into my eye, I blinked—and he was gone. Or the illusion shattered. I turned to see if the created man had seen what I'd seen, but he sat at the tiller, directing us towards the middle of the lake, oblivious.

So I said nothing.

Floating through the night, there is little to do but wait.

I sat in the bow, facing the created man, watching him helm us across the Dead Sea. After a time, he nodded to me, then gestured at the seat next to him on the other side of the rudder post. I climbed cautiously over our gear (though I needn't have, since the skiff rode smoothly) and settled beside him, the transom at my back. He lifted his arm away from the tiller, then gestured that I should put mine there, and I did my best to bear us in the same direction.

As I steered, the created man laid a cup and small cloth on the bottom of the boat. In the cloth he placed dried fruit and cheese, and in the cup poured water, making a tincture of the *entheogens*. He brought both back to me, placing the cloth on my lap and handing me the cup, then sat next to me again, our shoulders touching.

With one hand on the tiller, I ate and drank.

As if in a dream, the Holy Lands slid by.

On the edge of the sea, against the white of the salt, I saw a shape that might have been the hermit I'd seen before. He raised a hand.

Something stirred in my chest. Only I was mistaken: it was not in my chest, but on my chest, where the pouch of skin and bone hung.

"*Father*," the created man whispered to me, "*I would be saved.*"

When I woke, shortly after sun-on, the created man's arm was around my shoulders, cradling me, while his other hand held mine steady on the tiller as we sailed in utter silence towards dawn.

Bethabara

Just past sun-on and the heat was already unbearable. We sat in the stern, shoulder to shoulder, and sweat ran into my eyes; it stung, and I blinked furiously.

"The heat does not overly affect this other," the created man said, and I could see it was true, for although my clothes clung to me wherever I perspired, his were dry as a bone—save where my arm touched his and my sweat gathered. "You must get out of the suns."

I nodded, and released the tiller to the created man.

Sometime during the night, he had rigged a simple tent with rope and a sheet of canvas facing the stern. Under this he'd put the rucksack containing food, a gourd of water, and my book. I crawled into this makeshift shelter, and although it provided little relief from the sweltering day, I was grateful, at least, to be out of the fulgent light.

I settled back into my cocoon and opened my book, running my finger along the edge of the title page. I read the hand-written words one more time: *To David, as my father gave me the Good Book, now I give you the One True Book.* "Why David?" I looked up at the created man. "Why not Thomas?"

"Two boys came to Rome with Kite, and were involved in the assassination of Cardinal Adolpho and two *Cent Suisses*. Two boys of the same description killed another *Garde* as they climbed the tower and preceded the Church into Heaven. The names of these boys were never a secret. It is only prudent to assume the Church is searching for a Thomas."

"How do you know they are searching?"

"This other used the *teleidelon* to watch as they found evidence the boys stayed in the house of Zeracheil for an extended period. And then were helped to flee. The Church knows you are involved, and that you are special to the Angels. But it doesn't understand why, and what the Church doesn't understand, it fears."

"I don't believe the Angels would tell them anything," I said, thinking on the fall of the burning Angel.

"Nor does this other. But the Angels are not men and do not understand the ways of man. It is possible they might have given away things without realizing what they were doing."

"Like my name."

"Among other things."

"But why David? If we are to be wary of discovery, should you not have given me a different name?"

"David is your real name, is it not?"

"Yes."

"When you are amongst people again, it will be more natural for you to use your own name, rather than to learn to answer to a third."

I saw the wisdom of this, but told the created man that if the Church was sufficiently interested in me, they might uncover my true name by connecting me to the Orphanage at *San Savio*, and from there to my father's inquisition.

"Ignatius kept no record of where he obtained his boys, and he is dead. Did you tell anyone else?"

"Just Ali."

"She is dead, too."

I know he did not mean to hurt me, but I flinched nevertheless; for a moment I was seized with a compulsion for the consoling oblivion of the *entheogens*. Ignoring this urge, I said, perhaps a bit too sharply, "When we are amongst people again, we will need more than just a new name for me."

The created man looked at me blankly, as I should have guessed he would.

"You can't call yourself *this other*. It's *I* or *me*."

"God did not see fit for this other to have a soul, and hence this other is different from men. It would be vanity to use the personal pronouns of men as if this other might be one of the blessed."

"You do have a soul," I pointed out.

"It is not this other's soul. This other only shelters it temporarily."

"Didn't God command that you should help me in whatever way you could?"

"Yes."

"Then I ask that you do this to help me, even if it be just for the time you harbour my son's soul. Can you?"

He contemplated this for a moment, then said, "Yes."

"From time to time, you should call me by name, as people do."

This he assented to doing.

"And we should give you a name, too, so that I might call you something." As I spoke, I realized that naming him was only a starting point. "We must have a story."

"A story?"

"A fiction. About us. Where we come from and where we are going."

"*The false witness will not go unpunished, whoever utters lies will be destroyed.*"

"You quote from Proverbs," I said. "Yet the Church tells us that not all the stories in *The Bible* are literally true, that it uses allegory and metaphor to convey truth. As do the fictions in *The One Book*, albeit to a greater extent. Both do so to get to larger truths."

"*I,*" he paused here, as if tasting the word, "am bound to the truth in all things."

"What if I concoct something that is essentially true, metaphorically true. Would this, and God's command to help me, suffice?"

"If I were not required to reiterate the falsehoods."

I took this as an assent of sorts. "Then I can think of only two reasonable possibilities. In the first, we would be a father and son, pilgrims travelling to the Holy Lands and then Rome. In the second, I'd be indentured to you, just as I was indentured to Ignatius; and a man travelling with an indentured boy is as likely to be a panderer as anything else. In this case, you would be seeking a better market for your wares, where the troops have been massing near Rome. I've no doubt the city has been overrun by camp followers, and so you would be just one more profiteer amongst a thousand."

"You do not think the first will work," the created man said, "or you would not have offered the second, which you know would be unacceptable to me."

I shrugged. "The second is better. People want to think the worst of others, and so distrust the stories of those claiming higher intentions, but rarely question those who freely admit their greed."

"Why do you think the first wouldn't work?"

"We look nothing alike. No one would believe we were father and son."

"When God created me, he created me so that I might mimic men. Although I can't change my general size and shape, I can change the external appearance of my flesh, and so seem to age as men do. Given time, I can grow fatter or slimmer, thicken or thin my hair and change its colour, make my skin dark or light, wrinkled or smooth. And I can manipulate the contours of my face, to a degree."

I should have been astonished by his revelation, but I was long past astonishment. "Then, I suppose we will be father and son," I said. "What name would you take?"

"What was the name of your father?"

"To make it easy for me to remember?"

"Yes."

I turned away, pretended to look through my book, so that the created man might not see my face. "His name was Thomas," I said, the familiar disorientation and nausea of my withdrawal blurring the words on the page.

Through the heat of day, I read.

The One Book was not comprised solely of fictions. Within were treatises on nature, philosophy, and theology, as well as histories of the Spheres and biographies of famous men and women. Alongside these, however, were what seemed to be fictions *masquerading* as histories and biographies, for they were of remarkable people I'd never heard of, or spoke of places that didn't exist. Like a vivid, imagined history of the Popes, at odds with what I had learned in several details, including a fallacious description of Rome not being immediately on the coast, as it is and has always been, but a march of four hours from the sea. And this wasn't the only discrepancy—there were numerous mentions of journeys whose duration seemed inordinately long, as if the distances had doubled or tripled (as anyone who'd travelled the same roads would know). By this time, I'd read enough works in *The One Book* to understand that stories sometimes used real places and events to blur the line between fiction and reality, lending verisimilitude to the story, and so drawing in the reader. But to get such glaring details wrong? I couldn't fathom why an author might choose to undermine his credibility in this way. . . .

The One Book itself was no help—in no way did it distinguish between works of fact and those of fiction. Perhaps this was purposeful. Perhaps the distinction between fact and fiction might itself be artificial. After all, histories and biographies were written by men and women who could not have had a perfect understanding about what they wrote. And no matter how hard they strove for the truth, the lenses of time and distance—and their innate prejudices and limited apprehension—would have invariably distorted the truth. Perhaps this is why *The One Book* didn't distinguish. Because there was no distinction. Or if there was, it was not a difference of kind, but a much smaller one of degree.

Later, I came to find this notion comforting.

But when it first occurred to me all those years ago, I found myself distressed at the idea that there was no clear dividing line between what was real and what was imagined. For my entire life I had believed that there was only one true book, the word of God, *The Bible*. But now I wasn't so certain, for not only did *The One Book* contain *The Bible*, which I knew cover to cover, but it also held variants of the Holy Book numbering in the thousands.

Peering over the edge of the boat, I was startled to see the shore lined with a dozen or more hermits, standing perfectly immobile in the swelter of the day. Only we were close enough to the shore now for the illusion to be shattered—their forms were too varied, too rough, and too different for them to be men.

"Beneath us the salt collects on the bottom of the sea," the created man said. "The weight of the air and the water forces this layer out towards the shore, where it emerges in columns."

Not columns, I thought. *Pillars. Pillars of salt.*

I was still in the shelter, *The One Book* in my lap, when the mouth of the River Jordan swallowed us. No rivers or streams drain the Dead Sea, only into it, for it lies at the lowest point in all the Sphere, though springs bubble up here and there along its shores.

Whatever mysterious force powered the skiff continued to push us forward, against the current and, as far as I could tell, we didn't slow as the landscape closed around us. For a time I watched the denuded banks slip past on either side. Whatever foliage they might have once borne had now burned off completely, the only evidence of any former growth the skeletal remains of trees. The river was about twenty metres wide, and we were close enough to the banks that had any living thing moved, I'd have seen or heard it. But there was nothing, not even the buzzing and clicking of insects one might have expected.

The Jordan meanders much of the way to the Sea of Galilee, and it was through these twists and turns the created man navigated our vessel, until we came to a place where the river bent back upon itself. On either side, greyed pickets had been driven into the shore. I scrambled out of the shelter, alarmed at their martial appearance, but realized almost immediately that they were not fortifications, but pilings that had once held back the river banks, now permanently above the reach of the water. Ahead, on our right, driven into the slope above the pilings, was a single pillar bearing a cross made of iron; behind it I could see the remains of a dilapidated structure that might have once been a Church. From its narthex descended, through a gap in the piles, a set of broken marble stairs, ending in a broad platform. Once, the bottom of the stairs and the platform must have been submerged. *Why*, I wondered, *would anyone want to walk into the river?*

"Stop," I said.

The created man lifted his hand from the tiller; whatever force impelled it fled, and the boat slowed, drifting to a stop.

"Take us to shore."

"I do not think it wise to—"

"If you don't take me over, I'll jump in and swim."

The created man frowned—a tiny knitting of his brows, a subtle gesture most people would have missed—but he steered the skiff as I had directed until it gently scraped bottom.

I vaulted over the side and splashed onto shore, then scrambled over loose rocks that had once been part of the river bed and, wheezing with the effort, hauled myself onto the platform. I was certain I knew this place. *Unless a man be born again of water and the Holy Ghost, he can not enter into the Kingdom of God.* Letting myself down, I stepped from stone to stone until I was knee-deep in the river, next to our boat. "Bring me my cane and a cup," I said. "And climb into the water."

He did as I asked, and I took the cane and withdrew the vial. He said nothing as I tipped two drops into my palm and lapped them up.

Though the created man watched me closely, he did nothing to stop me. The metallic taste of the unadulterated *entheogens* was so strong it stung the tip of my tongue.

We stood there, he and I, waiting.

For a moment I was afraid the Gift of Water would fail me, or that it might overwhelm me and I would suffer a seizure. My greatest fear, however, was that it would work—but that I might not be able to control what it would bring.

All at once, the oppressive heat lifted, and the unendurable glare of the suns, a glare that washed out everything, fell away. The world became so sharp and clear it hurt. I could see every pore on the created man's face, every strand of hair on his balding head; behind the translucent skin on his temple spun intricate gears of gold and silver. And, perhaps, behind that, moved something that might have been a soul. I took the cup from his hand, dipped it in the water of the Jordan and poured it over his head three times, saying on each, "I baptize you, Thomas, in the name of the Father, and of the Son, and of the Holy Spirit." With each, his features shifted, so now I stared into a face not unlike mine or my father's—or what my son's might have been.

I felt another presence. Without looking, I knew it to be the hermit of the wilderness, bedraggled and dressed in sackcloth, he who had haunted the shores of the Dead Sea. In his hand he held the unstoppered vial containing the Gift of Water. Putting a dirty thumb over the top, he tipped it up and back, leaving a drop on his thumb, which he pressed against the small leather pouch that hung from my neck. In a stern voice, but one not lacking compassion, he said, *I baptize you, Thomas, in the name of the Father, and of the Son, and of the Holy Spirit.*

Then light fled, and it felt as if a great hand closed over all of us, gathering us up from the river, comforting and suffocating at once, and I felt an indescribable ecstasy radiating out from my son's soul—and from the mind of the created man, now inextricably bound to him—an ecstasy known only to those who, born in original sin, experience that sin being washed away.

Out of the Wilderness

All at once the dark peeled back, as if God Himself had pulled a mantle away; above me hung the spine and curved ribs of a long dead beast, black against the grey firmament. For a moment I thought myself caged inside the remains of a leviathan, as trapped as Jonah had been. Then I realized the bones were not bones but staves of aged wood, and that I lay beneath the carcass of an overturned boat.

"Can you travel?"

My eyes had been open for several moments, and the created man, with his exceptional vision, must have seen this. I sat up, almost bumping my head on a length of rotted wood that might have once been a bow seat. There was a throb in my temples, and my stomach grumbled, but otherwise I felt far better than I had any right to. On my left lay my backpack and cane; on my right, outside the skeleton of the capsized boat, the created man had turned his back on me and now knelt, folding the tarp which he'd pulled from its ribs. We were on sand, which inclined gently towards the Sea of Galilee, where our skiff was beached. In the other direction, past the scattered remnants of innumerable sailing vessels, were the jagged ruins of a lightless city.

"You and I will travel at night and shelter during the day," he said over his shoulder, opening a rucksack beside him.

"*We*," I said, tasting the staleness in my mouth. "It's *we*." I crawled from between the staves, dragging my knapsack and cane. Pushing myself to my feet, I brushed the sand from my knees.

"*We* will travel at night and shelter during the day," he said, shoving the tarp into his bag, and then turned—dumbfounding me.

"Your . . . your face."

He ran his hand lightly across his nose and cheeks, and I noticed his wispy hair had thickened and was several shades lighter. A face I knew at once, and one I had loved: that of my father.

"Why do you stare?"

I ignored his question. "What happened at Bethabara?"

He had still been feeling the contours of his new face, but dropped his hand. "A mad hermit of wilderness came upon us and you had a seizure. I took you back to the boat and sailed on."

"Nothing more?"

"You poured water over my head."

"I baptized you."

"You said no words."

"No, I baptized you."

"Perhaps in your vision. But not in this world. And I am solely a creature of this world. If you baptized anyone, it was your son."

"When I did it," I said, thinking back, "I didn't think of you as separate—and I don't now. I believe you are one body and one soul, sanctified by the sacrament of baptism, and inseparable—unto death."

The created man said nothing; but his new face contorted in a way that his old wouldn't have, mirroring the contradictory feelings that only a human could have: the shock of attaining something long coveted but thought impossible, and the sudden, awful understanding of what it might mean.

We made for a large dock whose piles had not touched the sea for many years, and at its foot found a broad avenue which we followed into the city. Tiberias was long abandoned. Few buildings still had roofs; most, in fact, had been reduced to rubble, unrecognizable as homes, save for the regularity of the foundations and the stones themselves. Nowhere could I see any sign of habitation, save when we passed rocks ringing a fire pit. Between two of its stones, a small cross made of two twigs bound by dried palm leaves had been wedged; it fell apart at my touch.

Though strewn with debris, the avenue was passable, and only twice did we have to clamber over the remains of the upper stories of houses that had collapsed into the street. Within an hour, the city had fallen away on either side, and we crossed a stone bridge. Ahead lay a perfectly straight road, made of rectangular stones embedded in mortar. In this devastated land, there were no weeds with the strength to push the stones awry or to crack the mortar between, so the road remained whole and level, reminding me of nothing so much as the well-used road Ali and I had taken in our flight from Rome.

The created man and I walked the night, pausing only twice so that I might eat. We said little; as was his wont, he rarely started a conversation, and I didn't want to, for it disquieted me to hear his voice, so unlike my father's—coming from a man who now bore my father's face. *How*, I wondered, *has it come to this, that I walk the Holy Lands beside a man who is both my father and son?*

When we crested our last hill, my heart beat faster, not because of the daunting mass of the Mediterranean stretching out in all directions before us, but because of the semi-circular shadow on its margin, in which I could see the familiar, geometric shapes of buildings and, here and there, the gleam of shuttered light. Soon, I would be back amongst the living.

Abraham and Isaac

We camped in the hills above the port of Akko. The created man tried to persuade me to sleep for a few hours while we waited for the city to wake; he wished to arrive well after dawn, so the inhabitants would not think us the sort who skulked in darkness while honest citizens slumbered. As heavy as my eyes were, I couldn't sleep. Instead, I lay flat on the ground, head propped on my hands, watching as the city stirred. At first I had to squint to make out the small black dots of rowboats as they separated from their docks and sculled across the harbour, mooring next to their fishing smacks. Within minutes, the first smack had lifted canvas, weighed anchor, and tacked out to sea, leaving behind an anchored rowboat. By sun-on, all the vessels had put out, save for one larger ship that looked to be a trading cog.

Until now, smoke had threaded upwards from scant chimneys; but sun-on was like a signal, and hundreds of kitchen stoves must have been lit almost simultaneously, for the sky quickly filled with black filaments that twisted, one round the other, into rising braids. As cities go, Akko wasn't large, certainly nowhere near the size of *Los Angeles Nuevo* or Rome. I guessed it to be a home to perhaps ten thousand souls. But I soon revised my estimate downwards, for there was little evidence of activity in or about the outlying areas and buildings, especially those most landward—and nearest us—where virtually no strands of smoke were evident.

Shortly, I picked up the movement of people, not in the city thoroughfares as I'd expected; rather, in an ant-like stream to either side of the city where there were long, parallel lines of the oddest tents I'd ever seen, end-to-end in rows, and whose peaks appeared to be as high as the roofs of the nearest houses. Tiny specs of humanity moved slowly back and forth in the aisles between the tents, but never entered them. I watched, trying to puzzle out their meaning. . . .

I felt my father's hand on my shoulder, gently shaking me from sleep. "Time to go, David," he said.

I blinked in the mid-morning light, then rubbed my eyes, not quite sure where I was. Fuzzy-headed, I dragged myself to my feet, fumbled on my pack and picked up my cane, following my father back to the road.

Not my father, I chided myself. *The created man.*

The illusion was almost complete. His voice had changed and was now more akin to my father's. And, thinking back, I realized it had been changing all along, ever since Tiberias.

How did I not notice?

I suppose I didn't want to.

He wasn't my father. That was a lie. But a lie I wanted to fall into with all my heart. If a liar believes his own lie, and there is no one to say otherwise, does it become truth? I suspect this is the way for most men. But not for me. For I am cursed by a memory that will never let me forget—or forgive.

My recovery had been faster than could be expected. Although I no longer required the cane to walk, it had other uses. I'd also grown accustomed to its comforting weight beneath my hand. So I used it as we approached the city, effecting a small limp. Though I don't think we looked particularly dangerous, I reasoned a man of middle age accompanied by a lame boy would look even less so. Nevertheless, the denizens gave us a lukewarm welcome, and we were met with sideways glances, suspicious stares—and a palpable silence. Who could blame them? We'd emerged unscathed from the wilderness, when no man in living memory had, startling them from their circumscribed existence. But I didn't care about their cold shoulder. It was enough to be back amongst people.

We secured lodging at a run-down inn adjacent to the docks (the only inn we could find) and ate in the common room amongst a scattering of locals who glared over their tankards at us, if they bothered looking in our direction at all. When the proprietor served us a stew with a thin broth and a few small withered and tasteless vegetables, it came as no surprise—save for a handful of carefully tended gardens, we'd seen no attempt at farming as we'd entered the city, doubtless because the surrounding land did not lend itself to cultivation. Yet the broth had been seasoned strongly and contained substantial chunks of sea bream. Although I had at first relished the food the created man had provided, I'd grown tired of it, for it was always the same. So I revelled in the exotic spicing of the stew. And the created man surprised me by eating a modest portion of his, too, before pushing it away. My surprise was not that he could eat, but that he did, until I remembered we were among strangers, and wished to pass as father and son—as much as was possible.

I was still hungry; I took his bowl for myself.

I was so engrossed in my meal, I didn't notice the old man enter the room. But before I'd properly tucked into my second portion, he stumped up to our table. His clothes were tattered and unkempt; a cracked leather belt held up canvas pants several sizes too large for him, and a second belt, with a scabbard for a seaman's knife, crossed his narrow chest. Following on his heels was the proprietor of the inn, who I'd not seen leave his establishment. His face was ruddy, and he was out of breath, as if he'd just run a distance.

"G'day," the old salt said. "Might you be looking to book passage?"

The created man, whose back had been to the door, turned. "We might," he said. "But how is it you know our minds when we haven't yet spoken to anyone about it?"

"You're a stranger here, is what Abel—" the old man jerked his thumb at the proprietor "—told me. A stranger in a place where a stranger is uncommon. Coast road's not much passable these days, with the bandits and all. Them what comes and leaves this place does so by ship. I'd wager a bishop you'd be wanting passage, sooner or later." He put his hand on the back of a chair tentatively.

The created man nodded, and the old salt seated himself; the proprietor remained standing behind him, waiting, it seemed, for something.

"Sooner," the created man said.

"Beg pardon?"

"Sooner rather than later. Is that your cog moored in the harbour?"

"Aye. Abraham's me name. And that's my cog, *Isaac*, out of Messina." He smiled, revealing the remnants of caries-riddled teeth. "I'll grant me dad had a peculiar sense of humour in naming both ships and sons."

If the created man understood, he showed no sign. "Thomas," he said, then nodding at me, "David. Where might you be headed?"

"Good Christian names," the captain acknowledged. "To Sidon, then Messina after."

"When would you be weighing anchor?"

"Sun-on."

"Might you be persuaded to sail directly for Messina?"

"It'd cost." From his tone I knew he thought it unlikely we could muster the funds necessary to defray his loss at not securing his cargo in Sidon.

The created man withdrew two gold popes from an interior pocket in his robe, and placed them side-by-side on the table. The captain's eyes widened—as did every other pair of eyes around the room. What conversation there had been, stopped.

"Would this do?"

"Might," the captain said, tongue flicking over cracked lips. "Just might."

"One," the created man said, pushing a pope across the table. "Another when we arrive in Messina." He put the second piece back in his pocket.

"But, father," I exclaimed, "that's all we have!" I didn't want any of those listening to think otherwise.

The captain squinted at me, as if seeing me for the first time, then looked back at the created man. "'Course," the Captain said, his eyes never leaving the gold. "Goes without saying the two o' you'd have me cabin. Ain't much, but better'n nought." He smiled. "Do me good to bunk with the lads again."

"Then we have an agreement," the created man said.

"Aye." The captain leaned forward, his scabbard ticking against the edge of the table. In a soft voice only we four could hear, he said, "A piece of advice. You ought not flash gold like that. Bandits needs to live somewhere, and I'd reckon more than a few live here. Though they be generally reluctant to shit where they eat, they might forgo that nicety if the amount were great enough." The captain stroked his beard in thought. "Best you and young David sleep aboard, and I warrant your chances of waking will be much improved."

He means to protect his investment, I thought. *Or relieve us of our gold before someone else might.* I'd heard of such unscrupulous captains, whose passengers were thrown into the sea, and sank the more slowly for having been lightened beforehand. But I didn't see we had much choice.

Apparently, I wasn't the only one who had misgivings—the proprietor's face had grown progressively redder during the negotiations; he took a step forward, and seemed about to say something, but before he could, the captain turned his crooked smile on him. "Now I understand why you asked a commission rather than your usual fee, Abel. I 'spect this good man overpaid for 'is room, too."

"Ten percent of the arranged fee. As promised." The proprietor's words were almost a snarl.

"You know my word is good. I'll pay. But perhaps you're afeared you'll lose a rich goose ripe for the plucking. Or," he said, looking significantly around the room, "another commission, but from a person a mite less reputable."

This took the innkeeper aback, whether because he was incensed at the accusation, or because this was his plan, I couldn't have guessed. "I ain't giving back what he paid for the room."

"He wouldn't ask that," the captain said, turning to the created man. "Would you?"

"No."

"All parties satisfied?" The captain grinned as if he was amongst old friends, but his right hand now rested on the hilt of his seaman's knife.

The proprietor said nothing; by the look in his eyes, though, I judged that he still felt cheated.

"Then it's settled." Captain Abraham extended his hand. I was afraid the created man might not know what to do, but he reached across the table and shook it. Below their clasped hands, the gold pope had somehow disappeared.

Sun-off was a scant hour away. Leaning over the aft rail of *The Isaac*, I watched as, one by one, the fishing smacks returned to their moorings and bone-weary fisherman transferred their catch into row boats and rowed slowly back to shore. From there they filled carts on the docks and dragged them over to what I had taken to be tents, but now realized were long rows of fish flakes, all manner of sea creatures drying on them. Men pulled the carts along the rows, and others toiled, cutting down an old catch and hanging the new catch.

The Isaac reeked of fish, so much so that I feared I'd never get used to it. Particularly bad was the captain's cramped quarters, where the stink of a thousand voyages commingled with the smell of our captain—and likely the smell of all those captains that had preceded him.

I'd told the created man that I wanted some air before sun-off, not caring if he believed my lie, and left him in that suffocating space to do whatever created men do when they are alone.

"I've no design on your father's purse." Captain Abraham stood next to me; I hadn't heard him approach. "Nor do my men. There are eight lads aboard, nine if you count my boy, and none's a saint, but they're as honest and loyal as can be expected of such men, and they will do as I bid them."

"We made our choice," I said, wondering if it had been the right one.

"You 'ave." Captain Abraham said. "You'll not be needing that on board." He nodded at my cane, which I'd leaned against the rail next to me.

"I need it to walk."

"If you say so." He opened his fist and I saw the coin the created man had given him. The captain spun it on the rail, snatching it up as it began to wobble. He opened his hand in front of me. "Old coin," he said, letting me look. "Long dead pope. For all that, shines like it were freshly minted."

I said nothing.

"Know what else strikes me as odd?"

"No."

"A son more worldly than his father."

I started to concoct what I thought was a reasonable explanation, for the gold and the odd relationship between the created man and me, but he waved away my words.

"Stow it," he said. "'Spect it's believable. Might even be true. But there's no need to waste it on the likes of me." He pocketed the coin. "I think you know what I know, or guessed at it, so I'll speak frankly. Abel saw the coins just as much as I did. And he'll wonder, just as I did, if you might'n have come across such an old piece in the wilderness, and whether or not it might have friends."

"You think we found a treasure?"

"It makes no matter what I think. It's what them in Akko thinks. That's what has you worried. That's what has you standing at this rail. But you needn't worry. As brazen as the thought of a chest might make 'em, they'll do nought this evening."

"So we're safe?"

"Safe enough—least till we sail."

My thoughts had travelled along the same lines, but I'd been more concerned about the immediate threat; I'd decided to save those worries for the morrow. "You said they're road men. I suppose there are pirates, as well."

"Aye."

"Are they likely to have heard already?"

"Half of them what listened to us strike our bargain was sailors. If I was the inquisitive sort, I'd wonder if they had some sort of other work that kept them from working on the smacks."

"Then," I said, "wouldn't we be better served weighing anchor immediately?"

He shook his head and pointed to a spit of land. "Just now I seen a small skiff sail out that way, round the point. Lots of inlets on t'other side big enough for a sizable vessel, offering good cover for them what's inclined to hide. Best we wait a few hours after sun-off and our chances of slipping past will be much improved."

"Why are you telling me all this?"

"Can't outrun them. Not this old cog, sturdy as she is. Not with our hold almost full."

"You think our chances would be better if we were to dump the cargo."

"Two gold pope's was more than fair enough for our original arrangement. But if we throw away our profit on the cargo, I'm thinking another pope wouldn't be out of line. . . ."

"When I was in Rome, a gold pope would buy enough fish to fill four holds the size of yours."

"Rome is a long way off."

"I've no idea how much gold my father has."

"Gold is like rats and cockroaches," Captain Abraham said. "You see one, and you know there's likely others nearabouts."

"What if he doesn't wish to pay more?"

"We keep the cargo, and hand you over—if we're taken. But I expect your father will do as you suggest."

"I'll ask," I said, "but only if you agree to sail to Rome. The extra pope should cover that and your cargo, too."

He thought on it for a moment. "Crew won't be happy. But you give me the second pope now as a sign of good faith, and a promise that you're good for t'other, and I'll convince 'em."

I could conceive of no reason why the captain would bargain—especially now that he had us at his mercy—unless he was a man of his word, so I agreed.

Inside the cramped cabin, the created man was sitting on his berth, just as I had left him, but now the contents of his purse were spread out on a crate before him. The coins gleamed, looking, as Abraham had observed, as if they'd never been touched by a human hand. Amongst the brass deacons and silver bishops I counted eleven gold popes—a small fortune by anyone's estimation.

"Take one for the captain," the created man said, and I realized his hearing must be as acute as his other senses. "And three more to hide on yourself. If anything should happen to me or my purse, at least you'll have those."

To Rome

Quieter than I believed possible, the crew of *The Isaac* ran up the square-rigged sheets three hours after sun-off. They padded across the deck in bare feet, no more substantial than shadows, never uttering a word, yet working synchronously. I stood next to the captain, who observed all from his post at the tiller. Once, a dark-skinned boy, his chin without even the hint of the beard all the other men wore, glanced my way as he drifted past, appraising me in the way one boy might appraise another who has inexplicably fallen into his orbit, a look filled with both curiosity and wariness—the same look, no doubt, I returned. I remember thinking that had my life taken a different turn, this might have been me. I watched the boy climb the mast, his movements fluid and cat-like, executed with a surety born of repetition in this small, circumscribed world. For a moment I envied him the boundaries of his existence, the simplicity of life. But only for a moment. I knew that if I were to ask him, he'd likely have judged his life very differently, speaking instead of mind-numbing repetition and long stretches of isolation. And, just as I envied what I thought to be his life, he might have envied the less restricted life he thought to be mine. But we both likely would have been wrong, for it seems to me that the less one knows of another's life, the easier it is to envy.

The sail caught wind, and the vessel slipped away in the darkness.

On the open sea and well away from land, the crew threw open the hatches, and two descended into the hold. The three who remained on deck, including the boy, lowered leather buckets on ropes, then, after a moment, hauled them up, dried fish spilling over their sides.

The men staggered over to the rail with their buckets, and tipped their contents into the sea—except for the boy who hadn't the strength. Instead, he waddled backwards, dragging his bucket across the deck, then grunted as he wrestled it up to the rail, nearly losing his grip, but managing to dump it all the same. By the time the boy dropped his bucket into the hold for the second time, the others were already on their third load.

"Have you no winches or hoists?" I asked.

"Aye," he answered, "only they are fixed to the mast and boom when we're at anchor. Can't use 'em and sail at the same time. We might have rigged somewhat else, but, being as how time was an overriding consideration, this is the fastest way of lightening our load."

I watched as the boy dragged his bucket over to the rail. By the time he'd returned for his third, I stood next to the hatch. I helped him as best I could, a second pair of hands on the rope, hauling up a bucket of dried fish, together dragging it across the deck, together tipping it over the rail. We did this, load after load, until my palms and fingers were rubbed raw and bleeding, until my back ached so badly I thought I might never stand straight again. Despite my resolve, when I next wrapped my hands around the rope, and the weight of the bucket bit into my palms, I strangled a cry of pain, though not completely; what emerged was a pathetic whimper.

As soon as we let the bucket down onto the deck, the boy wrapped his fingers around my wrist and turned my hand up. My palm shone darkly with blood. The boy let go and elbowed me aside, then began dragging the bucket by himself. I took a step towards him, intending to help, but he looked up and said softly, and without rancour, "Best see to your hands, or you'll be of no use to anyone."

Though we were of the same age, his voice still held the sweet note of youth.

Returning to the cabin, I showed the created man my palms. He pulled a vial from an inner pocket of his cloak that contained a viscous, grey salve. He applied it my palms, then tore two strips of cloth from the sheets on his bed and wound them around my hands. Within moments, the burning diminished to a mild tingling. Shortly after, I made my way back on deck and watched as the crew continued to dump cargo for the better part of the night.

Of the four days and four nights at sea, there is little to say.

I sat on deck from sun-on to sun-off, reading and watching the sailors go about their work, only returning to the cabin to lunch with the created man. My hands mended faster than was possible, the abrasions healing over by the evening of our second day. But I kept the rags wrapped about them so as to not raise any eyebrows.

There is a rhythm to a life at sea, and it is marked in watches.

The sailors were divided into four groups of two, each of which took a watch of four hours, as measured by a large sandglass fixed to a stout wooden stand midships. The cabin boy was bound to no group, but rather stayed by the captain, his regular duty being to turn the glass every half hour, beginning at sun-on. Eight turns and the watch changed. When on, one of the men would climb to the crow's nest, while the other would busy himself with routine tasks: scrubbing the deck; mending and stowing sails and ropes; pumping bilge water. Those off watch would loll about on the quarter and main decks, smoking long curved pipes, carving blocks of wood or bone, a few idling away their time gambling; at noon, one man, hunched over a small stove, would cook the others a hot lunch. Sometimes they sang. Shanties and the like, rhythmic work songs, for which they seemed to improvise the lyrics, and to which those on watch laboured. What they may have lacked in technique and talent, they more than made up for in gusto. So would go the day until, not long after sun-off and a cold dinner, the captain settled into a hammock on the forecastle, the boy on worn blankets beneath him, while the men would find a place on the main deck, some sleeping on bare planks, while others would make nests for themselves in the coils of rope. I'd leave them in peace, then, and repair to the cabin where I'd find the created man preparing my supper.

During this time I first experienced unsettling feelings about the works contained in *The One Book*. I have already mentioned that many of the stories got significant details of the world wrong. But as I thought about these errors, I was struck by their consistency—even between fictions. Rome, when it was not on the sea, was always a four-hour march from the sea. Never three, or two, or ten. But always four. Like wheat from chaff, it seemed as if I could separate the works in *The One Book* into one of two groups: those set within this world and those set in another world—one similar to this, but in which these errors were not errors, but the way of things. A shadow world, consistent within itself, that lurked beneath this one.

But who was to say which was wheat and which was chaff?

Perhaps this other world was real, and ours merely a poor reflection of it. Like the way in which the Spheres were imperfect reflections of the Kingdom of God. And perhaps it wasn't just two worlds, but more. An infinity of worlds, nested one within the other. And a strange thought came to me: I wondered if in this other world there might be a boy named David, who sat on the deck of a trading cog, as I did, reading works set in yet a third world, one that was neither mine nor his.

As I was reflecting on this infinite regress, it also occurred to me that the works it contained might be no more constrained by time than by place, for I'd read remarkable tales clearly set far in the future, and wondered if this remarkable book might, in fact, contain works not yet written. I opened *The One Book* to its title page, and imagined the list of works that I would write. My heart skipped a beat when more than a dozen titles filled the page. I stared at the first title, *The Book of Thomas*, and with no small amount of trepidation, called up that book—and found myself staring at a blank page.

On our fifth night, I woke to hear one of the men humming a slow, mournful song; a moment later a second voice joined in the dirge. Soon it seemed as if every man hummed, the wordless threnody of a mournful giant, and bare feet stomped on the planks in counterpoint. And then the boy sang. His high voice cut through theirs like a knife, his words the sharp lament of a sailor for a family left behind, of a mother for sons lost at sea, and of those who passed into a watery grave without a soul to mourn them. In another life, Father Paul had declared that I had a voice that would make Angels weep. He'd been wrong, of course. Ignatius, for one, knew the limitations of my talent, and helped me understand them, so that I might compensate for them. Back then, before my voice changed, I was good. Perhaps great. Yet even with the benefit of Ignatius's tutelage, I knew I'd never have had a voice to match the one I heard that night.

I crept from my berth and pushed open the door. I found the sailors in a circle on the main-deck, the boy standing in their midst, his eyes closed, head tilted back, singing Heavenward. I listened, rapt, thinking of Ignatius, of what he might have done with such a voice—the untrained voice of a boy I knew for only a few days, and whose name

I'd never asked. Behind the boy, I saw what I thought was an island, then realized it was a spit of land, one protecting the harbour which we were entering. Running along its base was a chalky white stripe of rock, exposed when the sea had receded. We tacked around that solitary point, revealing a harbour, behind which a black silhouette rose, a dark headland upon which I could descry the regularity of crenellated walls, here and there lit by torches; behind the walls rose the unmistakeable dome of Saint Peter's. The boy sang on, oblivious, as they all did, and I wondered if this was a ritual they performed before dropping anchor; I knew by now that sailors had their share of such customs.

In the midst of the refrain, light slashed out from the lantern at the apex of the dome and hit the surface of the sea two hundred metres from the bow; a geyser of water and steam erupted with a great hissing like the sound of meat thrown in a heated frying pan, only magnified a thousand fold. Drops of boiling water pattered the deck around us.

The light winked out. Silence fell.

"What is it?" The boy looked at me, his voice filled with fear—of the light, and of me, too—as if somehow I'd conjured this—as perhaps I had. I'd read of such things in *The One Book*, in those stories set in that phantom universe. I turned to the forecastle, where the captain stood, mouth agape. "Douse the running lights," I screamed, "come about hard!"

But it was too late.

The blade of light snapped to life again, this time shearing off the top of the main mast; splinters of burning wood and rigging rained down, and a thousand tiny fires burnt on the deck. Glowing flecks settled on my head, face and arms, singeing me, and heat buffeted us from the canvas that burnt above. I didn't see the created man, just a blur in the periphery of my vision, felt him slam into me and lock his arms around my chest. I caught my last glimpse of *The Isaac*, the thread of light back now, gouts of fire erupting where it scythed over the deck, and those sailors not fortunate enough to have died already, dancing a mad jig, garbed in flame, and we plunged into the sea.

My Interrogation

A small fire of sticks and twigs crackled, ribbons of smoke rising past the remains of a ceiling, drifting out into the dark. Despite the fire and the mild night, I shivered in my sodden clothes. On the other side of the hut huddled the men of this picket, whispering amongst themselves the way men do when they find themselves uncomfortable, perhaps even shamed, by an order they are given to do harm to another, and don't see the sense of it. A thick-set thuggish fellow watched me while the others conversed. I guessed he'd been given this task since he was the least likely to have any compunction in following orders, sensible or not.

"You're irregulars."

The guard glared at me where I sat, my back against the embankment which formed one of the walls of the hut, but did not deign to answer.

The tallest man broke away from the group and walked over to me. Only it wasn't a man, but a broad-shouldered woman with a narrow face in which were set tired, grey eyes. She crouched in front of me. Like the others, she was dressed in a poor leather cuirass stamped on the front with the device of a beggar holding out his bowl and on the back with a lamb; but this was the only sign of uniformity, for they were all armed with a motley collection of weapons: long and short swords, mauls, picks, war hammers, daggers, and knives—one even clutched a pitchfork. The rest of their kit was similarly mismatched and, for the most part, appeared hard used, as if scavenged from the field of battle rather than issued from a quartermaster's stores.

She regarded me without malice—but equally without compassion.

"Yes, we're irregulars. Stand up."

I did.

"No need to be scared." She spoke in a voice which I'm sure she meant to sound friendly, though I doubted she'd much practise in that.

"I'm not scared," I said, giving her the answer she'd expect.

Her slap, when it came, shocked me, more for its suddenness than for its sharp sting—of which it had ample measure, too. I tasted blood in my mouth.

"I had a son once," she said. "He died when he was thirteen, about your age, I reckon. Mostly, he was a good boy. Honest, well-behaved. Loved his mother, he did. But boys will be boys, and I reluctantly learned how hard I might hit him, without knocking him senseless, so that he might experience his punishment as he ought, and so that he might have a chance to offer his repentance. For his own good, you see." She cuffed me on the side of the head again, staggering me back into the earthen wall, momentarily blinding me and setting off a ringing in my ear that made it hard to hear her next words. "But you're not my son, and I've no misgivings in a less gentle handling of the Popish bastards that killed him."

I'd thought them irregulars on the side of Rome, volunteers for the war on Heaven; only her words held no love of the Church.

She cupped my chin in her hand. "You'll answer my questions straightaway and truthfully, won't you?"

She tilted my head up and down, nodding it for me—though I would have, had she not.

"Good lad," she said, releasing my chin and clasping my shoulder, giving me a friendly shake. "Now, then, you and the man you were with, be you with the Angels or be you with the Church?"

"Neither," I answered honestly.

"Then," she said, "you are an enemy to both."

"I'm not sure the Holy See thinks enough of me to count me as an enemy."

I fully expected her to hit me again. But instead her lips crooked up in a smile. "I warrant these days the Church doesn't think of much other than its own self."

"Why'd your ship run the blockade?"

A blockade? I was taken aback. "Is the Vatican under siege?"

She stared at me, as if weighing the sincerity of my reaction. Then slapped me so hard I dropped to my knees, my other cheek aflame.

"Let *me*, lieutenant," my guard hissed. "I'll give 'im more than a love tap, I will!"

The relish with which he said this raised goosebumps on my arms.

"Shut up, Abel," the lieutenant said casually. She helped me back to my feet, brushing the dirt from the knees of my pants. "You neglected to answer. Shall we try again?"

"I . . . I don't know. We, I mean my father and I, we booked passage for Rome. We didn't know there was a blockade." I hadn't seen anything that looked like a blockade when I'd scanned the area using the *teleidelon* a fortnight earlier. "Nor did Abraham or he'd've never agreed to sail to Rome."

"Abraham?"

"The captain of *The Isaac*, sailing out of Messina."

"There's the problem, boy. That wasn't no passenger ship. Abel told me it was a trading cog. The sort that might be used to spirit supplies into the city."

"The hold was empty."

"*Liar!*" my guard hissed.

The lieutenant shot Abel a sharp look, and his mouth snapped shut. "A trading cog, far off its route, with empty holds, its only cargo two passengers. And in a place where no man is to go save upon pain of death." She stroked her chin, a gesture of mock contemplation.

"My father hired the ship."

"That man on the beach, he was your father, then?"

"Yes."

"He hired a trading cog to sail you from Messina to Rome?"

"No. He hired *The Isaac* in Akko. We were on a pilgrimage to the Holy Lands, and from there to Rome."

"Then why did your father flee?"

"He didn't."

"We ordered him to stop."

"There were others who were still alive, clinging to flotsam. He went back to help them." I had no idea if this was true or not. I was as confused as they were, for the created man had no sooner dumped me on the stony beach then he'd turned and calmly walked back into the sea, ignoring the shouts of the ragtag soldiers who'd emerged from the scrub.

"You don't seem overly distraught," she said. "Not for a boy that watched his own father drown himself."

"He's a strong swimmer."

"I posted men up and down the beach, a kilometre apart, and none have seen him come back, or we'd have had word." She spat into the fire, and it sizzled, a tiny echo of the sound the light had made when it struck the water. "He's drowned, all right."

I thought of my first father, of how I'd watched him die at the hands of the Black Friars. "No." I braced for another slap, but none came.

"Believe what you will. It won't make him any less drowned." I had an irrational compulsion to tell the lieutenant about the created man, about how I knew he wasn't dead, how he could slip past those sentries with ease. But that would certainly earn me another slap. She shrugged. "What you believe is your own business. What troubles me, though, is why an innocent man might run."

"He didn't run."

She raised her hand as if she was going to hit me again, but didn't. "I suppose you're right, in that he didn't run into the water. But you don't have to run to flee."

"The fire that burnt our vessel, it came from the walls of the Vatican. Why would the Vatican burn a ship running it supplies?"

"It's a conundrum, all right." But by the way she said it, she didn't sound like she really cared much one way or the other.

"We'd had running lights. Would a ship trying to slip past a blockade at night have lit itself?"

This, at least, seem to catch her attention. She turned to Abel. "Is it true?"

Instead of answering, the thick-set man glared at me.

"Abel, was it lit or not?"

"No," he lied. "It were all dark, like a smuggler would be."

"Then how did you see it?"

"What?" Abel seemed confused for a moment. "I tole you, it were on fire! Thas how I saw it!"

"When you reported, you said you saw the cog *before* the Fiery Sword cleaved it. How could you see a cog that far out without running lights?"

Abel stared at me with hate in his eyes, as if I'd made him lie. I recognized that look, for I'd already seen it many times, most often on the face of clergymen who visit the punishment for their own sins on others.

"Abel?" The lieutenant raised her hand, looking this time like she was about to strike him.

"P'haps," he said, and I could tell the word tasted vinegary in his mouth. "P'haps I were mistaken. Now that I'm thinkin' on it, I'm thinkin' it just might'a been lit."

The lieutenant turned her attention back to me. "As you can see, I've had more than my fair share of sorting truth from lies. There are times I wish I was still a soldier, like Abel here. It's kill or be killed, and there's never a need to sort out if the other man is sincere." She sighed. "Still, there're details in your story that don't make sense."

Despite the violence she'd visited upon me, the lieutenant seemed a woman willing to listen and think things through before making a decision (a quality, I learned later, rare in an officer of the militia). But she also seemed the sort who, once she'd made up her mind, there'd be no swaying—except to a less favourable disposition. "We're for the Angels," I declared.

"I'd like to believe you. But the Spheres have been turned upside down and inside out, and it's difficult for a woman to know what to believe in these days."

"God," I said. "Believe in God."

She barked out a laugh at that. "True enough. But it isn't God I doubt, just those that claim to speak for Him. Do you claim to speak for Him, boy?"

"No," I answered, sensing we shared a frustration at those, both well-intentioned and not, who'd been manipulating us in the name of God. "I can only tell you what the Angels told me."

The lieutenant looked startled. The other men, who'd arrayed themselves around the room, and been following my interrogation with more or less interest, now all stared at me, intent.

Abel stepped forward. "He's lyin'. Two boys, we were looking for. Not one and a man."

"What's your name, boy?" she asked me softly.

"David."

"See!" Abel seemed almost gleeful.

The other irregulars seemed relieved; but it didn't seem to assuage my interrogator. "Might you go by other names?"

In that moment I knew the created man's dire prediction had come true, and this officer had been told to keep watch for a pair of boys travelling from the Holy Lands. But this woman and her men were not for Rome. On a threadbare hope that perhaps they might have been ordered to watch for us on behalf of the Angels, I said, "Thomas. My real name is Thomas."

The others had fallen silent again; the lieutenant chewed her lower lip, taking the measure of me—and my lie.

None of us heard him approach; what drew our attention was the piteous moan.

In the splintered doorway stood the created man. He was soaked. In his arms he cradled the limp body of the cabin boy, whose clothes had been reduced to a few charred rags, and whose left side, from mid-calf to the tip of his ear, was burnt black beyond recognition.

A Prayer for
Nameless Boys

The created man put the boy in a corner, where he lay in a foetal position, so immersed in his pain that I'm sure he did not know we were there. His eyes never opened once, and he drew ragged breaths for perhaps an hour. A few minutes after sun-on, he expired.

Even though I'd never learned his name, I wept, and the created man comforted me.

The lieutenant had dropped any pretence of interrogation, and now treated me solicitously. At her insistence, the irregulars kept their distance and effected a respectful silence. I suspected that the lieutenant's newfound concern arose because, along with being told to keep watch for us, she'd been given orders to see that no harm came to us.

The picket had no shovels amongst them, so the lieutenant ordered her men to scratch a shallow grave into the rocky soil using their weapons. I wanted to help, only my hands shook and my knees felt weak. I'd forgotten, but my body hadn't: it was well past the time at which I'd normally have taken the Gift of Water. Only there was no way to remedy my condition, for my cane now lay at the bottom of the Mediterranean with the remains of *The Isaac* and her crew.

"Are you unwell?" the lieutenant asked.

"I'll be fine," I said, almost believing it.

When they'd finished digging, they laid the boy in this poor hole, then carried larger stones from the beach, making a cairn, and fashioning a makeshift cross from two timbers we pulled from the roof. The lieutenant mouthed a silent prayer, and one of the irregulars, who claimed to have once served as a deacon, said a few words of consolation.

Shortly, a runner she'd sent during the night returned, and with him half a dozen men, dressed in the same strange variety of gear as our captors, only the leathers these men wore were well-oiled and their weapons clean and meticulously honed. Their bearing, too, was hardened and sure, that of seasoned troops. One, a sergeant named Jotham, commanded our escort; beneath his cuirass, he wore the remains of the uniform of the *Cent Suisse*, from which all emblems of both Rome and the Papacy had been meticulous removed. Though he revealed no more humanity than Kite was wont to do, I nevertheless took some comfort in his company.

Before we departed, the created man and Jotham spoke privately, and a man of our escort was dispatched—to where, I couldn't have said. As we gathered outside the hut to take our leave, the lieutenant pulled me aside. "I believed you, but you lied. He's not your father, is he?"

"No," I answered. "Nor am I your son."

"You are not," she agreed. "He couldn't lie so well. Perhaps had he been able, he might not have died trying to hide a few scraps of food from the Church's tithes." I could see the pain in her eyes, though I knew she was long past shedding tears. "I know little and understand less of all that is happening, but if what you do might save another woman's son, I wish you God's speed." Then she essayed a curt nod, turned on her heel.

Behind the hut, a narrow trail threaded its way through a sparse forest; we followed this inland until we came to a small clearing, where we halted. Lucky we did, for my body was now slicked with perspiration, and intermittent tremors shook my arms and legs like a palsy.

I let myself down.

A moment later, the man who'd been dispatched caught up to us. Under his arm he had a long bundle wrapped in cloth, which he laid on the ground and unwrapped—and I realized it wasn't a cloth, but the created man's cape. Within, dry and whole, lay *The One Book* and my cane.

On hands and knees I scrambled over to the cane and snatched it up, no longer caring who might see; I tried to twist off its head, but hadn't the strength. The effort so dizzied me, I slumped to the ground.

Somehow, I found myself in the created man's arms.

"Your canteen and a cup," the created man said to Jotham.

In a few heartbeats, both appeared. Making no attempt to hide what he was doing, the created man unscrewed the head of the cane and prepared the tincture, then raised it to my lips. I drank. Immediately, the alleviating effect of the drug flowed through my veins, and a warm haze enveloped me.

I looked up into the face of the created man. "You left me on the beach," I mumbled, "to retrieve the book and cane from the sea." And then I think I said something else, though I might have just imagined I spoke aloud: "Was finding the boy a coincidence?"

An uncharitable question, and if he heard it at all, he didn't answer. If I'd had my wits about me, I'd have known he wouldn't answer, not in front of our escort, for his silence would have kept his secret—and made my words seem even more like the raving of a drugged mind. The next thing I remember is being lifted and cradled like a child, and watching the scrawny forest drift past as if behind a gauze.

I never asked the created man what excuses he made to Jotham, about the Gift of Water he gave me or about my accusation. It's quite possible he made none—unlike a man, he felt no compulsion to explain his behaviour. And, if my estimation of the escort was correct, they had all seen worse and said naught. How else would they have survived this long?

I drifted in and out of sleep, and had several dreams, most of which are lost to me now. But I remember one. In it, I stood between two open graves, one for the lieutenant's son, and one for the boy from *The Isaac*. I wanted to offer a prayer I'd heard at *San Savio*, when we'd buried a fellow student who'd succumbed to a fever. It seemed fitting, for it beseeched God for the departed, that He would not deliver this soul, *"into the hands of the enemy, nor forget it unto the end, but wouldst command it to be received by the Holy Angels, and conducted to Paradise, its true country; that as in Thee it hath hoped and believed, it may not suffer the pains of hell, but may take possession of eternal joys."* But my tongue stumbled on its first line, for the prayer began by naming the departed, and I, a boy with two names, had no names to give.

Sword of the Angel

Rome is girded by hills, and it was up the back of one that Jotham led us. Near the summit, the trail snaked between emplacements for two large artillery pieces, which protected the city behind. Trenches had been dug on each side, and in these were powder kegs and balls of iron shot stacked in pyramids. No *Garde* manned the cannon. Around the emplacements and as far as the crest of the hill, the brush had been cleared, and I realized this had been done as a firebreak, for lapping over the summit were the splintered and blackened remnants of the pines that had once bearded the crown, a few still standing, leaning like monstrous, ebony pickets. Into this charred wasteland we walked, our feet and the tip of my cane stirring the carpet of ash, a fine layer of grey powder rising and clinging to us.

We came to a low stone wall near the summit over which we had to vault. I did so with my cane in one hand, and when I landed I caught my foot on something that snapped like dried kindling, and I went down. The created man was there almost as soon as I had fallen, lifting me solicitously. As we brushed the ash from my clothing, I glanced back to see what I'd caught my foot on—and felt sickened. The attenuated black leg of a burnt corpse. But that wasn't the worst. There were bodies tangled within bodies. Six in all. A family—or what I supposed was a family. Two of the largest corpses covered four smaller ones, as if trying to shelter them. Even so, the firestorm had burnt all beyond recognition, their jaws agape in silent screams, frozen forever in their agony. I wondered that no one had given them a proper Christian burial.

"We best keep moving," Jotham said.

Only I didn't, for as I turned, I stopped in my tracks. From this vantage, the siege of the Vatican unfolded before me like a surreal map.

The Holy City sat on a low prominence jutting above the *Tyrrhenian Sea*, and was encircled by a massive wall, wide enough at its top, I guessed, that half a dozen *Garde* might walk abreast. At its heart, haughty and unassailable, stood Saint Peter's Basilica, its immense dome dominating the cityscape. The Vatican was a city within a city, and outside its walls lay the other Rome, where those who were not God's anointed lived and worked and died. Wide swaths had been blackened by fire. Near the walls of the beleaguered Vatican, the city had been laid waste. So thorough was the devastation, it was impossible to relate the piles of smouldering debris and rubble to the streets through which I'd once walked. A kilometre from the Basilica, and outside the ancient walls of the Holy See, the *Castel Sant'Angelo,* once the Pope's fortress, had been cut off and overrun by the besiegers, and now the cantonment of *The Meek* lay sprawled behind it, stretching as far back as the crook of the Tiber River. Despite my antipathy towards the Church, and those who claimed to speak for God, it nevertheless unnerved me to witness the assault on the Vatican first hand. It felt like an unforgivable affront, a slap to the face of God.

"The Church isn't God," Sergeant Jotham said, no doubt guessing the source of my disquiet, "no matter how much the Pope would like you to believe so. If you need proof, look no further than those poor souls back there. It wasn't God who burned them, it was the Church. And if we don't move on, the Papists will be happy to oblige us, too."

I nodded, trying to take the sergeant's point to heart; but I couldn't, not fully anyway. Through years of lessons and exhortations, through countless studies and sermons, the Church had seen to that.

We walked in silence for a time.

At last I said to Jotham, "Our ship was burned by a blade of light. One that came from the lantern at the top of the Basilica's dome. The lieutenant called it the *Fiery Sword*."

"So it is called."

I recalled the passage from Genesis, of God's expulsion of Adam: *He banished the man, and in front of the garden of Eden he posted the great winged creatures and the fiery flashing sword, to guard the way to the tree of life.* I realized the weapon had been named this not out of reverence, but out of hatred for those who wielded the sword and would bar them from the earthly garden that was the Vatican.

"The Fiery Sword cuts a straight line from where it's mounted," Jotham said, pointing at Saint Peter's dome. "No matter how distant, what they see, they may burn."

It occurred to me the obverse was also true: those who could see the peak of the dome could be burnt. I suppose that's what made Jotham nervous.

"When we first saw the light," he continued, "no one knew what it was. But coming from the Basilica as it did, it seemed like it was the light of Heaven, God Himself extending his welcome. Some even took their children towards it, hoping to have them touched by the finger of God." Jotham stared for a moment into his memory. "Mothers held up their infants," he said, "like offerings."

For a time I held my peace, concentrating on keeping pace with Jotham's long strides.

The trail switched back down the side of the hill, and soon stone houses rose up around us and the dome was lost to sight. Our footsteps echoed up and down empty streets. We passed into a section of the city that had been scoured by fire; here and there blackened corpses littered the street, and in a few places posts had been driven into the ground, the dead stacked like cords of firewood between. If there were people about, they'd hid themselves well, giving no sign as we passed.

"*The Meek*'s encampment," I said, hurrying to catch up to Jotham. "It lays in the shadow of the *Castel Sant'Angelo*, hidden from the Angel's Sword."

"Yes."

"And that's where we're headed."

"Yes."

"The city seems abandoned."

"Most fled. Nowhere is safe."

"But the camp could still be struck by canon shot?"

"You needn't worry," he said, misunderstanding the purpose of my question. "Sometimes the Papists loft a shot or two into the camp to rattle us. But they're shooting blind. Nor do they have an inexhaustible supply of powder and shot. They're likely conserving what they have until it might be used to more effect."

I hadn't asked the question because I was worried for myself; I'd asked because of those six poor souls up on the ridge. They'd reminded me that *The Meek* wasn't an army so much as it was a throng of desperate people. Husbands and wives, fathers and mothers, daughters and sons. I was afraid for my son. I'd been mad to bring him here. He could have been killed at any time on our descent from the hill; and he would be no safer in the camp. I brushed my hand over the pouch at my neck to assure myself it was still there; and then I looked over at the created man. He strode forward, his gait measured, his expression imperturbable, showing no sign of the weariness that dogged everyone else. Nowhere could I descry a hint of my son. Had he fled? Or might I no longer be able to conjure him? My fingers twitched on my cane.

We passed an alley, and out of the corner of my eye I thought I saw movement. I peered down the narrow lane, and realized there was, indeed, a child standing there, watching me. He was covered in soot, and was little more than a shadow against a backdrop of the identical colour. Only his eyes stood out, a startling blue, baby-blue as it is called, like my mother's had been. Like mine were. Then he was gone, vanished back down the hole from which he'd crawled.

If anyone had noticed, they'd made no sign.

We trudged through the charnel house that was Rome. I watched the backs of Sergeant Jotham and the other gaunt and grim-faced men of our escort. Unlike me, they were not taking ones they loved towards danger. They were returning to those they loved. Hatred of the Church and the love of their own carried them forward. But when I had looked at the encampment from above—how insignificant it appeared next to the expanse of the Vatican and the weight of its ancient walls, how *The Meek* cowered behind the *Castel Sant'Angelo*—it seemed to me that no matter the depth of their anger, nor the extremes to which their love for their families would drive them, they had scant chance of success.

Beloved of the Angels

After crossing the Tiber at the *Ponte Cavour*, we halted on the edge of the chaos that was the army of *The Meek*. Before us was a sea of tents (and other structures that could only charitably go by that name) spanning the gamut from rickety lean-tos to elaborate multi-peaked marquees. Most were old and discoloured, many tattered and scorched, like they'd been part of one campaign or another since the beginning of time. The wind gusted, and with it came the choking stench of nearby latrines that poisoned the Tiber. Here and there a few scrawny animals bleated and lowed in hastily assembled pens, and a thousand communal cooking fires sent threads of smoke heavenward. Between the disorderly rows of tents were makeshift thoroughfares, where planks had been laid down haphazardly; garishly painted camp followers strolled on their margins trying to capture the attention of the would-be soldiers who idled in and around the tents: haggard boys and men—and even a few women—clad in a confounding variety of armour, bearing a miscellany of weapons. There seemed no order, no sense to the cantonment, certainly none of the regularity one would have expected of an army. But this came as no surprise. This was an army of the poor and dispossessed, which acknowledged no rank, no authority, other than the weight of its own momentum—a juggernaut of desperate men, of hungry women and children, that had swept up through two Assumptions, then over the Papal palace, only to impale itself on the outworks of the Vatican walls—where it now slowly bled to death.

Without a hint of irony in his voice, Jotham told me that they called it Purgatorium.

Those who noticed us crossing the bridge stared, their eyes filled with equal measures of hunger and desperation—the same hollow look I'd been met with when, so long ago, we'd first followed Kite into the camp of *The Meek*. Two armed irregulars had been lounging to either side of the bridge; when we stepped off, they rose. Jotham strode over to them and exchanged a few words I couldn't hear. One of the sentries turned; sprinting away, he was quickly swallowed by the camp. Jotham rejoined us.

"Will we be staying here for a few minutes?" I asked.

"The General asked me to bring you to him direct, only he could be in half a dozen different places right now—or in none of them. We'll wait here until we have word on his whereabouts."

To our right, at the foot of the bridge, was a kind of market, where items had been laid out upon threadbare blankets: Bibles and rusty daggers and foodstuffs—mostly slivers of mouldy bread and cheese, and slim rinds of dried meats. Nearest us, a crone perched on a crudely constructed wooden bench that seemed to teeter beneath her; one of her eyes was brown, the other an undifferentiated milky white orb. Bibles of various sizes and different bindings were spread out at her feet. I'd never seen such a variety. Curious, I asked Jotham if I might look at her wares.

"Please yourself. Just stay close, where I can see you."

I walked over to her, the created man on my heels. "Good day," I said.

She didn't respond, her good eye moving from me to the created man and back.

I nodded towards the Bibles. "May I?"

She gave a curt nod.

Putting my cane under my arm, I picked up a Bible and opened it—and almost dropped it in surprise. Where I'd expected to see the words, *In the beginning God created Heaven and the Spheres*, I read this: *As Gregor Samsa awoke one morning. . . .* Taken aback, I put the book down and picked up another, and another after that. None had the words I'd expected, none was a Bible.

"Where did you get these?"

"I traded for them fair and square," she said. "And anyone what says different is a liar."

"I meant no disrespect." I hastily replaced the third book.

She rolled forward off her bench and snatched up all three volumes, waving them in my face. "You took 'em, they's yours." Her good eye was fixed on me expectantly.

"I've no coin to pay," I said, hoping to blunt the anger of what I thought was an imbalanced mind. "I've nothing to trade."

"A blessing," she hissed. "That's the price."

A blessing? I took a small step back, waving away the books.

"Tryin' to cheat an ol' woman?" A note of hysteria had crept into her voice. "A blessing is the price, and a blessing it will be!" She tottered forward, thrusting the books at me.

People were openly gawking at this exchange; some began edging closer. Not wanting to draw more attention, I took the books and, though I had no idea why she might want my blessing, I mumbled one.

The old woman lowered her head; I was taken aback to see tears well in her eyes. "Praise God," she whispered, as she prostrated herself before me, "and he who is Beloved of the Angels."

The crowd pressed in, converging on our exchange, and in the periphery of my vision I saw the men of our escort come alert. At my elbow was a middle-aged woman in homemade armour; around her neck a tattered tin cross was suspended on a leather thong. "And me," she said, "Bless me." She touched my shoulder lightly, tentatively.

Immediately, the created man's hand shot out and clamped on the woman's wrist, twisting it back. I heard the sickening snap of bone; the woman let out a strangled shriek, and her knees buckled. She went slack, the created man holding her entire weight by her broken wrist. He loosed his grip, and the woman crumpled to the ground.

For a moment there was silence. Then, from somewhere in the back, a man shouted, *Bless her!*

The faces of most of those I could see registered the same confusion I felt; yet I heard a few cries of agreement. People jostled one another, trying for a better view.

I wanted to tell them I didn't understand. To beg their forgiveness for the created man's unprovoked reaction. But before I could do so, the created man snatched me up like a sack of grain, lifting me off my feet and bulling past half a dozen people, scattering them like bowled pins. In a heartbeat, he deposited me in the midst of the escort.

"Stay behind us," Jotham said, drawing his sword.

From the back of the crowd someone shouted, "Give 'er your blessing!" To my ears it seemed as much entreaty as a threat.

Jotham levelled his sword, but those nearest him didn't step back. A few even edged forward.

The men of the escort looked uncertain; I knew they were all wondering the same thing: whether or not they had it in them to drive a sword into the bellies of those who, until this moment, they'd been fighting to save.

Jotham must have sensed their ambivalence, too, for he shouted an unequivocal order: "Any comes a step closer, stick 'em!"

Most of his men drew their swords. Not all, though.

In front of Jotham, a rough-cut man in rusty armour shuffled forward, and though he had a sword and knife stuck in his belt, he drew neither. "Stick me," he said, "if you're gonna stick anyone."

Jotham raised the tip of his sword until it hung just in front of the grimy flesh on the man's bare neck.

Bless her! someone shouted from the back of the crowd; and, right after, another voice, closer, barked, *Stick him!*

My heart sank that the latter comment had garnered more murmurs of approval than the former. Moving deliberately, the man wrapped his fingers around Jotham's sword; blood oozed from between his fingers. "Stick me," he said again, smiling, exposing blackened gums and a few lonely teeth.

From where I stood, I could see the woman laying on the ground, rocking back and forth in her agony, seemingly forgotten, and next to her the three books that had been forced on me, and which I'd dropped when the created man had grabbed me up. The old crone was on her hands and knees, trying to force her way through the crowd to retrieve her books. *They'll both be trampled*, I thought. And for what? For the chance of my blessing? And the foolish pride of two men both believing they were doing right. How could God let such an absurd scene play out?

"No!"

My shout, when it came, was of such volume and intensity that it surprised even me. And those in the crowd, too, if what I could see on their faces was any measure. Into this vacuum, and in as calm a voice as I could muster, I said, "Put me down."

The created man turned to me; in his eyes I saw confusion.

"They mean me no harm," I said.

"Father?" His voice was filled with a small boy's remorsefulness, uncertain what he'd done wrong.

Ignoring the astonished stares of those around us, I said again, "Put me down."

He did. I handed him my cane. Then I shouldered my way through the ranks of the escort, and stepped between Jotham and the man who gripped his blade. I pried his hand from the sword, and I directed Jotham's blade down until its tip scraped the ground. Jotham didn't resist. Leastwise, not much.

When I stepped into the crowd, those nearest shuffled aside to make way. Kneeling next to the woman, I rolled her onto her back. She was conscious, but her skin was clammy and her pupils dilated, her breath coming in pained gasps; she stared, but was unseeing. I bid the created man bring me my cane. When he did, I unscrewed the top, withdrew the vial, and tipped two drops onto her lips. Her eyes focused on mine. "Beloved of the Angels," she murmured. Then her eyes fluttered shut and her breathing assumed a more peaceful regularity.

My hands shook when I capped the vial and returned it to the cane. When I'd administered the drops to the woman, a small amount had trickled onto the tip of my index finger; I stuck the finger in my mouth, tasting the metallic tang of the Water. Nowhere near the amount I usually took, but enough that within a few heartbeats the world grew brighter, my tremors subsided, and the panic I'd been fighting fell away. I felt calmer. More in control. I looked at the circle of faces surrounding me. "Her wrist needs mending. Is there a surgeon nearby?"

"There's a field hospital in the centre of the camp." Jotham stood next to me; beside him was the man whose throat he would have cut. "We'll take her there."

I directed the created man to lift her gently. The men of the escort took up a protective formation. I caught Jotham's eye and shook my head and, much to my surprise, he ordered his men to stand down. In single file, then, Jotham led us, the created man following him and bearing the wounded woman. The crowd parted to let us through.

On my right was the man who'd grasped Jotham's sword, and whose hand was now bound with a dirty rag. I paused to urge him come with us to the hospital, but he declined, asking, as the old woman had, that I bless him. So I muttered a few words to satisfy him, and hastened to catch up. Walking between the ranks of people, the same whispered supplication, *Bless me Bless me Bless me*, swirled around, and I was grateful that I was several paces behind the created man, where he couldn't see the hands that reached out to touch me as I passed.

An Old Friend

"I shouldn't have picked up the books."

Jotham shrugged, as if it didn't matter. And I suppose it didn't. Not now.

We were in a triage area outside an immense tent, housing one of half a dozen field hospitals. I sat cross-legged on the ground. The sergeant stood in front of me, my cane in his hand, *The One Book* tucked in his belt, while the men of our escort fanned out behind to keep the gathering crowd at bay. "I thought they were Bibles." I'd been trying to make sense of what had happened, but as I spoke I realized I was trying to assuage my guilt by making the old woman and her books somehow complicit. Shamed, I stared at the dirt just beyond the tip of my sandals.

"If anyone's to blame," Jotham said, "it's me. Ought to have taken you straight to the *Castel Sant'Angelo*."

A few paces away, the injured woman lay on planks set across two upright barrels while a weary man in a blood-stained apron examined her. She was semi-conscious, likely delirious, swept up in her pain and the visions the Gift would bring. When she moved her lips wordlessly and nodded, I wondered if she might be conversing with my son. "I should have never touched those books."

"Got nothing to do with the books," Jotham said. "After we took the Castle, we laicized all of value we found, giving it out to the people. Food and coin and weapons, mostly. No one thought there was much of value in the library when we discovered it—until word got out. Then we had a group of the older ones, the ones that remembered, at the gates, demanding the books, which we gladly gave them. I reckon they won't fill their stomachs so much as their minds, but the Church created an appetite, and they were starving for them all the same."

"If it didn't have anything to do with her books, why did the crowd react the way they did?"

"Lots of reasons. But the main one was they knew if we brought anyone back, it'd be you."

"*Me?*"

"They're desperate, and desperate people will look to any hope."

"How could I bring them hope?"

"You're Thomas, who went to Heaven and came back. Thomas, beloved of God and the Angels."

I was appalled. Not just at this misbegotten belief, but at the violence it had engendered on my behalf.

"I regret causing this inconvenience." The created man's words startled me; I'd forgotten he was standing behind me. I glanced over my shoulder, but whatever sign I'd seen of my son had long since fled.

Jotham didn't look at him, not directly anyway. His eyes were on me—save when they flicked to the growing crowd.

"He doesn't understand," I said.

Jotham nodded, but I had no idea what was in his heart.

Time distended or contracted, the way it always did when I took the Water, so I couldn't have said how long it was before the man who'd been dispatched to find the General found us. Only he didn't push his way through the crowd, as we'd expected, but came from the other direction, emerging from between tent flaps. Jotham spun around, hand on the hilt of his sword.

The man looked taken aback. Collecting himself, he said, "Someone already told you?"

Jotham frowned. "Told us what?"

"The General, he's here, with the wounded."

"Other circumstances brought us here," Jotham said, his words clipped. "Take us to him."

The sentry nodded, and we followed him between thick canvas flaps.

Inside, row after row of cots bore the wounded. There was a hush, like that in a Cathedral, the only sounds low, reverent whispers. Men and women nursing the injured moved between the cots, changing the dressings on wounds and administering tinctures, while deacons in modest vestments (so unlike those pompous ones favoured by the

Vatican's clergy) walked slowly and solemnly up and down the aisles, offering what spiritual comfort they could. Many of the wounded were burnt, and with them came the smell, a scent at once both nauseating and sweet, like different meats all cooking on a griddle at once, threaded through with the odour of heated charcoal and sulphur. In all, a smell so thick that I could taste it—and, even now, as I write these words, still can—the same smell that had curled off the hapless boy we'd buried.

From the outside, the tent had looked large; from the inside it seemed endless, and I realized that it wasn't a single tent, but several of the same width joined end to end. After a few minutes we came to a man with a plaited beard kneeling next to a cot, a man so tall that, even on bended knee, his head was level with mine. His eyes were closed and he prayed silently, hands folded over those of the burnt man who lay before him, and who laboured for each breath. Jotham motioned us to stand behind him and keep our peace.

As we waited, the created man put his hand on my shoulder, in the way a father might, and I took comfort in it the way I might have from my father's touch.

By and by, Jotham approached the General and, bending, whispered in his ear.

Laying the wounded man's hands on his chest, the big man made the sign of the cross, and rose, towering over me. Jotham and the sentry stood at attention. The General regarded me gravely for a moment through dark, deep-set eyes. Then, in a slow, sonorous voice, spoke my name: "Thomas."

He'd changed so much that I wouldn't have recognized him had he not spoken; nor, I suppose, would those who'd known him far better than me. When we'd parted, he'd been dressed in rags and a small step from a cadaver; now, fleshed out, he cut an imposing figure, no less for bearing a full set of leather armour: manica, greave, and a cuirass, all stamped with the same two devices the irregulars bore. A few months ago this armour would have looked ridiculous, hanging on him as it would on a skeleton. "Samuel."

"Sam to them who know me."

He extended his hand, and I shook it, my hand swallowed in his, just as when we struck our deal at the Babel Tower, though this time neither of us spat on our palms.

A hint of a something—a smile?—played over his lips, but was gone almost as quickly as it had appeared. "Last time I seen you, you were with another boy," he said, turning to the created man. "Not a man."

"He's my father, Sam."

Sam raised his eyebrows. I expected him to ask the created man how he'd managed to find me, but he asked something else instead: "And your friend, Ali?"

"Dead." Saying it aloud made my stomach lurch.

"It's true," Jotham said. "The lieutenant showed me where they buried him."

They believe the boy we'd buried was Ali.

"He'd some salt in him," Sam said, "but I think he loved you."

I nodded, having decided not to disabuse them of their mistaken notion.

"Your father, eh?" Sam moved his hand to the hilt of his broadsword and scrutinized the created man, taking his measure. His gaze had no kindness in it, and I think had he looked at me that way, I'd have bolted.

"He's a good man."

"Perhaps," Sam said. "Learned it's best not to judge a man by what he says or what is said about him, but by his actions."

"He saved me from drowning," I said. "And tried to save Ali as well." It wasn't a lie—or not much of one, anyway.

"So I heard. War changes a man, Thomas, and rarely for the better." Lifting his hand from his sword, he extended it to the created man. "Much as I owe your son for freeing me, owe you for raising him to be the man he is."

"My name is David," the created man said, surprising me with how easily the lie rolled off his tongue. *Perhaps*, I thought, *he's becoming more human.*

"Samuel is mine, Sam to them who know me."

As they shook, I felt a twinge of guilt, the same sort I'd experienced when I'd struck a bargain with Sam at the Babel Tower. He was as honest a man as I've ever met, and it troubled me that I had lied to him again—even if Sam saw through my lies.

"Come," he said. "There are better places for talk, and some folks that'd like to meet you."

"But what about your comrade?" I asked, nodding at the man on the bed.

"Neither here nor there to him," Sam said, picking up a large, leather helmet from the floor and tucking it under his arm. "Already gone ahead of us, to Heaven."

Company of the Condemned

Sam bade us wait while he and Jotham stepped outside the tent; a moment later he returned alone. So it was only the three of us—me, Sam, and the created man—who slipped from the far end of the field hospital, picking our way through the camp towards the *Castel Sant'Angelo*. Understanding my concern with the crowd that had gathered outside the hospital, Sam told us we would enter the castle through a little-used postern gate. But the gate wasn't the issue; with a man of Sam's stature (both in height and reputation), it was hard to be inconspicuous. It didn't help that soldiers everywhere snapped to attention, or that Sam seemed to know many others and felt compelled to nod or raise a hand in greeting as we passed. I feared it wouldn't be long before a second crowd began to accrete. But I needn't have worried. For all they stared, people kept a respectful distance, and no one followed us.

As we made our way, Sam questioned me gently. Without Jotham or other men nearby, I felt strangely free to talk, and told him much of my time in Heaven with the Angels and their behest; and of my flight with Ali and our journey through the wilderness. But I didn't want to lie to him, so I said little of the created man, and nothing of the Gift of Water, or my son, nor of Ali's real death, letting Sam think what he might and being grateful when he didn't press me on it. If I offered him any further lies that day, they were ones of omission.

"And you, Sam," I said, after it occurred to me we'd been talking about me the entire time. "How is it that you ended up here?"

"Not something I planned," he said. "No more'n I planned to meet you at the Babel Tower."

"I'm glad you made it out."

"Owe you for that."

"No. We struck a deal and you lived up to your end of the bargain."

"Leading you through a dark tunnel is too small a price to pay for freedom."

"If anything, Sam, I am indebted to you."

"Can't see how you figure that."

"The lieutenant who found us, she was looking for two boys named Thomas and Ali. The Church might have known our names, or discovered them, but few others. Save you."

"Didn't expect you'd get up the tower," Sam said. "Didn't expect you'd get into Heaven. And didn't expect you'd turn up here neither. But when I heard the Church was looking for two boys, thought I'd have the men keep an eye out, all the same."

"Then if we're not your prisoners—"

"You're not!"

"—you've saved us as much as we saved you."

"Your words are generous, Thomas, and I thank you for them. But I've done nothing to save you, and maybe just the opposite, for I've dragged you from the frying pan into the fire." He waved to indicate the cantonment and its hopeless siege.

"If you feel you owe me a debt," I said, "you can repay me by answering some questions."

"Gladly, but not in repayment. It's poor recompense."

"Most men overvalue their words," I said. "But I suspect you undervalue yours."

"Seems to me there's no more or less value in wind, no matter the direction from which it blows."

I laughed at that. "How about this: I'll ask some questions, you answer them, and when you have, I'll judge the worth of your answers."

"Do as you please," he said, "and so'll I."

Taking that to mean we'd reached an accord, I asked him, again, how he'd ended up here.

"That's a story," he answered, "started back at the Babel Tower." As we'd been talking, Sam had glanced at the created man several times, as if expecting him to join in the conversation, as most fathers would. But, of course, he hadn't.

"Go on," I said. "I told my father what happened at the tower."

Sam nodded, without looking convinced. "Found the backpack,

where the other boy said it would be, but before striking out on the old road, decided I could do with some company. So I helped some other fellows, just as you helped me. Together we lightened the stores of victuals and weapons, and left our chains by way of payment. Not a soul pursued us across the bridge and into the forest, though when they seen what we were up to, they shouted after us something fierce."

He told me the black egg I'd given him worked as it had for us, keeping the wolves at bay, and that they'd walked four days through the forest, always close together. They ate the food they'd pilfered, and drank out of whatever streams they happened across. "All in all," he said, "it was better'n most of us had in a long time."

On the morning of the fifth day, they reached the river where I'd lost my backpack.

"Before we crossed, made sure I put that black egg back in its nest, case it might be useful to the next fellow. Wasn't long after we struck a path on the other side of river, and in an hour or so it took us right back to a stone road. Can't say I recognized it, but some of the lads claimed to, and swore it was the same one they dragged us down to the Babel Tower by. The fifteen of us sat in a circle in the weeds aside the road, and talked on what to do. I was for splittin' up, keeping to the trees and out of sight of the road. Less likely to get caught that way, figured. Most of the others, though, wanted to stick together. So I suggested we do both, and send a scout ahead and one behind, so they could warn us if there were troops coming our way.

"We took turns, only no one came from behind, and what was ahead was empty. You been down that road, Thomas. You know there's guard posts every few kilometres. But the first four were abandoned. When it was my turn to run ahead, just before sun-off, I spotted the fifth post, only this one was garrisoned. Three men held it—boys, really. Went back and told the others. Could see nothing to be gained in trying to sneak past, so we strolled by them like we had every right to, all fifteen of us, whilst they watched us, nervous-like, looking like they'd tear out of there in a half a second if we took a step towards them. Don't blame them, for I'd a done the same, too, if the numbers were that much against me.

"We walked the road the next day unmolested, and we passed two supply waggons and a prison cart, like the one that had brought each of us in the opposite direction. Though they seemed surprised to see us, and though we couldn't a been mistaken for anything other than what we were, none of the soldiers that drove them rigs seemed inclined to challenge us.

"When the road to the Babel Tower joined up with the highway, it wasn't just the Pope's carts we seen, but ones laden for market, and empty ones heading back, as well as clutches of other travellers: merchants and pilgrims and young lads who, knowing no better, hankered to be soldiers. *Dulce bellum inexpertis*," he said, surprising me with his Latin. War is sweet to those who have never experienced it. "But no more soldiers, save the few that drove carts heading for the Tower. We agreed amongst ourselves to leave them travellers be, so as not to draw unnecessary attention. A couple of the men saw it differently and struck out on their own, and I can't say I felt good about that or what they might do. But most stayed.

"When trouble came, it wasn't the Pope's men, but other companies like us.

"Twice we crossed paths with highwaymen waylaying travellers, and helped out those travellers as we could. Each time we were paid for our kindness, though we asked nothing. And when we scared off a gang of armed men besetting a freeholder's farmhouse, the freeholder provisioned us handsomely, then proposed a bargain: if we would be inclined to escort his waggons to market, he'd pay a good commission on everything sold. With the Tower and all, I guessed Rome to be overflowing with recruits with empty stomachs—and thousands of others of those kind of men and women who ride on the skirts of war. So after hashing it out with the rest of the company, I shook on it with the freeholder. Turned out a good bargain, too, for both sides. The road was rough and, without us, I think it unlikely the freeholder would have made it to Rome with his goods—or his life. Nor would he have been much safer once in the city, on account of the *Garde* was thin there, too. But he had us, and his waggons emptied in less than an hour with nary a problem. His purse fit to bursting, the freeholder tried to hire four of the company to see him home, but the men wouldn't have it. Luck runs good and luck runs bad, and I suppose it all balances out in the end. But, to a man, we'd all had a long run of bad, and not a one of the thirteen of us wanted to break up the company with our luck running to the good. So thirteen, it seemed, were our lucky number.

"We helped him find other men, and the freeholder left us in Rome, our pockets sagging from the weight of his silver. That night we toasted our fortune and named ourselves The Company of the Condemned." Sam smiled, then, no doubt remembering that night.

"They voted you their leader, didn't they?"

"I guess they did," Sam said, chuckling. "Tried to talk them out of it, but they'd drunk too much to listen to sense.

"Next day, when we were all a bit more sober, we talked over what we might do.

"Some were for staying in Rome, some for leaving. But on account of the Papist's struggles with *The Meek* in the Spheres below, and its battle with the Angels in Heaven above, there weren't but a few *Garde* left in Rome, not nearly enough to keep the peace. And most that were left were garrisoned inside the Holy City. Which meant there was plenty of room outside for bandits and thieves, and other men without principle, to flourish—and opportunity for those who'd stand against them to profit. Before he left, the freeholder give me a letter with his wax seal on it. Thought it a good gesture, but didn't think it worth a damn, until I showed it around, and it brought us our choice of commissions."

Sam told me of their first few contracts, the details of which I will not relate here. Suffice it to say they did well, as such companies do in uncertain times, and developed a reputation, both as honourable and capable adventurers. And though they faced a skirmish or two, they'd acquitted themselves well, a cut to the thigh the worst of the wounds they'd suffered. After three contracts, they no longer had to look for a commission, for work came looking for them in the form of a Bishop. He told them the *Cent Suisse*, who guarded the Roman Assumption, were being redeployed. "It was a sweet job, and we'd no misgivings about relieving them of their duties," Sam said. "Nor did anyone in the company raise an objection to lining our pockets with silver from the Church, even though the Pope had sought to crucify every one of us— if anything, that made it all the sweeter. As good a job as we had, and probably the last, for we weren't there a week when *The Meek* overran the lower Assumption.

"Couldn't bring myself to raise my hand against them. Nor would any of the other men. They were people no different than us, just thinner and hungrier and more desperate. So I brought back the purse to the Bishop, and tendered the company's resignation. Never seen a grown man's face turn as white as his. Thought he might beg me, or offer more gold popes, or threaten me, only he didn't do none of those things. Thought he mightn't let me go, for he had four *Cent Suisse* with him who could've done for me easy. But he didn't stop me when I took my leave. Guess his mind was other places. And I suppose things might have fallen out different if he'd known all the time we'd been talking, *The Meek*'d been rising into Rome.

"Word spreads fast in a place thick with people, and many of those that lived in the city fled. The streets swelled with the citizens of Rome, some heading for the gates to the Vatican, to shelter within, whilst others were hurrying outta the city, hauling whatever possessions they could. A panic set in, and it was no small struggle to move against that current of people, and make my way back to the Assumption.

"Maybe a hundred thousand souls come through the Assumption those first few days. They flooded the streets and alleys, taking abandoned houses for themselves and their families; and those who couldn't find shelter that way lay down in arcades and markets and public squares. Some fought with citizens who'd stayed behind, others amongst themselves, skirmishes over scraps of food, mostly. Our company did what it could to keep order. *The Meek* had leaders of sorts, as much as you can lead a mob, and some of them helped out, too. But when people got nothing to lose, they ain't inclined to listen to anyone or anything, not even them that claim to speak in God's stead. Still, we found men who bore weapons, a few who served as *Garde* once, or worked as a sheriff for a Church magistrate or the like, maybe three hundred in all. We organized platoons, sent them out to do the best they could, and to recruit any other armed men they found. Keeping order was nigh impossible.

"The first day was bad; the second worse. The third was better, and I had foolish hope—until that night when the Church attacked.

"A few hours afore sun-on, half a dozen sorties of *Garde* spilled out of three different Vatican gates. They killed all who stood in their way, torched buildings and tents and people as they found them. By sun-on, they'd disappeared, rabbiting back into the Holy City. Thousands had been killed or maimed, most burnt alive. Of our company, one lay dead, three were wounded, and one missing.

"Two days it took to douse the fires. Another two to bury the dead. Rome stank like a charnel house, and rang with a weeping and wailing of thousands of new widows and widowers and orphans. And for what, Thomas? Still can't see what the Church hoped for. There weren't no scaring *The Meek* into turning tail and running. Where would they run to? They crossed the Sphere below like locusts, leaving nothing behind. They'd wanted to come to Rome, and here they were, still starving, still dying, stuck between the Vatican's walls and the desperation nipping at their heels. There weren't no going back, and no going forward, neither. It were here, or it were death—as I see it, though, weren't much difference 'twixt the two.

"Had the Church just left them alone, things wouldn't a come to this pass. As deep as their resentment of the Papacy run, few of *The Meek* would've stood up to fight. Likely, they'd a drifted off, or died quietly, for they'd no spirit left. But that changed the night they'd seen their kith and kin burn in front of their own eyes. Their anger became hard, like stone, changed them from a mob of refugees into a pauper's army. Tens of thousands came to us to volunteer—men and women and children, too—wanting to fight as best they could, wanting to tear down the walls of the Holy City stone by stone, even if it were only with their bare hands.

"Only we had no hope of taking the fight to them. Alls we could do was wait for them to bring it to us. So when the sorties came again, we were ready.

"The *Garde* poured into half a dozen of the biggest squares and plazas, as they had done before, hacking at tents and setting alight bundles with naught but rags in them. And when they tried to retreat, the streets they'd come up were blocked by carts we'd set afire, as were all the other ways in and out. From windows and roofs above, stones and arrows rained down on them like the wrath of God Almighty. We fought through the night, backing them bit by bit, until they burned in the fires they'd lit. Of the hundreds who'd come out of the Vatican, no more'n a score of them made it back, and I'd wager none made it back unscathed.

"From their ramparts the next morning, the Papists started a cannonade what went on for three days straight, smashing every building within arrow shot of the city walls, until there weren't nothing left but the pile of rubble you see. Maybe they were afraid *The Meek* might use the rooftops to fire over the walls of the Holy City, or maybe they wanted to flatten the buildings so there weren't no way to hide from the cuts from the Fiery Sword. Maybe they thought it their best chance of stopping an assault, though we hadn't any hope of launching one.

"Many good men and women were lost in that barrage. Even so, as much as we suffered, the people who hadn't fled Rome and stayed in those buildings suffered worse; and, though I suspect most'd been professed Papists, they did the only thing left them, and joined us who'd nothing to lose, either. When the Pope barred the gates of The Vatican, he as good as drew a line, with them on one side and us on the other. We were all *The Meek* now.

"So here we sit with two choices, Thomas: try and take the Holy City or lay siege to it.

"As stouthearted as they might be, *The Meek* ain't no soldiers. Leastways not the sort who could assault the walls of the Vatican. They've few weapons and less armour, maybe enough for a few thousand souls. Nor is there any way to reach the Pope's wall, save crawling over rubble. And the Fiery Sword cuts them what tries to ribbons. There's no hope of taking the Holy City that way, and never was. Nor can we lay siege to the Vatican, for we've no ranged weapons, no engineers nor sappers. Our supplies are thin and we can expect no more. At best, we've about a week on tight rations—while I'd wager inside the Holy City there's enough laid by for a year or more. We've lost a third of our people already to casualties and sickness—and that's not counting them who see the hopelessness of it and drift off every day. I've no cause to blame 'em, for I see it, too.

"We're like a ship, Thomas, a ship a thousand kilometres from shore what's hit a reef and stuck. Can't go forward. Can't go back, neither. Can only sit and wait and watch as the sea pours in and drowns every last one of us."

The Postern Gate

As we'd twisted and turned along the walkways of the encampment, my perspective of the *Castel Sant'Angelo* had changed, giving me glimpses of the Vatican-facing side of the fortress; what little I could see was scorched, and here and there bites had been taken out of the walls where cannon shot had staved in the parapets. Of the *Passetto di Borgo*, the passageway connecting the castle to Vatican City, little remained save one support, a solitary T that no longer spanned anything. On our side, however, there was relatively little damage, save at the top of the circular fortress inside the castle walls, where half of the highest level had been blown away, and the bronze statue of the Archangel Michael had been sheared off, leaving only the stump of one leg. As we drew close, the improvised wooden avenue on which we walked gave way to a cobbled road; this, in turn, intersected a stone plaza, perhaps fifty metres wide, ringing the castle. To our right, dozens of wooden shacks had been erected and laid out in a neat grid. I found it curious that no one had pitched tents here, or was hawking wares, until I realized that men had been posted around the periphery of the plaza to keep it clear—which meant it likely those shacks were the quartermaster's stores, and the open spaces reserved as a place of assembly for what troops *The Meek* might muster.

We passed a pair of sentries—who jumped to attention from where they sat on the ground rolling dice—and stepped into the plaza.

Sam led us not to the left, to the main gate, where troops milled, but to the right, towards the shacks. Once past them, we were at the curtain wall of the castle, and followed it to the bastion at its end. There, sheltered from the view of both the camp and the soldiers patrolling the plaza, we came to a small, unguarded postern with an iron-lattice gate. The entrance was narrow, barely wide as a grown man's shoulders. And it was low-ceilinged and gloomy inside—so much so that I could barely make out a short corridor, ending in an identical lowered gate. A shadowy figure stood behind this gate, and from the general size and shape, I took this to be Jotham.

"Mantrap," Sam said. "Inner gate can't be opened until the outer is shut, so only one person at a time can pass through." He barked an order, and the gate clanked and clattered as it was drawn up on chains by hands within the castle.

The created man insisted on going first—I suppose he was concerned about what he might find inside. He stepped into the small space, his head brushing the ceiling.

Jotham signalled, and the exterior gate grated shut.

I waited for the inner gate to rise. But it didn't. Instead, two figures materialized on either side of Jotham. I couldn't make out much detail, but enough to see they held bows with nocked arrows, both aimed at the place on the created man's chest where a heart should have been.

For a moment no one moved or spoke.

Then there was a sound, low and feral, and I realized, with a shock, it was coming from the created man.

He looked this way and that from within his prison, his face contorting. Then he launched himself at the outer gate, crashing into it with his right shoulder; there was an awful clang of metal on stone and clouds of dust shook loose from the gate's channels. The gate, however, remained steadfast, while the created men staggered back, his shoulder bent back at an impossible angle, his arm now hanging uselessly behind him. If he felt any pain, he showed no sign.

He threw himself at the gate a second time. This charge had no more effect than the first, save the created man rebounded and tripped over his cape, losing his balance and going down on two knees and one hand, his right arm flopping sickeningly at his side.

"Let him out!" I shouted.

But Sam paid me no heed. Instead, he drew his sword, eyeing the created man warily, as he might a caged animal.

I watched in horror as the created man dragged himself to the gate and crouched in front of it, his cape spread out behind him. One-handed, he tried to lift the gate—an object of such weight that no man could hope to lift it with two. He strained mightily, but managed only a few centimetres before it ground against something above.

"There's iron rods atop," Sam said to the created man, "that slide into place when the gate's down."

Oblivious, the created man continued to strain, his body shaking with the effort. I heard an indistinct pop, then a tearing sound—not from the gate or its mechanism, but from the created man as the flesh on his forearm parted. A strand of a clear, viscous fluid slipped out and ran down to the tip of his elbow where it quivered.

"Stop it!" I implored him, but the created man chose to ignore me.

I threw myself towards the gate, reached through the bars and touched the created man on the knee; the tension in his leg sang through my fingers. "Please," I said, trying to keep my voice steady, "You're going to harm yourself."

Still, the created man didn't relent.

"You'll hurt my son!"

All at once, the created man let go; he fell back into a sitting position, his right arm hanging behind him at an absurd angle, his left torn open and oozing fluid. From behind, Sam grabbed the fabric of my shirt and pulled me back from the gate; the created man shuddered, as if he wanted to lash out, to knock Sam's hand away, only he knew he hadn't the wherewithal.

I twisted free of his grip and looked up at him. "Why?"

"Dangerous."

"He wouldn't hurt anyone." Then I thought about the pain etched on the face of the woman whose wrist the created man had crushed, and knew the emptiness of my words. "Jotham told you about what happened at the bridge."

"That and other things. Like he don't he act like a person ought. *Ignorant of the ways of men*, was how Jotham put it. Even if he means no harm, that don't mean he won't cause some out of ignorance."

"He was only trying to protect me."

"Just as Jotham protects me. Only Jotham ain't going do no harm to an old lady who asks my blessing."

I peered across the mantrap at the sergeant; the two men on either side had lowered their bows, but their arrows were still nocked.

"Didn't think he'd react like he did," Sam said, sheathing his sword. "Regret that."

"Let him go."

Sam looked straight at me. "You lied, Thomas. He's no more your father than I am."

"He's a creature of God," I said, "bidden by the Angles to help me. He'll harm no one unless he believes he needs to do so to keep me safe."

Sam chewed on this a moment, then said, "I believe you."

"Then free him."

"Believing another person *thinks* something's true ain't the same as believing that thing's true."

"You don't trust me?"

"Do, far as I can. But I've a duty."

"To protect *The Meek*?"

"Yes," Sam said, then surprised me by adding, "You, too."

"Me?"

"Do you know why them people did what they did?"

"They think the Angels favour me. They want my blessing." As we all hope for the blessing of our betters. *But how many would wish my blessing*, I wondered, *if they knew the extent of my sins?*

"They think you were sent by the Angels to save us."

I was nonplussed.

"Inside these walls is a room, Thomas, and in that room are twelve men and women who speak for *The Meek*, who want to talk to you, to ask you if you've been sent by the Angels to save us. That's where we're going. And as much as I can't risk your life, I can't risk the lives of the Twelve, neither."

"He's no threat to them."

From Sam's expression, it seemed to pain him to say what he said next: "Know something of why the Church was looking for you."

This brought me up short. No more than a kilometre distant was the chapel in Saint Peter's—where I'd been party to the assassination of Cardinal Adolfo.

"The Twelve will question you, Thomas. I believe much of what you told me, though I'm certain there are things you've left out—perhaps with good reason. I tell you this on account of these men and women. They're sharp, as sharp as Jesuits, and won't take kindly to things left out."

"You're afraid they'll catch me in a lie?"

"Know you're too clever for that."

"Then what?"

"They'll have heard some version or other of what happened at the bridge, like I did. And they'll know he's locked up here. But if they meet this man you call your father, they'll be bothered by things that bother me. Like that you seem to speak for him as a father would for a son. And that he holds his tongue, like an obedient son in the company of his father."

"You're worried they'll see he's not a man like other men."

"People are afraid of what they don't know, Thomas. And there are those on the council who'd use this fear to their own ends."

"What would you have me do?"

"Leave him here. He'll not be harmed, unless he harms himself. On that you have my word."

"And what do I say if the Twelve ask about him?"

"Whatever you choose. Though if I were you, I'd say as little as can be said, and hope they don't press you on it."

"You won't say anything?"

Sam shrugged. "See nothing to be gained by it."

"And after I tell the Twelve I'm not here to save anybody, will you let us be on our way?"

"If it were up to me, yes. But it ain't. The Twelve make the decisions. Do what I can for you—that, I promise. But be lying if I told you I knew the minds of the Twelve afore they knew themselves." Sam's face creased; he seemed genuinely distressed. "I'm sorry, Thomas, really am. Poor payback, after all you done for me. But can't see any other way of working it."

Sam's promise heartened me, for I knew him to be as good as his word. Still, it worried me that he wouldn't promise our release. But what choice did I have?

The created man startled me by saying, "Don't leave me, father."

He'd risen to his feet and peered through the iron bars, his eyes wide and his pupils dilated. I'd seen this reaction before, many times and in many different people, but it was so unexpected in the created man that it took me a moment to recognize it: fear.

"Let me in," I said to Sam.

"No."

"I'll do as you ask."

"Know you'd do so, anyway," Sam said.

"You're right, I would. But back at the Babel Tower you said you owed me. And you repeated that today. If your word is as good as I think, then I ask you to pay your debt by letting me in."

Sam shook his head, only hesitantly, like he was considering the idea.

"He'll give you no trouble, I promise." I turned to the created man. "Step back." He did. "Give me your word you won't try to get past me."

The created man nodded.

I looked at Sam. "His word is as good as mine. Better even. Please let me in."

Sam frowned, and muttered something I couldn't make out. Then he drew his sword again, and barked an order for Jotham to raise the gate.

I walked into the mantrap.

"Your arm," I said, touching it gently just beside the wound. "Does it hurt?"

With an inhuman strength, the created man gathered me into him, folding his torn arm around me so tightly it hurt; I dropped my cane in surprise.

"It's all right," I whispered into my son's ear. His fluids felt cold as they seeped through the back of my shirt. "You know I care for you more than I care for any other living soul?"

In my ear, the created man's breathing was shallow, but steady.

"And that I'd never do anything that would put you in peril?"

When he didn't answer, I repeated the question.

"Yes," he said.

"Nor would I ever leave you." I squeezed him in what I hoped was a reassuring way, and felt his grip relax, ever so slightly. "You must let me go," I said, gently but firmly pulling away. Though he didn't attempt to clutch me tighter, he didn't let me go easily. "I need you to wait here. Can you do that for me?"

He made a small nod.

I picked up my cane and stepped outside; the gate squealed closed behind me.

The created man grasped the gate with his good hand, his face framed in the opening between iron staves, and in his eyes I could see him struggling to master his fear. He did so because I had asked him to, and because he believed I knew what was best. A thing all children believe—until they learn otherwise. *A forgivable deception*, I said to myself. *The sort all parents practise. The sort all children require.* Even so,

I experienced a sharp stab of guilt, as any father would.

Weighted by the worthlessness of my assurances, I turned my back on my son and walked away.

Council of the Meek

Four sentries snapped to attention as we passed beneath the main gate at the *Castel Sant'Angelo*. Sam and I made our way across a small courtyard and into the circular fortress that was the castle proper. My eyes took a moment to adjust to the dim interior whose only light came from small, intermittent holes in the straw-coloured wall. We turned right, into a corridor, and the floor angled up; I realized we were climbing a ramp that curved around the interior of the fortress wall. We followed this ramp a quarter way around the perimeter before it levelled off, then Sam led us under an arch on our left. He pushed open an iron-banded door. I followed him into a small chapel—and almost tripped over my own feet in astonishment. This chapel was a twin to the one in Saint Peter's, the chapel where Kite had drawn his last breath. Behind the altar the wainscoting had been torn off, revealing a low opening—exactly the same as the one through which we'd fled into the secret tunnels of the Vatican. From this opening came the murmur of voices.

Sam ducked under the low arch. I followed.

However, rather than giving unto secret tunnels, as had the hidden door in Saint Peter's, a few steps through a short passage led to a circular room, around whose circumference rose five levels of elaborately carved wooden arcades, each containing bookshelves, all bereft of books. In the centre of this once-library was an open space, perhaps ten metres in diameter, and here, on a parquet floor, stood a round, oaken table, on which maps, marked with lines and arrows and sundry notations, had been strewn. The Twelve stood or sat around this table, some studying the maps, others engaged in conversation—

all of which had come to an abrupt stop as soon as we entered the room.

"This be Thomas," Sam said, stepping aside so they might see me.

For a moment they stared. A thin woman of middle-age—with pale skin and blue eyes, her face framed by a halo of fine hair—opened her mouth, as if in shock, then quickly pushed herself out of her seat and went down on one knee, bowing her head, the silver crucifix around her neck ticking against the floor; within a heartbeat, two men followed suit. A few of the others stirred, as if uncertain what to do. Some looked to the end of the table, where an older man, heavyset, with a mottled face and bushy, white eyebrows, sat. I turned to Sam, perplexed—but to my great dismay, he, too, was on bended knee.

"Get up!" I said, stricken. "I beg you!"

"As you wish," Sam said. I could see the others who'd knelt looking to him for direction, and he gave them a small nod. They rose one by one, though none took a seat.

"Sam, what's going on?"

The woman with the cross didn't wait for him to answer. She stared at me, as if she couldn't quite believe I was there. "Are you not Thomas, Beloved of the Angels?"

At the time, I had not understood what happened at the bridge. How those in bad straits would venerate anyone or anything they believed holy, that might have vested in it power to help them. To be the object of such reverence again sickened me.

A short fellow near the end of the table squinted dubiously at me. "You think, boy, that by—"

The older man had barely lifted his right hand, the slightest of movements, but it stopped the other mid-sentence. Though his fingers were bare, I couldn't help but notice all four of his fingers were pinched at their bases, as if he'd recently removed thick rings, the sort of jewellery a Prince of the Church might favour.

"Let us not be inhospitable." His voice was stentorian, and he spoke slowly, as do those used to their own authority. He smiled at me, only there was no warmth in it. "Can you not see it? The boy is flummoxed. Let him sit and catch his breath." He lifted a hand and, from the shadows, two pages brought chairs before scurrying back, out of sight.

When everyone was seated, the man said, "I am Bishop Arrupe." I was surprised that a high-ranking member of the clergy was amongst the Twelve, who had more than enough cause to hate the rule of the Church; and I was even more surprised that the others seemed to defer to him. Back then, though, I didn't know the weakness of men as well as I do now. "The men and women before you speak for *The Meek*." Inclining his head at Sam, he said, "Our honourable General bid us be here to meet a special boy. And given that he bent his knee to you, I can only assume that you are the Thomas he witnessed ascending to Heaven."

"No," I said.

"No?"

"Not Heaven, Lower Heaven. And not the way people think when they say a soul has ascended. We crossed a bridge and walked through an Assumption, as I'm sure Sam told you."

"That Sam vouches for you is true, and none here would question his honesty. And Sister Angelina is equally respected, and she did not hesitate to bend her knee." The way the Bishop glanced at the pale woman made me wonder if he'd been caught off-guard by her reaction. "Even so . . ." Bishop Arrupe shrugged. "As you no doubt noticed, Thomas, we are divided. Some of us are sceptical, while others wish to believe you."

It had not occurred to me that the truth of my time in Heaven might be in question. "I . . . I was there."

Bishop Arrupe looked at me like he thought he'd caught me in a lie. "No man has seen Heaven, Lower or otherwise, and lived to tell of it."

No man? Why would the Bishop say such a thing? Ali and I had. As had troops the Pope had sent. "What of the Papists who breached Heaven? They were the reason we fled."

Bishop Arrupe continued to stare at me, unblinking.

"Two hundred thousand is our best guess," Sam said. "All that passed into Heaven are now dead."

Two hundred thousand. It beggared belief.

"We feared the troops the Pope sent to Heaven'd be recalled," Sam said, "and then there'd be troops to take us from two sides. So we decided to send scouts. Weren't long before we captured a soldier who'd fled the Babel Tower. Told us none of those sent to Lower Heaven lived. Not Priests nor Bishops what went with them, not even Cardinals. A few souls made it back, and this fellow we took had a hand in tending them. Said they was flushed and feverish, and spoke little sense. To a man they suffered from something like the flux, though worse than any he'd ever seen. A few days they hung on, some rallying, only to fall to a wasting disease, skin mottling with lesions and running sores, hair falling out in clumps. Inside of three days, all were dead.

"Those left at the Babel Tower was terrified. Of God's wrath. Of catching the disease that'd wasted their comrades. Most deserted."

I thought of the lesions I'd seen on the skin of Angels; and of how my own forehead and cheeks had tingled after I'd witnessed the souls in Heaven, like I'd put my face too close to a fire. "The radiance of God," I said. "The Archangel Zeracheil warned me it would be too much for men."

"But apparently not for you," Bishop Arrupe said.

"The Angels must have protected us." Even to my ears, my words sounded like a miserable excuse.

"Us?"

Sam took a step towards me. "I told you the other boy died."

"Yes, of course," the Bishop said. "My mistake."

I was pretty sure it hadn't been a mistake. I had been about to say, *He was burned*, to bolster the lie I'd let Sam believe. It's an instinctive thing, I think, cultivating our lies, repeating them often and with conviction, hoping they become the truth to others, sometimes even coming to believe them ourselves. Only I knew this was what Bishop Arrupe wanted me to do. "Sam told me I ought to speak truthfully, and so I will. The boy we buried wasn't Ali. She died of privation in the Holy Lands, trying to protect me. Trying to carry out the bidding of the Angels, even though she had good reason not to."

Bishop Arrupe didn't look surprised, not that it wasn't Ali in that grave by the sea, nor that I called Ali *she*. Or if he was, he didn't show it. Others around the table, however, looked perplexed—save for Sister Angelina, who nodded at me, as if to say, *Go ahead, tell them*.

"When we fell from Heaven," I said, "we fell to the Holy Land—Ali died shortly after. That is where I buried her." My stomach tightened when I thought of the poor grave I'd scratched in the dirt. "After, I wandered the Judean Wilderness, and that is where I met the . . . the man I call my father. The Angels bid him help me in any way he can. He guided us to the coast, and together we took passage across the sea— until our ship was burnt. The irregulars who captured me had been given a description of two boys. They assumed the boy we buried was Ali. I didn't say otherwise because I didn't know who these soldiers were or why they were looking for us." I turned to Sam. "I'm sorry I deceived you." And I was.

"Seems to me we deceived ourselves," Sam said, which I took to be a kindness.

"I thought Ali died of privation," I said. "Only now I'm not sure so sure. Maybe she succumbed to the same thing that took the Vatican's soldiers."

Bishop Arrupe said, "Why would she die and not you?"

"I don't know." I thought for a moment. "The Angels are cloaked in flesh like ours and bear marks of a similar affliction, but they do not die. Or I don't think so, anyway. If the radiance of God affects their fleshly incarnation as it does ours, then they must have the means to counteract it—or at least arrest its progress. Perhaps they protected me in the same way."

"But not her?"

Ali was dead, whether of privation or God's radiance, I couldn't have said. So I shrugged. "I broke my arm just before the Papists breached Lower Heaven." Although I'd made a pledge to tell the truth, I saw no compelling reason to say how I had broken my arm—and several good reasons not to. "For days I was delirious. I have no memory of what happened, but Ali told me the Angels treated me before we fled. Perhaps it was then that they protected me. Maybe in their rush they didn't have a chance to treat her. Or perhaps they just didn't care about her. Either seems as likely. If I learned anything of Angels, it's that no man can understand the workings of their minds." I looked around the table. "You brought me here to find out if I was the Thomas who'd been to Lower Heaven. I am. And, judging by your questions, I think you may also want to ask me if I'd been sent by the Angels to save you. I'm not. As far as I can tell, the Angels care for no one, not even themselves. They did not mention your plight, nor instruct me to come here. They gave me a different task, which I intend to see through. Not because I believe God has commanded me to do so, as others keep telling me, but because I think it the right thing to do." Saying it out loud, I realized my mind had been made up some time ago. "I've other reasons, too, but those are my own and I won't share them."

"What motivates you is not our business," Bishop Arrupe said coolly. "But your intentions are. Can you not tell us the task the Angels set you?"

"The Church seeks me. If they knew my intentions, there's a greater chance they'd able stop me. I'm not willing to risk that."

"You don't trust us?" The slightest note of hurt had crept into Bishop Arrupe's voice.

"No more than you trust me."

"Perhaps we have reason," the Bishop said. "The same reason the Church seeks you: you conspired to murder a Cardinal."

"It's true I was there when the Cardinal Adolfo was assassinated. But the Church must know that those who made use of me neither asked my leave nor told me of their plot."

Before Bishop Arrupe could ask me more about the Cardinal's assassination, Sister Angelina said, "We are not the Curia, Thomas. We do not pursue you." She turned to Bishop Arrupe. "We are all on this side of the wall and they are on the other. Only sometimes we forget that."

Bishop Arrupe nodded and smiled, but I sensed he was annoyed, perhaps even angry. From his dress and manner, I'd guessed him to be a Jesuit; from hers, that she was an Ursuline. It wasn't unusual for the two orders to work together, each busying themselves with the task of educating boys and girls respectively. So it would make sense that they were of one voice in most things. I thought again about Sister Angelina's reaction when she first saw me, and wondered if in that moment Bishop Arrupe had lost his allay.

"I would willingly help," I said. "But what could I possibly do to feed *The Meek* or breach the walls of the Vatican?"

"No person can know the mind of an Angel," Sister Angelina said. "You told us this yourself. Isn't it possible they intended you to come here to help us?" She looked at me encouragingly.

"I don't believe that," I said, "and I don't think Bishop Arrupe does, either."

"What you and I believe isn't relevant," the Bishop said. "It's what the people believe." He opened his hands in a gesture that included all the men and women sitting at the table.

"You mean to keep me here."

When no one said anything, my heart sank. I looked at Sam, but he, too, kept his peace.

"We welcome you as our guest," Sister Angelina said.

"This is madness," I said, looking from face to face. "What would you have me do?"

"Nothing," the Bishop answered, then gave a small nod towards the Sister. "Or everything."

"I have faith in you, Thomas." Sister Angelina looked at me like I was the crucified Christ, hanging before her in a Church, hope brimming in her eyes that her petition might be worthy of my attention. She said, "I see your face."

Her odd testament had an immediate affect on those around the table: some opened their mouths as if in disbelief, while others frowned. Even Bishop Arrupe seemed taken aback.

"I see your face, Thomas," she said again, beaming.

In a matter-of-fact voice, the Bishop said, "God didn't bless Sister Angelina with the ability to learn faces. To her, one face looks like another, as do rocks in a garden to us."

"Not yours, Thomas." She stared at me, rapt. "God has let me see yours."

I knew then that she saw it as a sign, that what she believed of me was true. "You think I have a miracle in me."

"Do you?" Bishop Arrupe asked this in a disinterested way, as if he could easily believe my answer, whatever it might be. Why, then, did I still feel he hoped I'd make a claim that would be easy to discredit?

"Not like those in *The Bible*."

"Then you *do* have something." He nodded approvingly—more for the others than for me, I suspect. "Not a miracle, perhaps. But an idea?"

I hesitated, reluctant to say anything, but now unable to see another way. "I may know how to breach the wall of the Vatican."

Bishop Arrupe blinked. "How?"

"I won't say. Not yet, anyway."

When the Bishop said, "More things you cannot tell us?" Sister Angelina shot him a sharp glance.

"If the Papacy gets a whiff of our plan, we are lost. As there are fourteen people in the room—sixteen including the two boys, waiting in the shadows—I am concerned that the more people who swear an oath of secrecy, the more likely that oath is to be broken. I'm also not sure breaching the wall is even possible. I need time to check some things out."

"And how long might it take you to gather this intelligence?"

There had been no hint of sarcasm in the Bishop's voice, but how else could his words be taken? "One night. As long as my friend is freed and we are allowed to move about as we please. Then, tomorrow morning, I will tell you if it is possible."

Bishop Arrupe arched an eyebrow. "Is that all?"

"I'd like my cane and Bible back." As I said this, it occurred to me that those who believed I'd been sent to them might fear I'd flee. "In return, I will swear an oath not to leave camp without permission of the Twelve."

The Sister nodded, looking relieved, while Bishop Arrupe's expression was one of studied neutrality.

"Know Thomas to be as good as his word, but others here don't," Sam said, and turned to me. "Would you be agreeable, Thomas, if I were to stick with you until this is sorted?"

"Yes. More than that, I'd welcome your help."

Sam turned back to the Twelve. "Then you'd have Thomas's word he'd not leave, and mine that I'd see to it."

"If we can't trust the word of Sam," Sister Angelina said, "and that of a boy who is beloved of the Angels, then I fear we are lost."

Only a few at the table looked to Bishop Arrupe then, and I remember thinking that I'd misjudged both the Bishop's sway and the weight Sam's words might carry with the rest of the Twelve, for it was clear that all but a few now sided with Sister Angelina. I wasn't surprised when Bishop Arrupe, seeing the odds tilt against him, said, "If Sam vouches for the boy, then who am I to disagree?" He smiled approvingly, like this was what he had in mind all along. As perhaps it was.

Sam pulled *The One Book* from where he'd stuck it in his belt, and held it out. I put my hand on its cover as if it was what it purported to be, *The Bible*. Lowering my gaze—more to hide my guilt than for any other reason—I swore an oath to do as I'd promised.

After, Sam handed me *The One Book*.

Of the rest of the meeting there is not much to report. As good as his word, Sam said little about the created man. There were more questions—a few from Bishop Arrupe, but mostly from the others, many of which I answered truthfully. As much as I was able (and thought wise), I posed a few questions of my own, to which I received answers I deemed mostly truthful. To my relief, however, nothing more was said of miracles before Sam and I took our leave.

Miracles

A few hours to sun-off, and I was growing anxious. Not just because of the dwindling time, but also because my hands had begun to tremble, the way they always did when I was too long without the Water.

"Can see you're itching to do the bidding of the Angels, Thomas."

We crouched in one of the upper chambers of the *Castel Sant'Angelo*, to the side of a gaping hole where cannon shot had staved in a window's wooden shutters and part of the surrounding wall. I'd asked Sam to bring me to a place high up, where I'd have a clear view of the ground that lay between the castle and the Vatican.

"I am," I said. "But I've given my word I'd stay."

The ragged edges of the window framed a view of the Holy City surmounted by the Dome of Saint Peter's. Though Sam had cautioned me to peer over the lip of the opening only for a few seconds at a time, he needn't have. Scorch marks left by the Fiery Sword were clearly visible around the opening and on the wall opposite. I'd already taken a couple of quick looks: nearest us, most buildings had been levelled. But adjacent to the walls of the Holy City, too close for canon shot, whole structures still stood.

"Don't think Bishop Arrupe would mind if you was to slip away."

I asked Sam why he believed that.

"Can see he don't believe you have a miracle in you."

"I swore an oath, Sam."

"Heard you afore." Sam looked away from me, stared at the burnt wall. "If Bishop Arrupe wants you to go, it ain't really oath-breaking, is it?"

"I gave my word to the Twelve," I said. "And to you."

"None of us would hold you to it."

"It's true I want to leave, Sam. Not because I'm anxious to do the Angel's bidding, but because I'm worried I won't be able to help. Or that my helping will only make things worse."

Sam shrugged. "Hard to know what good or bad will come of what we do. But can't let that stop us from doing."

"They want a miracle, Sam. A miracle! But a proper miracle requires the impossible be made manifest through the divine power of God. That's what the Priests at *San Savio* taught us. I've seen things, Sam, that men would call impossible. Yet, I hesitate to call them miracles. In every case, I got the feeling I wasn't witnessing the *supernatural*, but natural things that happened for reasons I couldn't discern."

"Loathe to claim I'm sharp enough to recognize God's hand in things. Leave that to the Church."

"Do you think I have a miracle in me?"

"Seems to me a miracle don't need God. Just something to happen that people think impossible, someone to witness the impossible thing, and the Church to name it a miracle. By those standards, 'spect you have a miracle or two in you."

I shook my head. "I don't."

"Ain't up to you to decide what's a miracle—just up to you to provide one."

We both smiled at that. "You want me to go, Sam?"

He considered a moment. "Think you can help us, even if it's just by your being here. But if what you told is true, then you serve the Angels and God. Not the Twelve or *The Meek*, no matter they think otherwise. Go, if you believe that's what the Angels wish." Sam frowned. "There's another reason you ought be on your way, Thomas. What you said to the Twelve is true. Spies are everywhere, and it's a fair bet the Church already knows you're here. They'll know *The Meek* are heartened by it. And likely what words passed between us in the council will reach the Pope's ears soon enough."

"Are you saying there's a spy amongst the Twelve?"

"Not unless he's a good one," Sam said. "I've my own, and they tell me otherwise. But the Twelve all have those they talk to, and them to others, until there's no telling where our words will end up. Right now, the Holy Father's more troubled over his losses in Lower Heaven and the mob at his gates than in a boy who might or might not have had a hand in assassinating his Cardinal. Only if he fears you might rally *The Meek*, his thoughts'll turn to you. He'll start wondering how it is that you were called to Heaven. Maybe even think on what task the Angels have set you. Might be he'll see it to his advantage if you disappear one night—or meet an assassin's blade."

"They wouldn't make me into a martyr."

"'Maybe," Sam said. "Only there's others who it might serve."

It took a moment to realize what Sam was hinting at: a dead martyr might suit Bishop Arrupe's purposes better than a live boy who could work no miracles. "I'm staying," I said, pretending a courage I didn't feel.

Sam nodded, disappointed, I think.

"One more look." I popped my head up again and squinted, then dropped back into a crouch, wishing I'd thought to ask for a spyglass. I considered asking Sam if there was one I could use, but then decided it wouldn't help. From this vantage, the Vatican seemed unassailable, my scheme a Pyrrhic victory at best, self-annihilation at worst. "If the wall comes down, many will die. More than if *The Meek* just dispersed."

"Maybe," Sam said. "Maybe not. Dying of starvation is dying all the same. Anyway, them who run things don't count bodies like that. Only number they care about is the one you get when you subtract your dead from theirs."

"What if God isn't on our side?"

"Ain't about God. It's about them that has and them that don't."

"I don't believe that."

"Know you don't. But gotta ask why God would set His faithful against one another."

"I suppose some men are foolish. Or vain."

"Can't disagree. But didn't God make them that way?"

Sam's point was hard to debate; after all, God was the source of everything. Even so, I still believed what *The Bible* told us, that God favoured the righteous. I said as much to Sam, then added, "The Vatican was built to honour God, and no matter how corrupt the Curia might be, there are still good men and women inside those walls. And here we are, beggars and thieves and murderers. How can God favour us over them?"

Sam shrugged. "Maybe He don't pick the righteous until after all is said and done."

"Are you saying he doesn't care?"

"Maybe he's like the Angels."

The notion that God didn't care about the affairs of men took me aback. A phrase I'd read in *The One Book* came back to me then: *History is written by the victors.* Could the same be said of *The Bible*?

"Would you hear my advice?" Sam asked.

I told him I would value it.

"There's no straight and simple here, Thomas. Do what your heart tells you. Only don't mix God up in it."

I could see the sense in Sam's advice, even if I couldn't wholly accept it. "Would you take me back to the created man now?"

Nodding, Sam rose from his crouch.

I walked past him and down the corridor, descending the ramp. Sam trudged in silence behind me. I could feel his unhappiness pressing at my back. I stopped where the ramp levelled, as it did periodically when we passed doors to inner chambers. "What troubles you?"

"Know you wouldn't insist on staying—not after what I just said. Unless . . ."

"Unless what?"

"Unless you think you can do what you claimed."

I shrugged.

"Why'd you want me to bring you up here, Thomas?"

"If I'm going to work a miracle," I said, "I need to see the lay of the land." I'd meant it to sound flip, but in the oppressive gloom of the corridor, it sounded like a guilty admission.

"Fear for you, Thomas." He put one of his huge hands on my shoulder, and I took comfort from it. "Fear for miracles that'll get you killed."

How long, I wondered, *had it been since anyone had expressed concern as genuine as Sam's?* "You needn't fear for me, Sam. You should pray for those souls who need suffer and die to save *The Meek*."

Sam said nothing, only looked at me oddly.

Perhaps he read in my face how what I planned sickened me. I'd death on my hands, and breaching the wall of the Holy City would multiply it a thousand fold. But wasn't that the nature of many miracles? Like those of Moses, for whom God killed every first-born man or beast in Egypt, and drown the Pharaoh's army. Or like Joshua's miracle, which brought down the walls of Jericho: *They enforced the curse of destruction on everyone in the city: men and women, young and old, including the oxen, the sheep and the donkeys, slaughtering them all.* Was that part of the miracle, too?

My miracle would be no different, save in the most important way:

I had no divine approbation.

So as we descended the ramp, spiralling lower and lower into the depths of the *Castel Sant'Angelo*, I prayed to God for His blessing—and heard nothing but the echo of our own footsteps.

Returning to the postern gate, we found the created man exactly as we'd left him, hand clasped around the iron stave. If there was any trace of the wound on his arm, it was thinnest of white lines, and his shoulder had almost set itself right. No doubt Sam noticed these things, too, yet he said nothing, other than to give the order to raise the gate.

Unlike the Twelve, who'd taken rooms in the *Castel Sant'Angelo*, Sam had chosen to stay amongst his troops in a modest tent, containing a simple cot and a camp chair, its only luxury a chipped wash basin on a wooden stool. In front of the tent, under a tarpaulin, was a trestle table where I guessed he gathered his officers for their briefings. We sat, Sam and I, across from one another on rough-hewn benches, the created man by my side, *The One Book* and my cane on the table in front of him.

An orderly set three bowls of a thin, tepid stew before us, better than most in the camp likely had, and I was grateful for it. Before he took his leave, Sam ordered him to bring cots for me and the created man.

Sam stared at his bowl, but didn't lift his spoon, while I ate slowly, mulling things over. For his part, the created man ate, though whether or not he required that kind of sustenance, I couldn't have said.

When I finished my meal, I pulled out *The One Book*. Within, I found several treatises on siege warfare and explosives, which I skimmed. After some words with the created man, I felt there was a good chance to bring down the wall. I explained my plan to Sam, and we discussed it until the day's light had faded and a pall of darkness crept over the camp.

There was still one thing that I needed to confirm, and to do that I'd have to get close to the Vatican wall. When I rose, the created man put a hand on my arm.

"I will go," he said.

I'd never do anything that would put you in peril. This was a promise I'd made him earlier in the day—one I meant to keep. "No."

"You are needed here," the created man said. "I will go."

I knew there was nothing I could say to dissuade him. "Then we will go together."

"Two cannot move as quickly or quietly as one. And I can see and hear things you cannot."

"He's right," Sam said. "You'd only endanger him."

I could think of no answer to that. Although it sickened me to break my promise only a few hours after I'd made it, I told the created man what he must do. A few minutes later, he slipped away in the dark.

Not long after, I followed Sam into his tent. I hadn't had a proper sleep, at least not since being woken by the cabin boy's singing. I dropped *The One Book* and my cane on one of the cots the orderly had fetched, and collapsed into the other, too tired (and self-conscious in Sam's company) to administer the Water. Nor did I desire its soporific effect. I lay there, tossing and turning, my thoughts going back to the created man over and over. I didn't believe he was in much danger—it was fully dark now, and how likely was it that his furtive movements, darting through the rubble, would be remarked? Still, he carried a precious cargo, and I couldn't help worrying, as any parent must. After a time, Sam began snoring softly. I stared at the ceiling of the tent, straining to hear the sound of the created man's return, turning over in my head all that Sam had said. Shortly before sun-on (or at least I guessed it was, for I think I heard the bells of Saint Peter's ringing for the morning *Angelus*), I turned on my side to face the created man's cot—and was surprised to see him there, lying on his back, face streaked with dirt, eyes open and fixed on me. My thoughts were disconnected and muddled, the kind we're given over to on the cusp of sleep. I stared at him, wondering why it was that I had tried to stay awake. When he nodded, looking proud of himself, all of it came back to me—and with it a vast relief. Then, exhaustion overtook me. I think I managed to nod back before lapsing into sleep.

In a dream, I crossed the *Ponte Cavour* once more, only this time I walked alone. When I'd first stepped on the bridge, the camp lay sprawled before me, sagging tents abandoned, the makeshift avenues empty, not a soul to be seen. But when I reached the far side, I saw the crone who I'd seen before, sitting on her rickety bench by the foot of the bridge. Her foxed and dog-eared books were arrayed before her on that threadbare blanket. Good eye closed, she squinted at me through her milky-white eye.

When she nodded for me to sit next to her, I did. She smelled faintly musty—or perhaps that was her books.

Where is everyone? I asked.

She shrugged.

Are they all dead?

Suffering is not increased by numbers, she said. *One body can contain all the suffering the world can feel.*

I didn't understand her answer, though the words were familiar. So I said nothing. For a time, we sat there, she and I, but no one came to look at her wares.

After a while, she asked me if I'd brought my book, and I told her, no, I hadn't, that she had it, for it was on her lap. She smiled, as if my answer pleased her. Lifting *The One Book*, she turned it over in her spotted hands, examining all its sides. Then she put it back in her lap. *I'm all but blind,* she said. *Tell me, what does this book contain?*

Stories, I said. *All the stories ever written.*

She nodded, the way people do when they already know the answer to the question they've just asked. *Are they true?*

I thought for a moment before saying, *As much as anything is true.*

She smiled, and put her arm around me. *The world not as it is, but as men describe it.*

I squirmed, but her arm was like iron and held me immobile. *I know that not all the stories are true,* I said. *Not literally, anyway. Their truth lies in what they say, not what they describe.*

The world is as men describe it, she said, *until it is not.*

I told her I didn't follow.

A hundred men may see a hundred different truths in the same story, or the same truth in a hundred different stories. But I am an old blind woman, and know only two truths that all women know: birth and death.

Unsettled, I stared into the fire.

Tell me, she said, *why would men write such stories?*

I'd not thought about this before. *To make sense of the world, I suppose.*

And what is the world, Thomas?

This place, and all other places in all the Spheres.

What is Heaven?

It is the highest Sphere, I said, *a place of perfection.*

And where is Heaven?

I pointed up.

And what is Hell?

I said, *The lowest Sphere, a realm of evil and eternal torment.*

Where is Hell?

I pointed down.

Is this the extent of the world?

Yes, I said, certain, at least, of this answer.

The crone opened *The One Book,* leafing through its pages, as if looking for something. *Do you know the story of the creation of the Spheres?*

I nodded, quoting Genesis: *In the beginning, God created the Heavens and the Spheres. Now the Spheres were without form, and void, and filled with darkness. And God said, Let there be suns, and there was light.*

When I finished my recitation, she put an arthritic finger on the page of *The One Book* and moved it slowly, following the words she read. *In the end,* she said, *those who spurned God came to rule the extents of Earth, and good men despaired. Thus, in a vision, God came to Francis-Munroe, commanding he build the Spheres of the Apostles where the righteous might live in peace.* She looked up at me, her blank eye unfathomable. *Which is true?*

I told her I didn't know a place called earth, unless she meant soil beneath our feet, and had never heard of the man she'd named, nor seen that passage in *The One Book.* But that men could not have created the Spheres, for men did not exist before the Spheres; and that even if they had, outside the Spheres was nothing, and that only God could create something from nothing.

Again, she asked, *Which is true?*

Despite what I'd just said, and what I'd been taught and thought I believed, I couldn't bring myself to supply the rote answer. Instead, I said, *I'm just a boy and no judge of these things.*

Yet you have seen the stars. She sounded sad, though I couldn't have said why. *Men hear only the truths they wish to hear. Until they are ready to write their own. . . .*

Her arm was no longer over my shoulder, and *The One Book* was not in her lap, it was in mine, open where she'd been reading. But the pages were blank and, when I looked up, I found myself alone in the midday brilliance of the Judean wilderness, standing at the foot of a beggarly mound scratched from parched soil, a makeshift cross leaning precariously at the head of Ali's grave.

Beneath the Wall

When Sam shook me awake, it was dark; sitting up, my stomach cramped, and I doubled over, feeling I might be sick. The created man proffered my cane, and I clutched it with a shaky hand. I considered asking Sam to leave, but at that moment I'd had enough of secrets (and, had I been thinking straight, I'd have realized Jotham had seen the created man administering the Gift of Water to me, and had probably informed Sam of my addiction). So I withdrew the vial, tipped a drop onto the palm of my hand, and licked it off. A few minutes later, after I splashed a bit of water on my face, I felt considerably better. Not enough, though, to have an appetite, and so waved away the dry crusts of bread the created man offered.

I'd slept the day through and it was now just after sun-off of the next.

While I slept, Sam had been busy. Early that morning he'd spoken to the created man, then returned to the castle, where he met with Bishop Arrupe and Sister Angelina, who had been chosen to stand for the council. Sam told them that he believed it possible, as I'd said, to breach the walls of the Holy City. I'd shared much of my plan with Sam, and he in turn shared what he thought necessary with the Bishop and Sister, warning them to dole out their words in measured doses when the full council reconvened that night, lessening the chance that specifics would reach ears within the Vatican. Sam then set a time and place where Bishop Arrupe and Sister Angelina would meet us that night with word of the council's decision. In the meantime, they told Sam to make what preparations he could.

Sam did, instructing Jotham to assemble a company of men he trusted. Then he returned to the table outside his tent, where he'd ordered his senior officers to gather, so that they might plan their strategy for an assault on the Holy City.

After they'd dispersed, he'd woken me.

We set out for the castle, Sam holding aloft a dark lantern that had been shuttered on three of four sides. The camp was as silent as it ever got, a few lonely souls lifting their eyes from the hiss and pop of their fires to stare at us. We walked into the plaza ringing the *Castel Sant'Angelo*, where Bishop Arrupe and Sister Angelina waited. The Sister smiled at me, and opened her mouth as if to utter a greeting— then snapped it shut, gaping at something behind me.

I turned, but could see nothing, save the created man. "What is it?" I asked.

"His face," the Sister said, the astonishment evident in her voice. "It's the same as yours."

Bishop Arrupe looked startled. "You can see them both?"

"Yes."

The confidence with which she said this seem to discomfit the Bishop. "Are they identical?"

Sister Angelina peered first at me, then at the created man. "No, there are small differences. One has lines at the corner of his eyes, and the skin looks tighter and more . . . more careworn."

Sam said, "Like a father and son."

"I've never seen the faces of a father and son before."

"Thomas told us this wasn't his father," Bishop Arrupe said.

Sister Angelina blinked. "But it's *Thomas* who has the older face."

Don't leave me, father. That's what the created man had said at the postern gate. And Sam had heard it. He'd also heard me imploring the created man to relent, so as not to hurt my son. I'd no idea if Sam had shared any of these things with Bishop Arrupe, but now the Bishop stared at me as if taking my measure anew. I wish I could say this heartened me, but it didn't.

The three of them waited for me to say something. But what could I say?

Behind us, Jotham entered the plaza, leading in the first group of thirty or so men, all carrying litters borrowed from the hospital, holding not the sick or the wounded, but kegs of black powder.

"The Twelve assent to your plan," Bishop Arrupe said to me. "No doubt you still have much to do."

I nodded, wondering why the Bishop hadn't pressed me further about what Sister Angelina had said. Had he done so for my sake? Or because he didn't want to discuss the issue before so many others? Whatever his reason, I was grateful, even if it seemed more a reprieve than a pardon.

"We will pray for you," Sister Angelina said.

Bishop Arrupe held out his arm to the Sister and, much to my surprise, she took it. Arm in arm, the Jesuit and Ursuline departed, leaving me to wonder if there might be something more between them.

Four gun emplacements guard Rome, one of which we'd passed as Jotham first led us into the city. *The Meek* hadn't bothered trying to move the big guns, knowing their range too limited and their shot too small to breach the walls of the Vatican. Moreover, dragging the cannon to new positions would have been foolhardy, for all four guns would have had to pass across open ground the Fiery Sword had already burned over. Having no use for it, *The Meek* had left the powder where they'd found it, and it was this that Jotham and his men retrieved.

To bring down the wall, we needed to place the explosives beneath it. But no sewers run under the walls of the Vatican. Nor did *The Meek* have engineers or sappers, or time enough to tunnel under the fortifications, a dangerous operation that would have taken months. However, there was an extant tunnel few knew about. Ali and I had crawled through it when we'd escaped the Holy City. War had worked dramatic changes to the cityscape, but I'd been pretty sure I'd recognized the *Albergo Roma* when I'd peered through the window at the top of the Castle. Only I needed to be sure. So the created man sought a path through the rubble to the inn. Fire had gutted its upper floor, which had partially collapsed, but the main floor had held, and in the cellar the oaken cask through which we had emerged remained intact. After moving the blackened timbers and rubble that blocked the entrance, the created man had crawled through the opening and stood in the tunnel that ran beneath the footing of the Vatican's wall.

What Sam had set in motion while I'd been sleeping was beginning to come to fruition. In all, Jotham and his men had collected two hundred and seven kegs of explosive powder. More than enough, the created man assured me, to bring down the wall. When the last of it arrived, we darkened our faces and limbs with soot. Then I shook hands with Sam, who would not be coming with us, shouldered my backpack, and followed the created man around the castle's bastion and into the blasted landscape.

Sister Angelina and Sam hadn't wanted me to go, but I'd insisted: the created man would have to lead those carrying the powder. Though I'd sent him alone the first time, when I thought there was small risk, I wouldn't allow him to go without me this time when the risk was that much greater. Nor, I think, would he have agreed to leave me behind.

For a single man, it would have been easy to dart from shadow to shadow and remain quiet and unseen. Sam's scouts did it every day. But it was a more dangerous proposition for two men carrying a stretcher loaded with a considerable weight of powder. The inn was about a kilometre from where we started. Of necessity, the route the created man had chosen wandered, taking advantage of cover and relatively flat ground so the men would be less likely to trip. At one point, we had to cross an open area a dozen metres wide, and which was visible from several points on the wall. Each pair of men carrying a stretcher waited until the created man—who saw things in the distance and the dark that no man could—signalled. Then two men would hustle across with their litter. All went well until the second last group. They stumbled; their stretcher tipped, and the kegs rolled to one side, thudding to the ground. The men threw themselves flat and lay perfectly still. For several heartbeats we all held our breath. When no alarm was raised, and the created man waved them on, the men crawled across the intervening ground, leaving the kegs and the stretcher where they had fallen.

As we drew closer to the inn once known as the *Albergo Roma*, we moved more slowly, afraid any sound might now be heard by those patrolling the wall. Time seemed to crawl, and every now and then, I had to remind myself to draw breath. But no shouts were raised and, with a suddenness that surprised me, we were there. The men laid the kegs down; then, one by one, they carried them through a front door that hung askew on one hinge. In silence, we formed a human chain, passing the powder through the opening and down the stairs into the pitch dark of the cellar.

I had the men bring half a dozen lamps, and these we lit in the cellar. Then we opened the cask that gave onto the tunnel and, laying blankets inside to dampen the noise, we rolled the kegs through. On the other side, where the tunnel was large enough for a grown man to stand, the men formed another chain, passing the powder twenty metres, and stacking it under a broad stone arch, above which, the created man assured us, was the wall of the Holy City.

From floor to ceiling, we filled that space, save for a path I'd instructed the men to leave in the middle. It had taken longer than I hoped (but less time than I expected), so it was still before midnight when the created man told us we'd stacked enough kegs to do the job, even though we'd used fewer than half of what we'd brought. Jotham asked me what we should do with the remaining powder.

"Fetch the stretchers," I said.

I'd told no one—except the created man—about this part. I didn't dare. If it were to work, it might save lives; but I knew there were those among the Twelve who'd happily sacrifice every last one of *The Meek* to preserve what I hoped these barrels would destroy.

After I told him my plan, the sergeant raised his eyebrows, but didn't move.

No one had said I was in charge. And, at the best of times, I'd never considered myself as being suited to command. But I'd been giving the orders until now, and hoped that would be enough. "Well?"

Jotham looked like he was going to say something, then seemed to think better of it. A moment later, he sent men to retrieve the stretchers.

Angelus

Buried under the Holy City is a second city, ancient and forgotten, a resting place of the dead, the burial place of Saint Peter. Leaving behind those men who no longer had kegs to carry, I led the rest of our contingent through the labyrinthine tunnels to this place. Few, if any, of Jotham's men knew the streets of the Vatican above us. And, in the uncertain light, and through the myriad turns we took, I thought it unlikely any of them had a notion of where we were heading. My memories of the tunnels, however, were like all my memories, undiminished, so I had little trouble leading us to the gate to the necropolis. Here, I instructed Jotham and his men to stack their kegs.

After they'd done so, I guided them back to their comrades, who waited beneath the wall.

Withdrawing a wooden cup from my rucksack, I handed it to the created man, asking him to fill it with powder. When he brought it back, Jotham and I walked a distance from the kegs. I held the cup just above the floor, and I took six big steps backwards; from a hole within the base of the cup, powder trickled out, leaving a thin black line of powder that stretched about three metres along the floor.

"If you pace yourself as I did, you will get a uniform thickness."

I pulled a taper from my backpack, and lit it, using the lamp. Touching it to the end of the black line, we watched as the powder caught, and the spark hissed along the makeshift fuse, filling the tunnel with smoke and a choking sulphurous stench.

"It'll burn two seconds for each step, so if you take sixty steps, it will burn for about two minutes."

Jotham stared at the blackened thread inscribed in the dirt.

"Keep your men hidden until the bells ring for the morning *Angelus*.

Count five minutes and have your men withdraw. After the last man has gone, light the fuse. When the powder goes off, the tunnel will be like the muzzle of a cannon and anyone near will be killed. So get yourself clear. Find a spot as far from the inn and wall as you can, one that will shelter you in case there's debris."

"It'll be dawn," Jotham said. "The men will be spotted from the walls."

"I'm going to try to create a distraction." I think he'd already worked out what I'd planned to do with those kegs, and understood how, though it might save the lives of many men, it came with a price.

"With the powder we carried into the Vatican?"

"Yes. I'll light the fuse as soon as I hear the bells. If all works as I hope, those on the walls will be looking in and not out when your men withdraw."

"What about you? Won't you be caught in the *muzzle* you warned me about?"

"I know the tunnels. We'll have time to get clear."

"You won't have time to get back here."

"There's a way out near the necropolis."

"But you'll be inside the Holy City."

I shrugged. "The Vatican is big. There are plenty of places to hide while we wait for you to arrive."

"And if we fail to breach the wall?"

"I suppose we'll both be in trouble."

Jotham said, "You didn't tell the General about your distraction, did you?"

I admitted I hadn't.

"Because you didn't think he'd agree to it?"

"Yes."

"The General ordered me to protect you, Thomas. I can't let you do this."

"Didn't he also order you to follow my instructions?"

Jotham reluctantly conceded this. "Even so, why not run the fuse back here?"

"It's hundreds of metres. I won't wager the lives of your men on such a long fuse."

"I'll send a man back," Jotham said, "to light a short one in your stead."

"No. I must do this myself."

"I'll accompany you, then."

I shook my head. "Your place is with your men, not me. I'd only be a liability in the assault. But you're a seasoned soldier. A good one if I'm not mistaken. Sam wouldn't trust you if you weren't, and I can see it myself in the way you lead these men. They need you, Jotham, and the truth is, I don't."

"You're wrong," he said. "It's true I've been in more than a few skirmishes, but being a leader isn't about experience. It's about honesty. And trusting the fellow who leads you as much as he trusts you. Even if you can't see the qualities in yourself, Sam does. And so do I. You're more important to us alive, Thomas, than you are dead. Let another man light that fuse."

"I can't."

It was Jotham's turn to shake his head. "Why not?"

"You're a soldier. You do as other men ask, without questioning the right or wrong of things, trusting those who command to not lead you into sin. Only I don't know if lighting that fuse is right or wrong. Maybe it's both. But if I had to guess, I'd guess it's more a grave sin than anything else. The sort that would condemn those who committed it to eternal damnation. That's why I didn't tell Sam, or anyone else. I won't knowingly lead other men into sin. And I won't have them do it on my behalf. If this is to be done, I will do it myself, and it will be my sin alone."

"Let it be your sin," Jotham said, crossing his arms. "But I won't break my oath to Sam. I'm coming with you."

I could see there was no more chance of talking him out of accompanying us than there was of talking me out of lighting that fuse. So I gave him the cup, and told him to lay the fuse under the wall and instruct his men what to do.

A short time later he returned to where the created man and I waited. Then the three of us turned our backs on his men and walked into darkness—and towards Jotham's death.

We had overwhelming numbers on our side. But the breach in the wall of the Vatican would be visible from the dome of Saint Peter's, and anyone attempting the gap could be cut by the Fiery Sword. The blade of light couldn't be everywhere at once, Sam reasoned, and if enough poured through the breach, some would make it—one in four was his guess. And that was likely all that would be needed to take the

Holy City. Even so, a horrific number would die; and those who didn't would forever be scarred, if not from their own wounds, then from their memories of that day, of the nauseating reek as the flesh of their comrades—their friends—was seared from their bones, the air rent by their agonized cries.

When I'd told Jotham I wished to create a distraction, that had been only partly true; I'd also hoped to bring down the dome of Saint Peter's—and with it, the Fiery Sword. Supporting the dome is a drum surrounded by peristyles; this, in turn, is borne on four massive, stone piers, each eighteen metres in diameter. Directly beneath the Basilica lies the necropolis. The created man had some remarkable qualities, not the least of which was his ability to know, indoors or out, in light or dark, exactly where he stood—and, if he could see a thing, knowing to the centimetre how far away it was. Even if he moved so the thing was out of sight, he could still tell you how far away it was. Which is why, when we returned to the gate of the necropolis, I asked him where we should carry the explosives so they were adjacent to, and below, one of the Basilica's great pillars.

He pointed.

I'd kept this part of my plan to myself because I knew that even if Sam consented, Bishop Arrupe or Sister Angelina—no matter that this might limit the casualties on both sides—would never condone the destruction of the greatest of all Churches and the centre of the Faith. In truth, I also had a selfish reason for trying to save lives: I hoped this would lighten my accumulation of sin. Every sin, the Priests had taught us, stained the soul. If bringing down the dome meant fewer would die, I believed my burden might be less. To my childish mind, there was a simple calculus of sin. But I was mistaken. *Suffering is not increased by numbers; one body can contain all the suffering the world can feel.* So I read in *The One Book* years later, and so I learned that day.

Why, I wondered, *does God ask us to make such choices?*

Jotham and I picked up the kegs.

The created man had told me the explosion would certainly produce the desired distraction; but, unlike the wall—for which he knew the dimensions and could approximate the weight—he had no way of knowing if it would sufficiently compromise the pillar. The blast would have to happen in exactly the right place, and displace enough material to undermine the pillar. He didn't think it would. As odd as it may sound, this heartened me. I thought, *Let God decide if there's to be a miracle*—and felt a flush of shame at trying to sidestep my responsibility.

I walked into the necropolis, Jotham on my heels, the created man on our heels, carrying two more kegs than we did while still managing the lantern.

Trying to go in the general direction in which the created man had pointed, I moved down a narrow street of mausoleums, each the size of a house, with square lintels and triangular roofs, many sporting columns on either side of their doors, above which some bore sombre Latin inscriptions, eulogizing those within. The street ran more or less straight for fifty metres, at which point it jogged around a bend, coming to a dead end at a brick wall. Here, I looked back at the created man and he inclined his head to indicate we should go right. I turned under an arched passageway and continued through a series of small chambers with various sized sarcophagi, emerging, finally, into a small grotto that contained a dilapidated stone altar.

"Here," the created man said, stepping past me and lowering his kegs next to the wall behind the altar.

Over the next hour or so, we ferried the remaining kegs into the rough chapel. Pulling the wooden stopper from the last of them, the created man poured powder into a cup identical to the one Jotham had left with his men, and handed it to me. I laid a fuse long enough to burn two minutes. With a taper held between clasped hands, I knelt on the ancient flagstones to pray for forgiveness; after a moment, Jotham knelt next to me. Above us, many Bishops and Cardinals would soon be kneeling, too, doing their morning obeisance.

I didn't hear the bells ring for the *Angelus*, but the created man told me it was time, so I lit the wick. Then the three of us ran through the darkness of the necropolis, towards the world of the living.

Between Two Armies

Forum Sancti Petri: Saint Peter's Square.

Not a square, but an immense ellipsoid *piazza*, embraced on either side by mammoth, semi-circular colonnades, four columns deep. At its centre stands a towering obelisk of red granite, surmounted by a huge cross and flanked by two identical fountains—the largest to be found in the city. Towards the Basilica, the colonnades straighten, framing a smaller plaza, trapezoidal in shape, broadening to encompass the Church's enormous façade. Hovering above this is the crowning glory of the Church, the monumental dome of the Basilica, dominating not just Saint Peter's, but all of Rome. The square is a place of grandeur, a place where the faithful might prostrate themselves on the vast expanse of cobblestone before the glory of almighty God.

Like any paved gathering place, there are storm drains. Above us, through a sewer grate, I saw the firmament was grey with the first hint of sun-on.

I'd tried to mark the time the fuse had been burning as we'd run through the tunnels, but had quickly lost count, forced to focus every bit of my attention on not taking a misstep in the wavering light, almost colliding with the created man when he'd stopped abruptly. I'd no idea how much time remained—nor was I wholly convinced the fuse would even do its job.

"Thirty-one seconds," he said.

He stood astride a small channel in the middle of the floor, through which ran a trickle of water, the grate directly overhead. Turning away from us, he went down on one knee, and Jotham stepped lightly onto his back and then his shoulders, grasping the iron bars now within reach. Clasping Jotham's ankles, the created man slowly rose. With a rasping sound, the grate lifted free on the side Jotham held; it angled up, pivoting, until it was perpendicular to the ground. Another few centimetres and it pulled free of his grip, falling backwards with a *clang* loud enough to wake the dead. Jotham hoisted himself out of the sewer. A moment later he extended his arms down towards me. The created man crouched again, and I climbed onto his back and and gripped Jotham's hands; before I knew it, I'd been lifted clear of the sewer and was on my feet. Almost immediately, the created man leapt through the opening and landed softly beside me, still absurdly clutching his lantern.

We'd emerged near the obelisk, the Basilica on the far side. At this early hour, the square was largely deserted. When Kite had brought us here, during sun-on, I'd been overpowered by the immensity of the square; in the pre-dawn gloom, its magnificence was muted, the plaza brooding, making it a morose place that spoke more of damnation than redemption.

"Fifteen seconds."

A hundred metres distant, a clutch of nuns, who'd been about to enter Saint Peter's, stopped to stare at us, while two *Cent Suisse* left their post before the great doors of the Church and hastened in our direction. The created man grabbed my hand and drew me away from the sewer.

"Ten seconds."

A few metres ahead of us Jotham stopped; he scrutinized a bivouac close to the Vatican City wall, likely for those *Garde* manning the ramparts. There would have been sentries at this encampment, and perhaps at other places around the square. No doubt they, too, had heard the grate, and were perhaps moving towards us. But if so, I hadn't caught sight of them in my cursory glances; rather, my attention had been focused on the façade and the dome.

"Five sec—"

From the drain through which we'd climbed—and a dozen others around the square—came a sonorous *boom*. Dust, thrown up into the air from between cobblestones, rolled out from the Basilica like a phantom wave; as it broke around us, I felt the ground shudder, columns of dust geysering from the sewers, ballooning out, making the square look like an orchard of giant, malignant mushrooms. I fancied I smelled sulphur.

The *Cent Suisse* had stumbled to a halt, no doubt taken aback by the tremor that had run under their feet and the disconcerting sight of the dust thrown up from the drains and now settling into moribund, earthbound clouds.

None of this mattered; the dome still stood.

Had it collapsed, I imagine the *Cent Suisse* would have quickly lost interest in us. Instead, they hustled towards us with renewed urgency. I thought of Kite, who'd been one of them, who'd been killed by them. They'd kill us with just as little compunction. I wanted to run, only there was nowhere to go, save back to the sewer, now choked with impenetrable dust that would make passage impossible—at least for me. I'd suffocate. But my son wouldn't. I turned to the created man, pointed to the sewer. "*Go!*"

He responded by placing his lantern on the ground and positioning himself between me and the advancing men. Jotham stepped up next to him, drawing his short sword, no matter that it would be little good against the halberds the *Suisse* carried. Around the square, alarms were being raised, and shouts issued from the camp behind us.

My mind raced, but I could think of nothing to do, save watch the men who closed in on us.

When the *Cent Suisse* were no more than twenty metres away, the shock-wave of the second explosion rocked us from behind, and I nearly lost my footing.

Debris pattered down and a gruel of dust lifted from the ground and swirled round me. Blinking the grit from my eyes, I turned. The wall, where we had mined it, had merely sagged a small amount. I stared as a *Garde,* who'd been patrolling the wall walk, picked himself up, as surprised as me that he was still alive. In that surreal moment, we looked across the distance at each other, and I felt a bottomless despair, at the lives already lost, and those that would be lost, because my plans had miscarried. I wanted to weep—

As if from a gargantuan beast, a hellish groan arose, followed by a series of ear-splitting staccato *cracks*, like the surface of the Sphere itself were fracturing. The wall of the Holy City dissolved, mortared stones shivering apart, clacking and grinding as they cascaded down like a waterfall into the cavity the explosives had left below, tumbling that hapless man who'd just regained his feet. If he cried out, his plaint was lost in the grinding roar that thrummed through my chest.

An angry cloud of dust billowed over the bivouac, stones burying the tents nearest the wall, and the rush of air and dust knocking others askew; some tore free of their stays and were thrown up into the air where the sheets snapped and danced madly. The wave scudded in our direction, too big and fast to outrun. Throwing myself to the ground, I covered my head with my arms as the pother swallowed us. Everything went dark and deathly silent. I couldn't see a finger length before my eyes. In the time it took to count to ten, a thick layer of dust settled on me like a funeral pall. I was surprised at how heavy it was, and at how I could hear granules of debris ticking against its surface like the sound of a perverse rain.

I lay that way for what seemed an eternity, but couldn't have been more than a minute. In that time I hadn't drawn a breath, and now that I tried, I found I couldn't. Alarmed, I thrust myself to my feet, hoping to attain clear air—and, to my surprise, the dust fell away from me in a single sheet. I found myself facing the Basilica in the midst of a murky sun-on, the air still hazed, but breathable and clear enough to see, the created man standing at my side, every inch of him coated in grey dust, all trace of colour washed out. Around my ankles lay his dust-covered cloak. To my right, Jotham was on both knees, hacking and coughing; he, too, was no less grimed, a grey figure kneeling in a charcoal landscape. He struggled to his feet.

I turned to the created man. His lips were slightly parted, his expression blank, eyes darting everywhere, as if he didn't understand what was happening. Like he'd just woken. I snatched up his cape and, snapping the dust from it, handed it to my son. "Put it on." As he fastened the cape around his neck, his hands shook, so I took one in mine to comfort him while I surveyed the square.

Grey shrouded everything. I spotted two mounds, watched as they stirred themselves and rose: the *Cent Suisse* who'd been moving towards us. Of the Sisters, there was no sign. The square was eerily silent, save for the creak of settling stone, and the ticking of smaller pebbles dribbling downwards—until a plaintive cry echoed. More joined, an escalating chorus of pain and disbelief.

The breach was far bigger than I'd expected. At least a hundred metres from side to side. Of the few tents that remained upright, all were tattered and lop-sided. The *Garde* who were still able rose from the debris like ghosts. Some were naked, others wore night clothes. On many was what I took to be the sheen of blood. A few staggered in confusion, while others rooted through the tatters of their camp, searching, I suppose, for their armour and weapons—or their comrades. From beyond the wall, from the broken and scarred city outside, a distant cheer arose.

The Meek.

This gave me small consolation. And less so when Papist troops, who must have been billeted beneath the colonnades or within adjacent buildings, began pouring into the square, many struggling to buckle armour as they ran towards their banners. Orders were shouted and, behind the fountains, ragged lines of infantry resolved from the confusion, archers taking up positions behind them, all looking towards that gap and thinking of those men who would pour through it.

I felt my son tug on my hand. "We must go."

But I stood firm, watching as *The Meek* clambered over the remains of the wall, scuttling like a horde of insects, from cover to cover. Hundreds, perhaps thousands. In places it seemed like the rubble itself moved. Just as in the dream I'd had so long ago, my son and I stood, hand in hand, between two armies about to clash.

Above us, a flight of arrows arced towards *The Meek*, and the air was cleaved by the Fiery Sword, hissing and popping as it burned through the dust, larger particles glittering as they combusted. Men and women screamed as it blinded them and set them afire. I'd expected those scrambling through the debris to hunker down, but they didn't. Leastwise, not most of them. Instead, they picked their way through the ruins of the wall with determination, those most forward now only a few metres from the cobblestones of the Holy City.

"We must go," the created man said again, his voice pitched higher than I'd ever heard it.

Still, I couldn't look away from what I had wrought.

The created man tugged more forcefully, and this time I staggered backwards.

I pulled my hand free of his grip.

To my left, Jotham coughed and spat loudly. In a voice so rough I could barely understand him, he said, "He's right."

"Where would you have us go?"

On the wall-walk, half a dozen Papists had overcome their surprise and scurried to the broken edge; they began showering down arrows on the *The Meek*'s vanguard.

Jotham pointed. "In the sewer we may suffocate, but we'll die if we stand here."

The Meek's advance had finally faltered, stymied by the Fiery Sword before them and by the arrows from behind and above. Here and there dead men lay in the rubble, burning. I felt sick. We'd failed to bring down the dome, and *The Meek* would pay the price.

"I can't protect you here," Jotham said.

Bowmen in *The Meek*'s rearguard loosed a storm of arrows towards the summit of the broken wall; under this withering onslaught, the Papists fell back from the edges of the parapet. The advance resumed. The vanguard was close enough now that I could see they carried odd shields: large and flat and squarish, requiring two hands to hold. Most remarkable of all, however, was that the surfaces of the shields seemed to change texture and colour as they moved. When those in the lead made the plaza, they drew together and formed a tightly knit wall of these shields, perhaps fifty metres across—a sizable target for the Fiery Sword. I thought them mad, and watched in horror as the Sword raked their array. But instead of igniting the shields, the light reflected, lashing back in our direction, crackling across the pavement a few metres in front of us, incising a thick black line.

Mirrors! I thought. *Sam had them bring mirrors!*

Held as they were, the line of mirrors wasn't perfect; there were gaps, and some also had frames of gilt or black, which would not reflect the light. Nor, I found out later, were the mirrors themselves completely immune to the effects of the Sword; any small imperfection in the surface, or in the mirror's silvering, were places where the Sword, if held steady, could penetrate.

The blade of light swept over them again, only this time the reflection hissed over our heads and back towards the Basilica—and I realized *The Meek* were angling them, aiming at the dome. Or trying to.

Jotham stepped in front of me; I suppose he was trying to shield me from the reflected light, as he'd tried, a moment before, to protect me from the *Cent Suisse*. And, in this, he succeeded, for I heard him gasp as the Sword cut back our way again. His clothes and armour ignited; flames sheathed him. He staggered forward a step, spun, and fell to the ground, writhing. Stunned, I stood there, the scent of Jotham's blistered flesh curling into my nostrils as he died at my feet.

Behind me, my son groaned.

I swung around. He lay on the ground, the left side of his face singed beyond recognition. His ear was gone, and there was only a black cavity where his eye had been; the left side of his mouth had crooked up into a black grimace. Smoke wreathed his head, and small licks of flame still danced on remaining strands of hair. He lay perfectly still. I knelt next to him, using my hands to smother what was still burning, feeling his skin adhere to mine, peeling from his scalp as I lifted my hands.

Tears clouded my vision.

How, I wondered, *could God let such a thing happen?*

I looked up at the great dome of Saint Peter's, dimmed by the dust that hung in the air, and held up both hands, my son's flesh hanging from my palms in accusation. For the first time in my life I cursed God.

As if in answer, the dome of Saint Peter's rumbled forward like a ponderous warship that had weighed anchor. There would be no hiding in the sewer or anywhere else from His retribution. Only on the peak of the cupola was a lantern, and atop this a cross that canted forward, when it should have been fully vertical. The dome wasn't gliding towards us as I'd thought, but rolling forward, like an immense ball. No sooner had I realized this, then it disintegrated into a cascade of thousands upon thousands of panels from which it was constructed, tumbling in on the Basilica with a deafening roar, a massive plume of dust jetting up to mark its passing.

Stunned, I knelt there, not seeing but hearing other sections of Saint Peter's Basilica collapsing, while the colossal façade stood unscathed and imperious—until a wave of dust rolled over the upper cornice and poured down it, obscuring it, and cascading into the square.

Behind me, the cheer that rose from the ranks of *The Meek* was exultant.

Glass shattered; I turned my head. Everywhere men cast down their mirrors and drew swords. Behind were ranks four or five deep. A squat, thickset fellow at the fore bellowed a wordless war cry and, as one, they charged.

The created man's arms closed around my chest, his face pressed close to mine, the odour of his burnt flesh dizzying me. I felt him hoisting me to my feet, dragging me away from that bristling wave of retribution. I lost my footing; he hauled me all the same, the heels of my sandals scraping along the ground. A few desultory arrows clattered to the ground around us, though such was the confusion, and my own preoccupation, I couldn't tell which side had loosed them or if they'd even been aimed at us.

I'd no idea how badly the created man had been injured; nor, for that matter, if he was in pain. But I could tell he struggled now. Three times he stumbled, grunting wordlessly, a sound I'd never heard from him before. I wanted to make it easier for him, to tell him to let me go, but his grip was so tight around my chest, I couldn't catch my breath enough to say anything. Abruptly, he dropped into a crouch, hunching over me; several thuds shivered through him, like he was being punched on the back. But when he rose, I could see no one who might have delivered those blows. He staggered—

—then the ground dropped out from under my feet. The created man opened his arms, and I fell into the sewer, darkness swallowing me.

When I hit, my left ankle turned; I gasped as a jolt of agonizing pain blotted out everything. I lay prone, ears ringing, my injury howling displeasure. Fingers of thick, cloying dust worked themselves into my lungs; a coughing fit shook me to the bone, sending aftershocks through my ankle. When the intensity of the pain abated enough for me to be aware of anything else, I heard the sound of cloth tearing, then felt the created man's touch on my hand. Gently, he pulled my fingers away from my mouth. In my palm he placed a piece of moistened cloth.

"Breathe through this," he said, voice muted.

Ignoring my ankle as best I could, I cleared my throat, spat out the grit that had accumulated, and pressed the cloth to my face. Sucking through the coarse material, I pulled in a small amount of air. After I managed to draw three or four breaths, I found a rhythm that seemed to promise I wouldn't suffocate.

Above us was the thump of running soldiers, the ring of sword on sword, shield on shield. There were incomprehensible shouts and screams—of ferocity and anguish—and, now and then, grunts of stupefied pain. Above all else, the blaring of marshal horns, exhorting those fighting to an even greater frenzy.

Cool hands slipped under me, arms cradled and lifted me. The created man seemed to sway as he took slow, careful steps deeper into the tunnel; with every movement, my ankle throbbed mercilessly. I tried to put my arm around the created man's back to support myself, but my fingers struck something hard. I moved my fingers around it—a wooden shaft. I ran my hand along it until I felt the arrow's fletching. Then I reached farther, felt more shafts. Through the cloth, I said, "You're shot."

He staggered forward without answering. When the sounds of battle were greatly diminished, he stopped. Although I couldn't see them now, I'd seen the niches before as we'd run through the sewer, carved in both walls and at various heights, many still rimmed with mortar that had long ago cemented stone covers across their openings. A sewer that had once served as a catacomb. The created man struggled to lift me higher, then set me down in one of the niches; my foot twisted slightly, and a bright spur of pain blazed from my ankle. I must have lost consciousness.

When I came to, I lay on my back, cold stone pressing in on me. The searing pain in my ankle had diminished marginally. My throat felt raw; a fit of coughing seized me, and jolts of pain blazed from my injury at each spasm. By the time it subsided, I'd remembered the cloth. But it must have slipped from my fingers, for I couldn't find it.

"Part your lips as little as possible," the created man wheezed, "and take slow, shallow breaths."

I did, found I could breathe. *He lifted me to get me above the settling dust.*

"You . . . you must relax." Though he tried to hide it, the hurt was evident in his voice. "Breathe . . . slowly," he urged.

Dust coated my tongue and throat; I tried futilely to strain it through my teeth, tried not to gag on it. I heard a small, pathetic mewling, realized it came with each of my exhalations.

"Hold . . . hold out your hand."

My fingers closed around a small cylinder, smooth as glass and cool to the touch. My heart skipped a beat: the vial which held the Gift of Water. We'd left both my cane and *The One Book* in the care of Sam's orderly, but the created man had the foresight to bring this. Because he'd been thinking of me. This was the reason he was here now, and why he'd stood with his back to the archers. To protect me. But I was his father; I should have been the one to protect him. Instead I'd dragged him here, into harm's way.

When I held the cylinder out to him, he said, "It . . . it will not help this other." Taking my hand in his, he closed my fingers around the vial, and pushed it back.

I wanted to weep, from my pain, and from my failure. *What good is a father who can't save his son?*

I found the stopper, undid it. "I'm sorry," I said and, hoping for an end to my pain, to our pain, I tipped the vial back, emptying it.

Moriah

No one who prefers father or mother to me is worthy of me. No one who prefers son or daughter to me is worthy of me.

Father? I say, straining against my bonds to see him.

Without remembering a single step, I know I've taken this path a thousand times before, wood cradled in my arms, carrying it up the mount as my father bid me, arranging it on the altar of our sacrifice. A thousand times, bound, I lie upon this bed of sticks.

Yes, my son, *he replies. In one hand, he holds the slaughtering knife; in the other, a wooden husk, within which an ember, wrapped in cotton, slowly smoulders. He is a young man clad in a breechcloth, whose body, like Saint Sebastian's, is pierced by arrows too numerous to count.*

Look, *I say,* here are the fire and the wood, but where is the lamb for the burnt offering?

My son, *I reply,* God himself will provide the lamb for the burnt offering.

Slowly, carefully, I place the husk on the ground. Or he does.

We wait, wondering when the Angel of Yaweh will call from above, David, David, do not raise your hand against that boy.

—or—

Thomas, Thomas, do not raise your hand against that boy.

But he never comes, not before I ready the knife, not before I make my decision. Never before the decision to honour God's behest.

I raise the blade.

Lying on the altar (or standing at its foot) I wonder if perhaps it's not a test of man's faith, but of God's. Of his faith in us. Does He still care enough about us to stay our hand?

Sometimes the blade will fall, piercing my son, piercing me. When this happens, I arch my back and scream, and blood runs; later, if I live, I watch it sizzle in the fire.

—or—

There are times the voice of the Angel implores me to stop before I strike. Do not harm him, for now I know you fear God. You have not refused me your own beloved son.

Which will it be this time?

Around my neck is the small pouch I carry, and within it something stirs restlessly, its movements echoed by the man-shaped machine that lies on the altar. Whether God has commanded me to sacrifice my son, or to be sacrificed by my son, I can't say. I stare into his eyes, my eyes, the tip of the knife poised above my breast, and wonder if he'll strike. If I'll strike.

Father? *I say.* Son?

Either way, it's an act of faith. I wonder: What kind of God would ask this of a father? What kind of God would both kill and save his Son?

I, Yahweh your God, am a jealous God and I punish a parent's fault in the children, the grandchildren, and the great-grandchildren among those who hate me.

—or—

Parents may not be put to death for their children, nor children for parents, but each must be put to death for his own crime.

I wait patiently on His Judgement.

Victory and Defeat

I woke coughing, still in the grip of the Water.

Looking up from the bottom of a well, across the lip of which hung a corpse, something too thick to be water running down the dead man's left arm, dripping from the tips of his fingers, *tick tick tick*, against the stone floor, a tiny warmth splattering on my cheek. Smelling it, tasting it.

My head pounded mercilessly; the nauseating stench of decomposing flesh wafted down from above, seeking its own level. Seeking the dead. Ghosts stirred on the periphery of my vision.

Not a well, a sewer.

When I tried to sit up, excruciating pain radiated from my ankle; I lay on my back, shivering, breathing raggedly. When the worst had faded, I gritted my teeth, and slowly, ever so slowly, levered myself until I was sitting. Perspiration beaded my forehead and my arms shook.

My ankle had been splinted.

Bending forward, I fingered the white fabric, proof that my son was still alive. God, it seemed, had granted me a reprieve. Through the bandage I felt two pieces of wood, smooth and square, immobilizing my injury, and my leg, bloated to twice its usual size. Oddly, I couldn't feel my own touch, as if the taut and distended skin was someone else's. But when I lifted my fingers away, pain flowered. I gasped, blinked back tears. I might have fainted.

The only illumination came from the inlet above. On either side, the tunnel faded to an impenetrable black within metres; if anyone hid in the shadows, they were as silent as the dead man above. Then it struck me that I shouldn't have been able to see anything. I brushed my hand along the floor and small dust clouds swirled. I wondered how long I'd been down here. *Long enough*, I thought, *for the air to clear.*

Above me, the corpse seemed to nod in agreement. Then it jerked back, and the created man's head and torso occluded the light, wreathed in a burning halo.

"Don't move," he said.

Dropping through the opening, he landed next to me; only his motion wasn't fluid, not like before, and he lost his balance, going down on one knee, grunting. On his back I could see the remains of a dozen arrow shafts, splintered a few centimetres above the point at which they entered his flesh. His shirt was discoloured below each wound, not with dried blood, but with a stain that might have been left by tallow. One side of his face was charred; the other was translucent. Beneath the skin, on his temple, a shadowy cog turned.

"I dreamt I'd killed you."

The created man nodded. In his arms, he held a rig of leather belts, rope and twisted cloth. He lifted it up and pulled it apart. "Put your arms through these loops."

I'd thought it a tangled mess, but I could see it was a harness of sorts. When I did as he asked, it fit me perfectly, encircling legs and torso, forming a crude seat. In the midst of my chest, a thick, braided rope had been knotted around two horizontal straps; he tossed the free end out of the sewer. Then he jumped—not out of the sewer as he might have done before, but just high enough to grab the sides of the inlet, struggling to pull himself out.

A moment later, he straddled the opening; in his hands he held the rope, its free end trailing over his shoulder. From the bottom of one of his sandals hung a strand of clear, viscous fluid.

"When I lift, the weight of your leg will exert a downward force on your ankle if your heel rests on the floor. Turn your leg so the end of one splint is the last thing to lift free."

I did so, wincing with the effort.

"When your leg lifts free, the weight of your foot may pull on your ankle. Prepare yourself."

Reaching up, I wrapped both hands around the rope, and closed my eyes.

He was right; it hurt so much I bit my lower lip and tasted blood. I felt myself being hoisted, and for a moment the pain washed away all sense of the world; when I opened my eyes again, I found myself chin-level with the ground, blinking back tears in the light of day. Holding the rope in one hand, the created man reached down with his other and grabbed the straps where they clustered on my chest.

Before, he might have easily lifted me; now he struggled to hold me aloft.

Then I was up and out—and cradled in his arms.

The created man said something, but I didn't hear—my attention was on the torn and shattered corpses littering the square. Many were twisted into grotesque positions and, upon all, feasted legions of flies and carrion birds. Here and there were patches of cobblestone, blackened with dried blood, everywhere the frenzied marks of the battle inscribed in grey dust like a mad man's scrawl. Near the obelisk, bodies had been stacked like cord wood, five or six deep, a plethora of feathered arrows protruding from them. With horror, I realized they'd been used to create a rampart. Of those uniforms I could make out, only a small minority were the colours of the *Garde*. My heart sank. This wasn't a reprieve, it was judgement.

"David?"

I nodded.

"In the left pocket of my cloak is a knife. Can you reach it?"

I pulled free a large, blood-stained dagger—a sacrificial knife.

"Cut the rope free from the harness."

After I did what he'd asked, I wanted nothing more than to toss the knife away; instead, I rested my hand on my stomach, clutching the dagger so hard my knuckles went white. On the created man's back, I could see the sheen of fresh fluid trails.

Scattered around the square, dark spirits hovered, vestiges of the Water. They wept or railed in unnerving silence. A few still fought, too foolish to know they were dead.

Struggling to keep his balance, the created man staggered towards the Basilica, moving past the legion of ghosts; I winced at each step. The great façade of the Church still stood, smoke drifting listlessly from three of its upper-story windows. Of the dome, nothing could be seen, not even the ragged edge of the drum that had once supported it. Slowly, almost drunkenly, the created man shuffled past countless broken bodies. When we passed the obelisk and the wall of corpses, a furtive movement caught my eye; I craned my neck to look back. There, a ragged looter tried to worry something from the wall of flesh.

"*The dead know nothing whatever,*" the created man said, quoting Ecclesiastes. His halo had vanished. "*Their love, their hate, their jealousy, have perished long since, and they will never have any further part in what goes on under the suns.*"

The created man wasn't looking back as I was; he was looking at my leg. I hadn't noticed in the darkness of the sewer, but the material binding my ankle was embroidered white linen, looking like nothing so much as cloth ripped from the hem of a choir boy's surplice, and my splints resembled the lacquered pieces of a cross that had been snapped apart. On one side, peeking above the bandage, I could see a tiny hand of gold broken off at the wrist, palm out, through which a miniature nail had been driven. I thought then of the blood on the cobblestones, dried from a battle long over, and wondered about the body at the lip of the sewer. The blood had run freely and still held the warmth of life. I looked at the created man, then away, not wanting to know what he'd done—what he thought he had to do—to keep me alive.

The smoke coming from the Basilica thinned for a moment, and I saw *Loggia of the Blessings*, a white balcony from which are announced canonizations and beatifications, and from which the Pope, after his election, grants his Apostolic blessing, the *Urbi et Orbi—To the City and all the Spheres*. A body hung from the rail of this balcony, one adorned in a spotless white cassock and *zucchetto,* on whose shoulders rested a red Papal *mozzetta.* Like a common criminal, the Pope's head had been blackened with pitch.

"*The dead know nothing,*" the created man said again, lurching right, staggering towards the great colonnade.

We passed under the massive columns, emerging on the other side, then cut diagonally towards the Apostolic Palace, a multistoried building whose upper floors were girded with evenly spaced, rectangular windows. Passing under an arched gate, the sentry posts on either side manned by the memories of those who'd once stood there, we entered a courtyard. A cloud of birds squawked their displeasure at being disturbed and took wing; startled, I tightened my fist around the knife, only to realize it was gone—perhaps had never been there. The birds had been feasting on a dozen corpses, all bearing the uniform of the Papal Guard and sprawled across stone steps leading up to open double doors. Someone had shoved aside those bodies to make a narrow way to the door. Through the ranks of these dead soldiers, their phantom hands extended towards us, the created man carried me into the *Palazzo Apostolico*.

Inside, there were no bodies. Other than the shards from a broken vase, there was scant evidence of violence.

Under a cavernous ceiling, the created man walked to a marble staircase, then struggled up to the second floor, each step jolting my ankle. He turned left into a hall—and I caught my breath, pain forgotten for a moment. Every space on wall and ceiling, every nook and cranny, was decorated with a fresco, each bordered in gilt, some no bigger than the palm of my hand, others filling entire walls. We passed several doors surrounded by opulent paintings of Heaven and Hell, filled with Angels and Saints, demons and sinners. Some scenes I recognized; others I did not. They were astonishing works, beautiful and terrifying at once, the torment and ecstasy written on faces so real that, if we stepped into the room beneath the painting, I thought it possible we might find ourselves in the places thus depicted.

At the end of the hall, a second staircase rose above the first, and the created man laboured up this. At its summit was yet another hall filled with frescoes, but we turned away this time, the created man's footsteps echoing. We passed through a small room and into another corridor, its walls adorned with only a few hung pieces of art. For a moment the created man wobbled, and I thought he might fall, but he caught himself. Unsteadily, he carried me down the corridor to a stuccoed wall. On this the created man placed his palm. I was startled to see the outline of a door materialize. Swinging inward of its own accord, it revealed a spartan, white room. This room seemed familiar— and I realized I'd been in here before. Or at least in its twin, for this room was identical to one in which I'd woken, under the Holy Lands.

The created man crossed the threshold, and the door sealed behind him. He stumbled just before the bed, half dropping, half-flinging me onto the mattress; pain radiated from my shattered ankle as I landed. I think I cried out, then, and wept in agony, though I can't remember for certain.

When my torment abated—enough, at least, to regain a semblance of rationality—I turned my head until I found the created man next to the bed, face down on the floor, his back bristling with broken arrow shafts. Though I called out, he didn't stir.

I hadn't the strength to get to him; nor would the bed (if it was anything like the bed in that other room) have let me. Already, ghostly fingers crept over me, strange pale strands exploring the contours of my body, finding ways to enter it. Perhaps they had already, for I experienced a wash of calm, as unnatural as it was sudden, and I hated myself for the relief I felt. I fought it, tried to turn my ankle to create a spur of pain, but felt nothing. I cursed myself for letting him carry me, but it, too, was a feeble protest. If he was dead, I wished myself dead, too, though I knew it an unforgivable sin.

All this death, I thought, staring at him. *And for what?*

At the end of the bed stood the hermit I'd encountered in the wilderness, only now he bore stigmata; he looked upon me sadly.

"Why?" I asked him.

Do not suppose that I have come to bring peace to the Spheres, he said, his voice slow and melancholic, his lips not moving. *It is not peace I have come to bring, but a sword.*

I opened eyes I hadn't realized were closed—and found myself alone in a soulless white room.

Memories Old and New

The infirmary had changed.

Before, the interior had been a seamless cube of uniform colour; yet now there was a door in one wall, a large, mullioned window opposite, and the floor had a grid of alternating white and black tiles. The mattress had none of the strange buoyancy of the one in the other infirmary, and the bed itself was narrower and sported an iron headboard and a rail on either side. To my right were two tall cabinets, the sort apothecaries use to hold their tinctures; to my left a narrow table, on which lay *The One Book* and my cane. I had been dressed in nightclothes, and the pouch had been removed from my neck. At the foot of the bed, Sister Angelina sat in a wicker chair, head bowed, snoring gently.

I let her sleep.

It may seem odd I did so, for I had a thousand questions; but every muscle in my body ached, and I felt disoriented. I wanted a few moments of peace to order my thoughts. I also knew the Water had tainted everything, and I'd no idea how much of what I remembered was real and how much was not. Once, I'd believed my memory infallible; now, every recollection was suspect—even ones I believed I'd possessed all my life.

We are our memories, and they are us. And though we may possess a multitude of memories (I, more than most), most lie dormant, until something—a sight, a sound, a smell—triggers them. As I lay there, examining memories new and old, a recollection of my childhood came to me.

At age seven, I'd discovered a hidden cupboard in our house whose door was made to look part of the wainscoting. A dusty, cramped space that extended no more than a metre—so narrow my shoulders scraped both walls as I squeezed in. In the back I found a stack of mouldering books with raised bands on their spines, and whose gilt letters had flaked off, leaving only enough ghostly characters so I could tell they weren't Bibles. They were forbidden. I remember thinking I should tell my father. But I didn't. Not because I was afraid he'd punish me for finding the books (by this point, I'd already come to the realization that children who bring to light their elders' sins are often treated as if they'd committed those sins themselves); rather, I feared in telling him, the secret of this cupboard would no longer be mine and mine alone. So I said nothing. And until I became too big to fit, I squeezed into that cupboard from time to time, pulling the door shut behind me, sitting in the dark, legs drawn up to my chin, one calf touching that small pile of proscribed books. Books I never dared open.

But I had another memory, too, of something else I'd found in that cupboard. A memory no less dim than of those books. Propped against the back wall, an old walking cane, missing its ferrule, its finish veined by a spiderweb of fine cracks. Save for its age, this cane was identical to the cane the created man had given me.

This memory shook me more than I can say, made me question everything. I wondered if the created man had brought me here. Or anywhere. Or had he, too, merely been a figment of the Water?

And if he had, then what of my son?

I couldn't stomach such a notion; instead, I focused on what I could see before my eyes, looking for proof of my past in the present.

More effort was required than I thought to raise the sheet; there were no splints on my left ankle and no apparent discolouration or swelling. Bracing myself, I flexed. My ankle was stiff, as if through disuse, and it seemed to me that my ankle didn't move quite right, but there was no jolt of pain, only profound soreness. I rotated my foot, turning it in circles. On each revolution, something inside went *pop*, like the crack of a knuckle. I let the sheet down.

The window had been thrown wide, and from the aspect I knew I was on the third floor of the Apostolic Palace, on the side of building opposite Saint Peter's square. If I had to guess, I would have said it was midday.

I recollected our steps, from the sewer to the courtyard, and into the building. Then up the two sets of stairs, and into the corridor. In doing so, I composed a mental map of the building and its dimensions—and realized that, if these memories were true, the hidden room had, in fact, been in the midst of the building where there could have been no window.

The room hasn't changed, I thought. *I am in a different room.*

Which meant the created man could have carried me into that other infirmary. Only, if that was true, then it was also true that he'd lain on the floor, mortally wounded. But I was *not* in that other room, whose door the created man, and no one else, could open. "*He* had to bring me here," I said, startled at the sound of my own voice.

Sister Angelina stirred; raising her head, she blinked away the cobwebs of sleep.

Before I could ask anything, she pushed herself from the chair so fast it toppled behind her, going down on one knee, bowing her head, the silver crucifix around her neck ticking against the floor, just as it had the first time I'd met her.

Resurrection

"Expect you'll have questions." Sam stood at the foot of my bed, his right arm in a sling. One side of his face was a tattoo of yellow and purple bruises, and he wore a patch over his eye. But he was dressed in clean clothes and bore no armour, save a modest dagger on his belt.

"I have one question. And, depending on your answer, perhaps a second."

Sam nodded. To his right, Bishop Arrupe clasped his hands behind his back; he was anxious, I think, to ask his own questions. Sister Angelina stood patiently behind, along with the short fellow who had first addressed me when I entered the council of *The Meek*. There was a fourth man in the room, too, who I didn't recognize—an ancient, bearded man, glasses perched precariously on the tip of his nose. A man, I later learned, who'd served as personal physician to three Popes.

"My father, is he . . . ?"

Sam shrugged. "No one's seen him."

"Then my second question is less a question than a request."

"Ask."

"I'd like to search the Papal Apartments for my father—and I'd like to do it now."

"Can't and won't stop you," Sam said. "Will even help as best I can. We owe you, Thomas, no mistaking that. But better if you'd rest first."

"I feel fine." I could see the scepticism in their faces. "A bit tired, is all."

"You've just woken," Sister Angelina said. "Doctor Lisi—" the ancient man nodded, pushing the glasses back up his nose "—

discovered you in the Pope's infirmary early this morning."

"Then I've already slept through a night and most of a day."

"Your father," the Bishop said. "He left you here yesterday?"

"Yes." Then I thought better of my answer. "Not here, exactly. He brought me to a place like this, but not this place. And I'm not sure he did that. It might have been a dream." I hesitated to say it might have been a hallucination.

"Why would he bring you here?"

"Perhaps he knew of this infirmary," I said. "I remember him carrying me to the Papal Apartments." I described what I remembered of the entrance way, the stairs, the galleries.

"Sounds right," Sam said. "About the building. But the timing is all wrong. Been ten days since the assault, Thomas."

"Your expression," Bishop Arrupe said, "suggests this comes as something of a surprise. No less than our surprise at your reappearance—after we'd counted you amongst the, ah, missing."

"Dead," the short man said. "We thought you dead."

"And we are pleased you are not," Bishop Arrupe said, turning to the short man. "Aren't we, Bishop Mazzarino?"

The Bishop nodded, but didn't look convinced.

"Is it possible that I could have been in the infirmary for several days before anyone noticed?"

Sam shook his head. "Doc was tending patients yesterday."

If the created man had left me in this room, it would have been in the last twelve hours. My heart beat faster. "I want to search the Papal Apartments," I said again.

When the others looked at Bishop Arrupe, I added, "With the permission of Bishop Arrupe, of course."

"It's Cardinal Arrupe," Sister Angelina said. "He's a member of College."

Arrupe nodded, as if his elevation was all but self-evident. "There was a spiritual vacuum which I, and other clergy," here he nodded at Bishop Mazzarino, "who'd ministered to *The Meek*, have humbly attempted to fill."

Sister Angelina stepped forward. "Allow Doctor Lisi to examine you and pronounce you fit, and we'll all help you in your search." She glanced at Cardinal Arrupe. "And after, perhaps we could answer more of your questions, and ask some ourselves."

She was right; a few minutes one way or the other would make no difference. And I'd welcome their help. So I nodded my assent.

Doctor Lisi opened one of the cupboards, and from it drew a device sporting an array of small, articulated mirrors that focused the light of a candle box in its centre. Lifting the lid of the box, he lit the wick and, adjusting the mirrors and a tiny set of louvres, scrutinized my throat and nose and ears. After extinguishing the candle and returning the instrument to the cupboard, he placed a palsied hand on my forehead, pulled my eyelids back with trembling forefinger and thumb, and squinted through his thick lenses at first one eye, then the other. Apparently satisfied, he tugged the sheet back and placed his ear on my chest to listen to my heartbeat. Then he lifted my arms and, flexing them different ways, tested the joints. I struggled not to wince. He did the same sort of thing with my legs. Only this time he spent an extra minute or two on my left ankle, bending my foot back and forth, feeling along my shin with his long, cool fingers, stopping every so often to press his fingers into the flesh around the bone. Then he traced an almost invisible white line that ran from my heel to mid-calf, one that I hadn't noticed before. He furrowed his brow. As he bent my ankle again, he asked, "Does this hurt?"

"No." It wasn't the truth, and he knew it.

The doctor's brow creased.

Sister Angelina said, "Is something wrong?"

"He has a recent scar from an incision. The sort that would be left by a skillful surgeon who set broken bones. And from the feel of the bones, I'd say he once had a bimalleolar fracture. But for it to heal up as it has, that injury would have occurred a long time ago. In childhood, possibly."

I told him I'd no recollection of ever breaking my ankle.

"You're a thin boy, and I can feel those bones quite distinctly. On the tibia and fibula I felt small fissures that circumscribe the bone, fissures I believe were once clean breaks. They've healed up nicely. Not perfectly, of course, but better than most I've seen. But the incision required to set them—"

"Is he well enough to walk?" Father Arrupe asked.

"I'd say so." The doctor pushed his glasses back up his nose. "A touch phlegmatic, but otherwise fine."

I was about to swing my feet over the edge of the bed when Bishop Mazzarino asked the doctor, "If he'd broken his ankle ten days ago, could it have healed by now?"

For a moment, the doctor seemed abstracted; he took off his glasses, rubbed the lenses absentmindedly with the tail of tunic, put them on again. He stared at my ankle and chewed his lip, uncomfortable, I think, to give an answer he didn't care to give. Until a few days ago, he'd been a physician to the Pope; now he was being asked to declare my healing, the healing of the boy who'd had a hand in the death of that Pope, miraculous. "No one heals that fast."

"Then you deem it impossible without divine intervention?"

Cardinal Arrupe stiffened. "Such things would be best discussed another time."

Bishop Mazzarino was having none of it; he locked eyes with Arrupe. "He is a Servant of God. You know I must ask these questions."

"When we thought the boy dead, yes," Cardinal Arrupe said. "But he isn't, is he?"

Bishop Mazzarino pursed his lips, but essayed no response.

I looked from one to the other, not fully understanding their exchange; but I understood some of what the Bishop was attempting to do. Others had tried to attribute miracles to me—or, at least, to situate me in their vicinity, as if my presence somehow precipitated them. "I fell down a ravine," I said. "When I was a young child, I wandered off and fell down a ravine. Broke my ankle. I remember it now." I didn't like to lie, but it was less of one than the Bishop had been formulating.

"There, you see," Cardinal Arrupe said.

The Doctor looked relieved, while Sister Angelina looked discomfited, perhaps because she was determined to see a miracle. Only there was none. The doctor's examination had persuaded me I'd broken my ankle. And that the created man had brought me to the Papal Apartments, to a different infirmary, a different bed from the one in which I now lay. A bed which had healed me. Though others might attribute miraculous qualities to that bed, to me it was a thing of the world, one whose dimensions could be measured and recorded, whose material could be touched and examined. Nor had its working been instantaneous as would be expected in a miracle; yes, my bones had re-knit quickly, but in a determinant amount of time. If my healing was miraculous, it was so in the way anything we don't understand is miraculous. I felt no sense of God in that bed—no more than I did in the *teleidelons*. Leastways, not after I'd become accustomed to them. I suppose familiarity will render things that seem miraculous prosaic. But true miracles are ineffable; they come from God and do not tarnish so easily.

If so, then I've been privy to just one true miracle: the resurrection of my son. Though I doubted many things, I believed this with all my heart. Otherwise, what would be left me?

Servant of God

With the aid of my cane, and the supporting arm of Sister Angelina, I managed to hobble from my sick bed. My ankle pained me, and I tried not wince with each step. Though he shook his head as he watched, the doctor kept his peace and, shortly thereafter, at my insistence, departed to tend to the wounded who still required his attention. Likewise, Bishop Arrupe begged our pardon and took his leave, citing other matters of importance concerning the healing of the Church.

That left me and Sam and Sister Angelina.

Pointing out the difficulty I would have climbing stairs, I asked Sam if he would check with his sentries whether there were no reports of my father. And, if there were none, then take some men and begin a methodical search of the first two floors. While he was doing this, Sister Angelina would help me search the third.

"Best dress first," Sam said, before leaving.

Sister Angelina asked if I felt capable, and when I answered in the affirmative, she left me to dress.

Like my leather pouch, my clothes had been taken away; this didn't surprise me, as they were little more than rags and likely had been given to someone whose were in even worse condition. A freshly laundered pair of pants and a shirt had been left on hooks behind the door and, when I tried them on, they more or less fit.

The Pope's private apartments were comprised of eight separate rooms on the third floor of the Apostolic Palace. But there was really only one place I wanted to look, and it was here I directed Sister Angelina. Taking my arm, she helped me locate the stairs to our floor, and from there I retraced the created man's steps to the white stuccoed wall, exactly where I remembered it. With the Sister still steadying me, I reached out, spreading my fingers as the created man had. The door didn't appear. I shifted my hand from place to place, while Sister Angelina watched with forbearance, never asking why.

After a few minutes, I gave up.

"What did you expect to find, Thomas?"

In answer, I rapped the wall with the head of my cane and said, "I want to see what's on the other side."

So we did a complete circuit of the floor, glancing into all the other chambers we passed, coming at last to a small room behind the wall I'd touched, a modest bedroom, perhaps for a member of the Pope's staff. If it had ever been anything other than what it was now, there was no evidence. Nor was there space between this room and the wall for that other infirmary, for as we walked, I'd also counted my steps, measuring out the dimensions of the floor, accounting for each square foot of space.

Nonetheless, I took my cane in both hands like a club and swung its weighted head at the wall, smashing though ancient plaster, again and again, until the air was hazed with dust. When there was a fist-sized hole large enough to see through to the hall on the other side, I stopped. Still, this proved nothing, save what I already knew: the other infirmary wasn't where I'd believed it to be.

I felt Sister's Angelina's hand on my shoulder—and realized I was crying.

Though I saw little point, we finished our circuit of the third floor, ending in the Pope's study, where we'd agreed to meet Sam. I was exhausted, and my ankle complained bitterly, causing me to wonder if the pain would trouble me the rest of my life. In the centre of the study was a lacquered cherry table, and onto this I dropped my cane before collapsing into a wooden chair. Sister Angelina sat opposite.

For a time, silence hung between us. Then she said, "I prayed you were alive, Thomas, though I didn't hold out much hope. Yet here you are."

I looked at her.

"I prayed for your father, as well. With God's will, we will find him."

I ought to have thanked her. Instead, I said, "And without God's will?"

"Despite what you feel, God has not abandoned you. I know He loves you both."

"Because you can see our faces?"

Sister Angelina looked like she'd been slapped, making me regret my words. "To me, at least, who can see no other faces, it is a miracle. There is another thing, too, that I've told no one. I think I should have, only now it's too late, and people would think I was making it up. But I'm not." A beatific smile creased her features. "It's not just your face that I see, Thomas, but a light which surrounds you."

Even though I couldn't fully accept what she told me, the strength of her belief made me feel ashamed for having questioned it.

"You feel lost, Thomas. Abandoned. I know that. But I believe I have glimpsed the hand of God in all this. In you."

I shook my head. "No."

"I won't try to convince you. But I will remind you of something from which you may draw comfort, if not now, then perhaps later: faith requires doubt or it is not faith at all."

My frame of mind was such that I could not be convinced. But this talk of faith, of miracles, had reminded me of something she'd said earlier. Something that had been bothering me. "You called me *Servant of God* when you spoke to Cardinal Arrupe."

She conceded she had.

"Before that, you'd called me *Beloved of the Angels*. At first I thought you were saying the same thing two different ways, but now I don't think so. I think you meant it in a more specific way."

"*Servant of God* is the term used to designate a person being investigated for sainthood. Bishop Mazzarino, who stood with *The Meek*, was to be appointed your *Postulator*, your *Advocatus Dei*—to gather further information about your life."

I shook my head in disbelief—then realized it couldn't be true. "A Saint must be in Heaven."

"We thought you dead Thomas. Now that we know you are not, the process of your canonization has been deferred, not annulled. The Bishop has been instructed to continue, albeit unofficially, gathering evidence as your *postulator*. And to that end, his Eminence has directed me to stay with you, so that I might document anything I observe."

"Even if I were dead, five years must pass before canonization may begin."

"The Holy See has the authority to waive the waiting period."

"There is no Holy See. The Pope is dead."

"That's true. And during the period of *sede vacante* the College of Cardinals has very limited authority, certainly not the authority to waive the waiting period. What they are charged with is convening a Conclave to elect a new Pope. Samuel ordered them to do so. In three days, they begin sitting."

I was going to ask her how, if a new Pope was yet to be elected, I was already being investigated for sainthood. Only I knew the answer. "You struck a bargain."

"The College of Cardinals understands that if the Church is to survive, that if it is to heal, then concessions must be made."

"Sam made them promise to make me a Saint."

"No. He asked that, when elected, the new Pope waive the waiting period." Sister Angelina reached across the table and took my hand between hers. "You need to understand that the battle of the Holy City lasted the better part of four days. Some of the Church's princes refused to surrender and were slaughtered. They died, Thomas, their blood staining the floors of holy places. It's something that will not soon be forgotten—or forgiven." Her expression crumpled; and in that moment I admired her for the dignity with which she bore such suffering. "*The Meek* may have won the battle for the Holy City, but they never had a chance to win the war. The Church isn't the Vatican, Thomas. It's the world. Those who've fled Rome will return—one way or another. And there are countless souls who do not live in Rome, never have lived in Rome, and who know little of *The Meek* or their straits. A thousand times the number of *The Meek*. Young men with nothing better to do, who would happily take up arms to escape their own misery or boredom, to grasp at the chance of glory, at the chance for martyrhood, that would accrue to those who'd free the Vatican from defiling heretics. How long do you think it will be before there is a new army camped outside these walls? Sam knows this, and is doing what he can to avoid further bloodshed."

"By making me a Saint? It's . . . it's blasphemy."

"Seventeen Cardinals died, Thomas. Fifteen of those are to be replaced by clergy who stood with *The Meek*. As a gesture of reconciliation. No different than your canonization. The College wishes to repair the rift as much as we do."

"Do they?"

"As much as it rankles, yes. Sam could have just as easily disbanded the College. *The Meek* would have supported him in this. But both Sam and the Cardinals understand that dismantling the Curia serves no one's purpose—and would likely lead to conflict and chaos."

"Then it must please those Cardinals to know I am alive, that there won't be a Saint Thomas."

"It does. And it relieves Cardinal Arrupe, too. He put your sainthood forward as a means to secure support of *The Meek*, even though he knew it would not sit well with the College. Now, it's one less point of contention."

After I'd first met Cardinal Arrupe, I'd wondered if I might suit his purposes better as a dead martyr than as a live boy who could work no miracles. Now, it seemed the opposite was true. "He means to be Pope."

"With your help."

"My help?"

"Before the Sistine Chapel is sealed for the Conclave, a sermon is given by an ecclesiastical designate on the qualities the new Pontiff should possess. You are to be the designate."

I was flabbergasted. "I . . . I can't."

"If you wish to help *The Meek*, you must speak on behalf of Cardinal Arrupe."

"You said *ecclesiastical designate*. I am not clergy."

Sister Angelina shrugged. "Some Cardinals believe you to be a living Saint—and who would deny a Saint the chance to give advice to the Conclave? Others are convinced you're a boy out of your depth and view this as an opportunity to see you fail. And the rest, well, they are curious."

"Those who wish to see me fail are the most likely to get their wish."

"You think too little of yourself."

I shook my head. "I won't speak for Cardinal Arrupe."

"He no more desires your sainthood than you, but he believes it is what he must do. As does Sam. As do I. For the Cardinal's reasons, yes, and for Sam's, too. But I also have my own reasons, Thomas. I would continue my investigation."

"Looking for miracles? You will find none."

"What might not seem a miracle to you might be a miracle to others."

"*Time turns our lies into truths*," I said, quoting a story in *The One*

Book. "I will not knowingly promulgate lies."

"Many of the Papal Court are aware of this maxim, too, and of its corollary: history is written by the victor. The Curia are as old as they are patient, and will bide their time, waiting to see what stories emerge, nudging them this way or that as best they can. Perhaps you'll become a saint. Or perhaps you will get your wish and be forgotten."

"With God's will," I said, trying to keep the bitterness from my voice.

"I have faith in you, Thomas."

I wondered, *Does God have as much faith in those who believe in him as they do in Him?* "I'm afraid it is misplaced."

Sister Angelina stared at me a moment. "There is something you are not saying, Thomas."

"I've killed men." I said. "I've caused many more to be killed. How could a Saint do such things?"

"You did so only when you had to, and always to save others."

"I've committed other sins that cannot be forgiven." I couldn't bring myself to say aloud I was a rapist.

"All Saints believe themselves to be sinners," she said. "But that is for God to judge."

My heart sank when she said this, for I knew there was nothing I could say to shake her faith.

Sister Angelina rose and walked around the table to where I sat. "It's not about what you or I think, Thomas. Or even what the College thinks." I let her pull me from my chair and lead me over to a tall window whose shutters were partially open. She swung them wide. From the sill, a red banner with gold borders had been suspended, and above this was a sweeping view of Saint Peter's Square. Hundreds of people milled in the square. The entire expanse had been cleaned, the bodies had been removed, the dust washed away. Save for half a dozen black lines that had been etched into the cobblestone by the Fiery Sword, the square was pristine. However, smoke still discoloured the giant order of columns of the great façade. Scaffolding had been erected on the left side of the pediment, and there men hauled buckets of water up to platforms to scrub away the stain. I wondered at their industry, so preoccupied in their repair of a façade that fronted nothing but a ruin.

"Why did you want me to see this?"

In the square, a few of the faithful had noticed the open shutters and were pointing. Others now turned to face the Apostolic Palace, craning their necks.

"I didn't," she said, stepping back from the window. "I wanted them to see you."

The first to bend knee was a man holding a child; soon, like a field of wheat being scythed, all went down, most on bended knees, a few prostrating themselves.

"They have good reason to believe in you," Sister Angelina said. "You saved them, Thomas. They are yours now."

Four Decisions

With the shutters closed and latched, the Pope's study was as dark as the hermit's cave had been; the gloom didn't improve my mood. I waited at the table while Sister Angelina left to find a lamp. As much as I liked her, I was glad for a few moments alone to think about what had transpired and make some decisions.

Principally, there were four things on my mind.

My first concern was for my son. If the created man was not dead, he was in hiding. As much as the former disheartened me, the latter gave me a sliver of hope. But only a sliver. Though I could think of no reason why he might want to conceal himself, I knew if he wasn't within the Papal Apartments, finding him would be next to impossible if he didn't want to be found. But there was one more place I wanted to search: Meussin's apartment.

When the created man and I had planned the undermining of the Basilica, I'd suggested we shelter in her apartment. Her rooms were proximate to the necropolis where we planted the kegs, yet still (I believed) a reasonable distance from Saint Peter's. The pillars near the apartment were broad, the arched vaults low and narrow, the course of thick stones as straight as the day they had been set. The place looked like it had stood a thousand years and would stand a thousand more. Even so, after hearing me describe it, the created man had balked, maintaining that no place underground (at least to which we could run in the time we had) would be safe from the shock wave generated by the explosion. He insisted instead that it would be safest above ground, and that we should exit the tunnels by the most expeditious route, placing as much distance as was feasible between us and the

Basilica. Which is what we did. But he knew about the apartment. If he was alive, and wished to hide, this was as good a place as any. There was a second reason, too, for going there, though this was a fainter hope than the first: I wondered if, as the threat from *The Meek* had risen, the Pope might have acted as a father would, and sent Cardinal Singleton to fetch his daughter, believing it safer for her behind the walls of the Vatican than on a far flung Papal estate. If I searched nowhere else, I would, at least, seek him in this one last place.

The second thing that weighed on me was what Sister Angelina had just shown me. I'd no desire for the attention of *The Meek*. Yet I could understand why they felt the way they did. The Curia had abandoned them and many believed that, by extension, so had God. In defying the Papacy, in laying siege to Rome, they'd betrayed God, hence imperilling their souls and subjecting themselves to eternal damnation—unless God sent them a sign to show He favoured them and that their cause was just. To show them a saviour who might work miracles to deliver them.

As much as it might have heartened *The Meek* to believe Heaven was watching over them, I shared no such illusions, and it disquieted me to be the object of such adoration. False idolatry was a grave sin, and to let such beliefs flourish was to further darken my soul. The right thing to do, it seemed to me, was to disabuse *The Meek* of this notion. Only I couldn't. Not because there wasn't ample evidence to the contrary—there was a superfluity—but because, even then, I knew enough about human nature to know that once a man accepts something as true, he will do everything in his power to defend this truth, even in the face of damning evidence. For a man to admit he was wrong, was fooled, requires a humility few possess (and, in this, I freely admit I am no better than any other man). Thus, even if I told *The Meek* the truth, few would be capable of hearing it.

I resolved I would not support the lie, but would do nothing to gainsay it, either. Although I knew this to be a grave sin, it was one which, for thousands of souls, rekindled a hope in life after death. For their sake, I resolved to carry my burden in silence.

The third thing that unsettled me was Cardinal Arrupe's ambition to be Pope. I had little faith in Arrupe, and less that the Curia would conduct itself any better than it had before. Perhaps, for a time, some of the Princes of the Church might try. But no matter how good one's intentions, true change is extraordinarily hard won and rare, even when circumstances favour it. And when that person serves the Church, an institution mired by both the weight of its history and a belief in its infallibility, how could anyone, no matter how well-intentioned, overcome such inertia?

From what she had told me, Sister Angelina didn't seem to share my concern. Nor Sam. But any objections they might have had they kept to themselves. I knew Sam was desperate to repair the rift between the Church and *The Meek*. No doubt the Cardinal was politically astute enough to navigate these dangerous waters. And installing him would be a recognition of the justness of *The Meek*'s cause, giving them the most powerful voice in the Church, a balance to those Cardinals who might still be harbouring thoughts of retribution. Even so, as much as I understood Sam's reasoning, I didn't share his trust (if that's what it was) of Arrupe.

But I could think of no better option for securing the peace. And even if I'd come up with one, what could I do? I decided that, if necessary, I would speak on the Cardinal's behalf, but only because I could think of nothing better that might be done.

There was one more decision I needed to make, but that was the easiest: I would depart Rome as soon as I could. Although there were many reasons for doing so, two overshadowed all others. The first was purely selfish: every day I spent in Rome was another day I would be forced to witness the death and destruction my actions had caused. The second reason was less questionable: I'd given my word, not only to the Angels, but to Ali and my son, that I would travel to the borders of Hell, and there do what I could to staunch the flow of God's Blood. With Ali gone, and perhaps my son, too, I was determined to be good to my word.

A hand shook me gently from a sleep into which I'd inadvertently fallen. Sam had returned, and he and Sister Angelina sat across from me, the lamp that the doctor had used in my examination on the table between, its louvres adjusted to brighten the room as much as possible. Sam gave me a moment to rub my eyes to try to clear the cobwebs from my mind.

When he did speak, he told me he'd found no trace of the created man (which didn't surprise me). I could see the concern on his face was genuine and seemed to be shared equally by Sister Angelina.

I told them I'd made some decisions, and then shared them, as well as my misgivings about Cardinal Arrupe. I spoke the truth, for the most part, keeping only what I deemed absolutely necessary to myself. When I'd finished, I said, "I wish to set out as soon as possible."

Sam frowned, and nodded at my ankle. "You capable?"

"On an even floor and with the aid of my cane, walking is manageable. But I wouldn't last long on a rough road. With your permission, I'd like to stay another week, maybe two, to recover." This wasn't exactly true, for I'd no intention of staying once the Conclave had commenced.

Sam frowned, although he didn't say no. I wondered if he saw through my lie.

"In the interim, I wish the freedom to continue my search for my father, wherever it might take me."

"I'd rest more easily if you had Sister Angelina and half a dozen of my best men for escort."

"I'd welcome the company," I said, almost believing it myself.

"Then tomorrow your escort will be waiting in the courtyard to accompany you."

Tomorrow? I was about to say something, then remembered I'd woken in the late afternoon; I glanced at the window but could see no light around its edges. Sun-off had already passed. And although I'd only been up for a few hours, exhaustion had settled on me like a mill stone, making the bones in my ankle seem to grind together with even the slightest of movements. I wished for nothing more than my bed in the infirmary. "Tomorrow," I agreed, dragging myself to my feet, wincing with the effort, and wondering if it might really be another two weeks before I'd recuperated enough to depart, thus transforming the lie intended into an inadvertent truth.

Old Friends

When I'd gone to bed the night before, I hadn't thought to shutter the window in the infirmary; the light of sun-on woke me and I sat up. Outside, the view was of a sea of peach-coloured roof tiles, amongst which rose intermittent islands of green, the crowns of tall stone pines (which the natives called umbrella trees). Although I couldn't see the Tiber itself, I could see the winding rows of pines that lined either bank and the gap between, where the river ran.

My head was clearer than it had been for a while, and I felt marginally better. When my stomach rumbled, I realized I hadn't eaten anything at all the previous day. Rising, I managed to dress, an awkward proposition because I was loath to put any weight on my ankle. As I hobbled towards the door, I caught sight of my reflection in a mirror: a haggard and dishevelled boy with dark circles under his eyes, whose clothes hung loosely and who leaned heavily on his cane, like an old man.

A stranger.

I straightened, but felt no better for doing so. Then I lifted my cane and stared at the end that contained the vial.

Nothing stirred in me.

No craving for the Gift of Water, no panic that the Water had been exhausted. A fortnight ago, my hand would have shook, and my forehead would have been peppered with perspiration. I wondered if, while I'd lain in that other infirmary, I'd been cured of my addiction— or if my addiction hadn't been an addiction at all, but a delusion of my own making. I gripped the head of my cane, twisting as I had so many times before. Nothing moved. If the cane wasn't a solid piece of wood before, it seemed so now. I looked back at *The One Book*, thinking for a moment of checking to see if its magic had also fled, but I had neither the energy nor the will.

Outside the infirmary, Sam's orderly waited. Waving away his help, I followed him into a dining room, a room which Sister Angelina and I had checked the day before. When I'd seated myself, he left, returning a few minutes later with a tray that held a plate of cheese and fruit, a loaf of bread (still warm from the oven), a small jar of butter with a wooden knife, and a steaming bowl of porridge from which arose the aroma of cinnamon.

My mouth watered.

"After you break your fast, Sister Angelina would meet you in the courtyard."

I told him I looked forward to it and thanked him.

He nodded and retreated to the hallway, leaving the door open and standing to one side. Hunger drove everything else from my mind; I ate ravenously.

When I was replete, I pushed the tray away and sat back; a moment later, the orderly, who I hadn't noticed slipping away, carried in a second tray, this time bearing a steaming mug of spiced mead. "The doctor asked that you drink it all," he said, then returned to his post by the door.

I took a sip—and was pleasantly surprised. When I was a young boy and took ill, our cook had made similar concoctions, the bitterness of the physic never wholly masked by the sweetness of the honey. But if there was medicine in this drink, I couldn't taste it. I sipped slowly, as much to savour the mead as to give myself a chance to reconsider what I'd decided yesterday. In *The One Book* I'd read about a people called *Persians*, who make every decision twice, once when they are sober, then when they are drunk. If they make the same decision both times it is held to be a good decision and adopted. If not, then the decision is discarded. I've no idea if these people ever existed, but it seemed sage advice. I'd no intention of getting drunk, but now that I was rested (or, at least, more than I had been), I felt my state of my mind was sufficiently different to reconsider my decisions. But I could see nothing that changed my mind.

In the courtyard, Sister Angelina waited for me, along with my escort: six soldiers of *The Meek*, armoured and bearing weapons. I nodded at the tallest of the group, the lieutenant who'd interrogated me in the ramshackle cottage on the beach, and who, like me, had lost a son. I was glad to see she had not been amongst the casualties. I asked the lieutenant if the Sistine Chapel had been spared in the collapse of the Basilica. When she told me it had, I directed her to take me there. She barked an order, and the soldiers fell into a loose formation around us, then she led us across the courtyard and through a set of high double doors, our footsteps—and the tick of my cane—echoing as we walked grand corridors with marble floors. A few moments later we crossed the threshold of the Chapel.

The lieutenant had been both right and wrong about the Chapel being spared. Though the structure itself had been preserved, many of the frescoes on the walls had cracked, and entire sections of the plaster on the ceiling had fallen. Even so, the effect was still breathtaking, so much so it took me a moment to notice that long tables had been set on each side, and on them every piece of plaster, no matter how small, had been gathered. Silent men hunched over the tables, squinting at the tiny pieces, moving and shifting them carefully, lovingly, working to fit together their near-impossible puzzle. So engrossed were they in their work, not one took heed of us as we passed.

Just as in the Chapel in the *Castel Sant'Angelo*, there was a waist-high panel behind the altar. I pressed the hidden catch, then stepped back as the panel swung open on a lightless passage; dust drifted out, eddying around our feet.

Sister Angelina took a step towards me. "Thomas, we can't—"

"Wait here," I said, stepping into darkness.

When I'd spent Lent in Meussin's apartment, there had been more than enough time to explore large extents of the tunnels beneath the Vatican. I'd discovered many chambers, some doors of which were locked by keys long lost, others open and containing sepulchres and niches, usually occupied, but not always, a few having clearly been ransacked by grave robbers. I'd also discovered eleven hidden entrances. The tunnels—leastwise, those near the apartment—like everything else in my memory, were indelibly impressed, but when I'd explored these passages before, I'd had Meussin's lamp. Now, a few dozen steps in, I pushed through utter darkness. In the distance, I heard Sister Angelina extolling the lieutenant and her men to follow me. I ignored the clatter of their weapons against the walls as they squeezed through the narrow entrance behind me.

I shut my eyes, there being no point in keeping them open, thinking this might help me focus on the sounds. Moving as stealthily as I could, my cane clutched in one hand, my other hand on the wall, I felt my way, shuffling my feet forward, barely raising them from the stone floor, in case there might be debris. My ankle troubled me enough that I knew I couldn't keep up this pace for very long. I turned left at the first junction I came to, then passed another two, turning right at the third. Half a dozen steps farther on I reached a stairway leading down. I paused to listen; what noise I could hear was distant and seemed to be fading. I descended slowly, feeling the edge of each step with the tip of my sandal, pausing at the foot of the stairs to catch my breath and to listen again. This time I heard nothing at all, save my own ragged breathing. I waited for the count of one hundred.

Hearing no pursuit, I pulled a tinder box from one pocket and, from the other, the candle I'd stolen from the doctor's lamp. In a moment the wick caught and a tiny flame fluttered to life. As feeble as it was, the light was a relief. As was the use of my cane. Another ten minutes brought me to Meussin's apartment.

I was surprised when I found the door open—and was taken aback by the stench of death wafting from the room. Bracing myself, I stepped inside.

Holding the candle aloft, I saw a kneeling man, gaunt and unshaven, head bowed and hands clasped, muttering hoarsely in Latin, a prayer imploring forgiveness. If he knew I stood an arm's length from him, he showed no sign. In front of him, arms pulled wide and shackled to the wall, was an immense shadow, human-shaped, but far too large to be a man, its milky eyes open and lifeless. Though ragged and molted, the tatters of wings still remained. The suppurating lesions and tumours that disfigured the corpse of the Angel made recognition impossible, save that the large growth on the left side of its skull was familiar, and I knew it to be the Archangel Zeracheil.

There was no sign my son had ever been to the apartment.

I sat on the bed, Meussin's bed. I knew Meussin, too, hadn't returned, for the shelves opposite were empty and coated with a fine layer of dust, suggesting an absence of months. I imagined her carefully hiding those books, the books Kite had given her, at the end of every Lent, then Meussin reshelving her beloved volumes when she was brought back the following year.

In the other room, the murmuring had continued unabated. Despite my presence, the man hadn't paused in his petition, hadn't even looked up to see who was in the room with him. After a time, I rose and walked over to him, placed a hand on his shoulder.

"Bishop Singleton."

His eyes remained closed, his cracked lips continuing to move. I don't think he was yet aware of my presence. I'd found no food in the apartment, and only a few gourds that might have once contained water or wine, lying at the feet of the Archangel Zeracheil. If the Bishop had taken shelter here when *The Meek* first breached the wall, he'd been several days without sustenance.

"Do you remember me? We met before, at the *Widow's Walk*, and then on *The Charon*. It's Thomas."

At the mention of my name his mantra stopped and Bishop Singleton opened his eyes; he swayed, blinking furiously, as if rudely woken from a dream. All I could see in his gaze was confusion, perhaps delirium. I titled the candle over the table until a small pool of wax accumulated, then placed the candle upright in that.

"You must stand, Bishop Singleton." I lifted his arm and put it around my shoulders, then clasped him by his waist. Pushing on my cane, I struggled to pull him to his feet. He was a tall man, at least two heads taller than me, only so hunched that when we stood, his face was almost level with mine. I was afraid he would be too heavy for me, but he was sickeningly light. I couldn't think of a way I could help him walk while I held the candle, so I left it behind.

In the tunnel, when the black had swallowed us, and the odour of the dead Angel had diminished, he whispered, "Thomas."

I paused.

"I . . . I know you." His voice was weak, but bore none of the feverish tendrils of his prayer.

"We met when you were escorting Meussin to Rome. I was with Kite."

"We wronged them," he said. "Forgive me."

"I cannot forgive wrongs you have done to others."

"Of course not," he said sadly.

Now that he seemed more coherent, I thought I might try a question. "What news of Meussin?"

I felt him shaking his head.

"Why did you bring Zeracheil here?"

"The Holy Father asked."

"When you got it here, and the Pope realized Zeracheil wasn't the heavenly creature you expected, you locked it away, hid it like you hid Meussin."

"Yes." Shame made his answer a whisper. "It got sicker and sicker."

Away from the ameliorating effects of its healing machine, the disease that plagued the Angels had run its brutal course. "Why were you in its cell?"

"The Pope bid me watch over the Angel. He was to send men with food and water, but none came."

"The Pope was killed ten days ago."

"When you spoke your name, I understood this."

"Bishop Singleton—"

"Not Bishop," he said, "Cardinal." He didn't say the appellation with pride, but with bitterness and self-recrimination. "I was afraid, you see. That the Pontiff wouldn't announce it before . . . before it was too late."

"Announce what?"

"My elevation."

Only a few steps from here, in her apartment, Meussin had told me that Singleton had been made a Cardinal *in pectore*, a secret Cardinal, appointed by the Pope to watch over her. Such an appointee was not allowed to wear the robes of office or exercise any of the powers of the Cardinalate. And his appointment was revoked upon the passing of the Pope—unless, before his death, the Pope announced the secret Cardinal publicly.

"When the Holy Father asked that I watch over the Angel," he said, "I demanded he announce my elevation. He acceded. And I witnessed the death of an Angel." In the dark, I could sense Cardinal Singleton sagging even more, as if his self-disgust had become too much to bear. "It is a title I no longer deserve or wish." He let himself go slack, slumping against the wall, feebly lifting his arm from my shoulder. "Leave me to my penance."

"You told me you wronged Meussin and Kite. And you believe you had a hand in Zeracheil's death. I also think you feel remorse for the way the Church has treated *The Meek*."

He said nothing, which I took to be assent.

"Do not renounce the title. Use the power you have been given to make amends to those you have wronged. Let the reconciliation of the Church and *The Meek* be your penance, and your offering to God."

"God has abandoned me."

I was taken aback, hearing those unlikely words from a high-ranking clergyman; it took me a moment to frame a response. "Perhaps," I said. "Or Perhaps God sent me to remind you of your duty." I let him think on that. When a moment or two had passed and he still hadn't responded, I said, "A Conclave to elect a new Pope begins sitting in two days. Will you be well enough to attend?"

Again, he said nothing, but this time he pushed himself away from the wall of the tunnel, nearly falling as he did so. I helped him put his arm back around my shoulders. Together, we shuffled through the pitch dark, both blind as Saul, and though it was hard to tell, I like to think the Cardinal, as befitted his station, carried himself straighter.

Conclave

Other men die in darkness, in confusion, and amid tears; the Pope, alone in the world, dies in ceremony.

So it is said.

After the Holy Father draws his last breath, the cardinal *Camerlengo*—his appointed Cardinal Chamberlain—takes a small silver hammer engraved with the seal of the Pope from a red leather bag. Three times the Cardinal Chamberlain gently taps the forehead of the Pope, each time calling the Pope's baptismal name. When the Pope does not respond, only then the *Camerlengo* declares him dead. The Chamberlain removes from the Pope's hand the Ring of the Fisherman—a gold band symbolizing the Holy Father's authority over the Catholic community. With a silver knife, the Chamberlain defaces the seal, once horizontally and once vertically, in the sign of the cross. The defaced ring is then placed on a lead block and the *Camerlengo* uses a silver mallet to destroy the ring, placing the pieces in a velvet sack to be interred with the deceased Pontiff. This ritual complete, the death is announced, and an *Interregnum* begins with a nine-day period of mourning called *Novendiales*. In normal circumstances, the first day is the funeral, followed by eight days of Masses celebrated in Saint Peter's Basilica.

Not this time.

The destruction of the Basilica and the battle for the Holy City made such Masses impossible—no less so than the affront such a celebration would have caused *The Meek*. After the passing of the Pope, by tradition there is a waiting period of fifteen to twenty days before the start of the Conclave to elect the next Pontiff. The exigencies of the situation made this, too, impossible. Thus, it was on the thirteenth day after the death of Pope Pius CXXIV that I passed through the *Sala Regia* and into the Sistine Chapel, where the Cardinals, new and old, had assembled for the start of the Conclave. Cardinal Singleton had taken a seat in the front row.

In the two days prior, as Cardinal Singleton had recovered from his ordeal, he and I had talked. He'd surprised me by evincing an empathy rare in those who hold high office, understanding what others thought of him, both good and bad. He knew that although he was not considered a personable man, he was nonetheless well thought of, his reputation being a steadfast and thoughtful cleric, well versed in canon law, and a passionate evangelist for the faith. Most considered him honest and honourable. That's why both the Pope and Meussin had trusted him, and the other Princes of the Church respected him. His return was welcome news to those Cardinals who felt themselves beleaguered. Whatever decision the Conclave made would sit better with its members for Cardinal Singleton's blessing. This was one of the things we'd discussed at length.

The purpose of the sermon I was to give immediately before the Conclave commenced was straightforward: to suggest the qualities necessary for the new Pope. I did my best, delivering my speech with candour and without equivocation. My words were greeted mostly with silence—and a few looks of astonishment.

I took an oath not to reveal the particulars of my speech (or anything else that transpired) so I cannot share its details, save to say it lasted only a few minutes. Then the Master of the Papal Liturgical Celebrations called out, *"Extra omnes!"*—the order for those not part of the Conclave to leave. After I departed, the Prince Assistant to the Papal Throne sealed the doors of the Sistine Chapel, chaining them.

Outside stood ranks of ecclesiastical and secular dignitaries, all absurdly watching those doors, some praying silently. After a moment, they began trickling away, though I'll warrant their thoughts were still on those sequestered within the Chapel. For the following days, or weeks, or however long it might take to elect the new Pope, all attention in Rome—indeed, throughout the enlightened Spheres—would be on the Conclave. Which is why I planned to slip away that night.

Although I trusted Sam to be as good as his word, he now shared his authority with others who were more likely to forget promises made in the past in the exigencies of the moment. I also knew that Sister Angelina would insist on accompanying me, and Sam would insist I take an armed escort. But the last thing I wanted was an entourage to draw attention to myself. I'd decided it would be better if I disappeared quietly and without a fuss.

For a bedroom, I'd taken one of the more modest rooms in the Papal Apartments, formerly occupied by a member of the Pontiff's household. Sister Angelina had taken the room opposite. After I'd left the Conclave, I'd closeted myself in the room, alternately praying for God to guide the Conclave and reading *The One Book*, waiting for sun-off. When sufficient time passed, I sat on the floor and pressed my ear against the door, waiting until I no longer heard Sister Angelina stirring. Then I rose and pulled from under my bed a leather satchel the room's last occupant had left behind. In it was a coiled rope I'd made by knotting half a dozen bedsheets I'd stolen from the infirmary's linen cupboard. I withdrew this makeshift rope, replacing it with *The One Book*, a knotted cloth holding the bit of food I'd managed to hoard, and a small stoppered gourd filled with water. Slinging the bag over my shoulder, I picked up the rope and my cane, then crept into the hall, careful to make as little noise as possible.

We were the lone occupants of the third floor, and there was no one on the floor below. But on the ground floor, sentries had been posted at every door of the Apostolic Palace.

Descending the stairs to the second floor, I walked a long hallway, stopping before a window, shuttered where the others were open. I undid the latch. At some point in the assault, this window had been shattered, and only ragged edges of glass were clutched tentatively in the frame. I wiggled free a few pieces of glass on the bottom of the frame, creating a gap. The window hung over a narrow alley, far from any of the guards who'd been posted on the doors, and pitch black at this time of night. Inside and beneath the window was a marble seat; I secured the rope around one of its thick feet. Tying my cane to the other end, I lowered the twisted sheets into the darkness until I heard the soft click of my cane against the cobbles.

Descending presented no difficulties, save that once I'd begun letting myself down into the gloom, I couldn't see more than a few metres in any direction. When my foot hit the ground, it took me by surprise. I'd only enough time to retrieve my cane before I heard, "You won't sneak away on me a second time."

From the darkness loomed two figures bearing the leather armour of *The Meek*: the lieutenant, whose name I'd never learned, and Jotham, whose death I'd witnessed.

My New Family

We drifted through the night like ghosts, I following the lieutenant, Jotham following me. In the pitch dark, footing was problematic, and I had to pay close attention to where I stepped; even so, I managed to glance back a few times at the face of the dead man. By the time we entered the Apostolic Palace, I'd almost convinced myself I'd been mistaken, that my guilt had conjured Jotham's ghost, but when lieutenant led us to a small, windowless room and lit a lamp, banishing the shadows, there he stood, outside the doorway, the man who'd been slashed by the Fiery Sword, who'd staggered forward, wrapped in a shroud of flame. Recalling that horror, the smell of his burning flesh curled anew in my nostrils.

Placing the lamp on a small table, the lieutenant turned to me. "You look unwell," she said. "Sit."

Behind the table and against the far wall was a bench, and onto this I slumped. When we'd entered the Palace, the lieutenant had dispatched the sentry posted on the door to fetch Sam, and we waited for him now; she stood at ease in front of me, hands interlocked behind her back. I stared past her, at Jotham, who'd spoken no word thus far, nor had the lieutenant acknowledged him in any way, not even with a cursory glance.

There seemed to be only three possibilities: the first was that I was imagining Jotham's presence; the second was that I'd hallucinated his death earlier, and he was alive and well, standing behind the lieutenant; the third possibility seemed both more and less likely at the same time, that Jotham was here, though not alive. I stared at him, and he stared back, while the lieutenant remained oblivious to both of us.

The first two possibilities frightened me, for if either were true, then my sanity was crumbling.

The third possibility, however, did not question my rationality: Jotham was dead and I saw his ghost. Although the Church discouraged the belief that the dead might return, *The Bible* is filled with spirits who wander the Spheres. In Matthew, do the tombs not open and the dead rise? And do these spirits not enter the Holy City and appear to many people? Perhaps Jotham's restless spirit was no different. . . .

Even so, I was afraid, afraid to say anything to the lieutenant, afraid of the possibilities collapsing into the certainty of my madness. Asylums are filled with men and women who insist they see what others do not. So I did as I suppose many of these men do and averted my eyes from the dead man who stood in the hallway, feigning I didn't see him.

When Sam and Sister Angelina entered the room, they startled me from a reverie; I'd been staring at the floor, and when I looked up, the corridor where Jotham's ghost had stood was empty.

Sam placed my leather pouch on the table. "Go on," he said. "Take it."

Sister Angelina still wore her bedclothes; arms akimbo, she frowned at me, no doubt irked that I had tried to slip away.

I pushed myself from the bench, hobbled over to the table and lifted the pouch, gently feeling, through the worn leather, the brittle bones and gristle. Nothing stirred. I slung the thong over my neck, tucking it inside my shirt.

"This, too." Sam dropped a second purse on the table, only this one made the tell-tale clink of coins jostling. "Put both aside for safe-keeping when we found you."

I stared at the purse, recognizing the one the created man had carried. He had trusted Sam—whereas I hadn't. "Too many people know my face," I said, feeling I owed him an explanation. "I was afraid that an escort would only draw unnecessary attention."

"What about the Assumptions, Thomas? Resourceful as you are, need someone older, and with a proper warrant, to pass through." Sam shook his head. "An ill-equipped boy travelling on his own is folly."

Although I recognized the sense of what he was saying, I was not immune to the perverse stubbornness of youth. "I'm leaving tonight."

"Gave my word we wouldn't try to stop you, and we won't. None of us. But wish you'd accept our help."

"I'd gladly accept it, but, as I said, I can't wait."

"For what?" Sam asked.

"For the conclusion of the Conclave." During the *Interregnum*, while the Cardinals were sequestered, the usual business of the Holy See was set aside. Getting transit papers would be impossible until a new Pope had been chosen, which might take weeks. By that time, there would be no slipping away.

"Conclave ended this afternoon on the first vote."

"I heard no—" I began, then stopped, realizing the bells of Saint Peter's had fallen with the Basilica.

"Cardinal Singleton took the name Pius," Sister Angelina said, "wishing no one to forget the sins of Pius who preceded him."

I hadn't expected such a swift conclusion to the Conclave, but it was as I had hoped, a man I judged to be both humble and contrite, who knew his own fallibility and had no ambition other than to atone for his sins.

"I'll accompany Thomas," said the lieutenant. "A mother with his son." I could see it pained her to say this, me a poor replacement for the child she'd lost.

"And his grandmother," Sister Angelina said.

I shook my head. "It's too dangerous."

Ignoring my protest, Sister Angelina turned to Sam. "You said the Pope favours Thomas. Can you get letters tonight?"

"Have to wake his Holiness."

I looked at the two of them. "You've discussed this already."

"We planned because we knew you wished to leave," Sister Angelina said. "Just not so soon."

I shook my head again. "Even so, securing letters might take some time and I don't want to wait."

Sam conceded this, then said, "How's this: you can leave within the hour, once you, the lieutenant, and Sister Angelina are properly outfitted. If it takes longer than that to get the papers, can send a runner after you—if you feel comfortable telling where you're headed."

I considered this offer for a moment, then asked Sister Angelina and the lieutenant, "Would you be willing to take direction from me?"

The lieutenant glanced at Sam then gave me a curt nod, while Sister Angelina said, "Yes."

My new family, I thought, looking between those two women who would be my mother and grandmother. "I can wait an hour." I was relieved, to tell the truth. I had misgivings about the lieutenant, but I could honestly say I would be glad of the Sister's company.

Stepping forward, Sister Angelina embraced me, as if I was the one who'd done her a kindness, though it was more likely I'd put her in harm's way. When she released me, I picked up the purse of coins and slipped it into my pocket.

I told Sam where I would go, and we made arrangements about where to meet his runner if he couldn't procure the letters before we departed. Then he caught me off guard by extending his hand, and I realized this might be the last time I would see him. Until now, the Conclave and the mechanics of my escape (to say nothing of the spirit that had watched me from the corner of that small room) had fully occupied my attention. Only now, standing here, my hand lost in his huge one, I was seized by a sudden melancholy, the sort that accompanies a true understanding of the consequences of our decisions. Though I had company of sorts, I was leaving behind the only friend I had. Worse, it was tantamount to an admission that, save for the inert bag of bones hanging around my neck, the created man and my son were forever lost to me.

We shook.

Sam unclasped my hand, and whether or not he saw the tears I fought to hold back, he said nothing more before departing.

The Book of Thomas

In my head was a map of the Spheres, and from this I'd worked out the most expeditious route to Hell. My initial plan had been to make my way to the Assumption in Rome in the hope there would still be a confusing and unregulated movement of people between the Spheres. In the commotion, few would notice, or much care about, a lone boy trying to return home. Truth be told, the Roman Assumption wasn't ideally situated and would necessitate a long journey in the Sphere below to the Assumption I'd need for the next descent. But I could think of nothing better—until Sam had handed me the created man's purse and agreed to provide letters of transit. With both, I'd decided it would be far faster to make my way to Rome's docks where I might be able to charter a ship to sail me close to a better-placed Assumption. With a favourable wind, and given my weakened ankle, a week on board would be the equivalent of months of travel by foot—and give a chance to convalesce. So I'd told Sam we'd be heading to the harbour (I didn't say I hoped to charter a ship, or which Assumption I hoped to reach, though I supposed he could have guessed both easily enough). He, in turn, gave the lieutenant the name of a public house that both knew, one perched on a little hill, overlooking the moored cogs and brigs, where we would be met by the runner who bore our letters.

Having settled the details, Sam, Sister Angelina, and the lieutenant departed to make their preparations. I'd given Sam my word I would wait, and I had every intention of doing so, at least for the promised hour; but I'd not expected them to trust me so completely as to leave me unguarded. I felt a twinge of guilt, for I knew I'd never have trusted them as far as they trusted me. My only consolation was that I was no better in this than most men, who foolishly put more trust in themselves than they do in any other.

True to their word, my travelling companions returned well before the hour was up. Sister Angelina wore the same modest clothes she'd always favoured, but had moved her silver crucifix inside her kirtle, a precaution any woman would take. She'd donned a hooded travelling cloak and carried a travelling pouch; and she'd braided her hair into cloth-covered plaits, as would a pilgrim. The lieutenant, for her part, had dispensed with her armour and weapons in favour of a simple tunic which hung from shoulder to ankle, belted in the middle like a man's. She, too, wore a loose travelling cloak; by the way it hung, I knew there were interior pockets housing an assortment of blades. Although the lieutenant was taller and broader than Sister Angelina, both had angular faces and fine hair, looking enough alike so they made a passable mother and daughter.

I agreed to wait for another fifteen minutes, but when Sam didn't return with the letters, I insisted we depart. Sister Angelina nodded, though I could tell she had misgivings; the lieutenant, on the other hand, slung her bag over her shoulder without a word.

When we walked to a kitchen, and from there through a door that gave onto a narrow alleyway at the rear of the Apostolic Palace, there were no sentries to be seen. I suppose Sam had dismissed them that we might depart unremarked.

I guessed it to be three hours after sun-off, and the city had fallen silent, the dark outside swallowing us obligingly. We moved cautiously, because I insisted on travelling without the aid of a lantern, at least until we were outside the Vatican's walls. We drifted through the night, the lieutenant leading us around the Palace and towards the Basilica—or where the Basilica had once stood. At the rear, the wall of the great Cathedral had fallen inward into a vast crater rimmed with debris. I was surprised to hear from within the cavity the clatter of stone and hushed, childish voices. When we passed a gap in the wreckage, I paused to peer down and saw bobbing lights.

Behind me, the lieutenant said, "The Priests lower orphans to search for relics."

I heard a high-pitched cry echo below, but whether it was the joy of finding an object of value, or a shriek of fear, I couldn't tell.

Appalled, I turned to the lieutenant. "Can't they be stopped?"

She shrugged. "Sam posted what men he could spare around the perimeter. So now the children are sent only after sun-off, when it's harder to catch them. But this also makes it more dangerous for them. Last night, a boy, no more than seven, fell to his death. His body is still down there, though it would be hard to see now." The lieutenant looked at me. "Perhaps it's best, even for a saint, not to be able to anticipate the entirety of the consequences of his actions."

I felt my face colouring.

Sister Angelina put a hand on my shoulder. "You did what you thought was right, Thomas. What *was* right."

The lieutenant shrugged. "You gave us a miracle." She kicked at a piece of shattered stone, which skipped over the lip and clattered out of sight. "There's nothing to be done here," she said. "Let's be on our way."

With any *postulant* there must be the antithesis, an *advocatus diaboli*. One whose duty it is to be sceptical, to debunk the miraculous. If Sister Angelina wanted to make a case on my behalf, it seemed the lieutenant offered to play the role of devil's advocate. I tried to convince myself that I welcomed the balance. Even so, I stumbled after her, seething with anger. At those callous believers who sent the children down in the name of God. And, unjustly, at the lieutenant, whose only sin was to speak the truth: no matter what Sister Angelina might say, I bore as much responsibility for this as anyone.

Just before we passed behind the ragged remains of a wall, I glanced back at that gap one last time—and was startled to see a man, his back to me, standing where I had stood only moments ago. Though I couldn't have said for certain who it might have been, his general size and shape was the same as Jotham's.

The smell of the sea now permeated everything as we descended towards the harbour. I looked out over the moored vessels to where a spit of land swept out to curl around the bay—the point past which we had sailed before the fiery sword had slashed our ship. I could see the same pale ribbon of white rock I'd seen from the deck of *The Isaac*, exposed over the years as the sea receded where the sea had permanently receded.

Still a few hours before sun-on, we stepped onto a narrow, cobbled street lined with shops and warehouses, and stood at last outside the inn where we'd arranged to meet Sam's man. The inn itself was closed, its fires banked, its doors barred. Behind it, row upon row of wooden houses, dark and shuttered, climbed in tiers towards the distant, looming walls of the Vatican. I supposed this part of Rome had escaped the devastation of the siege, largely because the pitch of the slope here would have made it suicidal to mount any kind of offensive against the Holy City.

We retreated to the shadows of a side street, where the lieutenant crouched on her haunches and Sister Angelina sat on a wooden crate, her back against the cladding of the inn. Impatient to be out from the shadow of the Holy City, I paced, knowing that the vessels weighing anchor would likely do so just before sun-on. I watched the docks closely. Once, in the periphery of my vision, a figure darted across the street, but when I turned, there was no one to be seen. If either Sister Angelina or the lieutenant had noticed, they showed no sign.

After another hour or so had passed, I detected the stirrings of a crew on a small cog, and could wait no longer. "We must go."

Sister Angelina started as if I'd woken her, which I probably had, while the lieutenant stared at me without venturing comment.

"We must go," I repeated.

Sister Angelina pushed herself to her feet, fighting a torpor. After a moment, she said, "The letters will be invaluable."

"We've no guarantee they're coming."

She said, "Sam promised to send a runner either way."

"We should already be trying to hire a vessel." I nodded at the cog I'd been watching; on the pier adjacent, a sailor was already slipping mooring lines from their bollards.

"The boy's right," the lieutenant said, surprising me. "Cardinal Arrupe would have been Pope, only now he's not. If we have to stay another night, it's possible he will find us."

I'd watched the Cardinal stir during my speech to the Conclave, his fingers (now bearing the rings he'd removed during his tenure on the council of *The Meek*) twitching slightly, as they had the first time I'd met him. That he was angry was a certainty, likely believing that I'd colluded with Pope Singleton to steal the Papacy. But I'd wanted to believe that, no matter the extent of the Cardinal's displeasure, he was still a man of God and would act as such. I suppose I would have dismissed the lieutenant's concern, had Sister Angelina not frowned. She knew the Cardinal better than anyone, and from her silence I knew she, too, believed he might wish me ill.

"If we have any hope of departing this day," I said, "We need to charter a vessel as soon as possible." Pulling my purse from my pocket, I extracted a single coin, holding it out to Sister Angelina. "No captain would talk to a boy. Take this and see if you can find a vessel willing to accept our commission. When you do, come back here to fetch me. If the runner shows up before then, I'll come down to the docks to meet you."

Rising from her crouch, the lieutenant said, "It's not safe for a woman on the docks, especially one with a silver crucifix around her neck and carrying a gold pope."

"You go with her. I'll be safe enough here by myself."

The lieutenant pondered this a moment, then seemed to surrender to the logic of it. Without a word, she pulled a short dagger from within her robes and offered it to me. In the dark, its blade looked like obsidian. When I shook my head, the lieutenant shrugged and returned the weapon to its place, as if it was neither here nor there to her.

I pressed the coin into Sister Angelina's hand. "You swore you'd help me as best you could. And this is what I wish."

Reluctantly, she closed her fingers over the gold pope.

Perhaps an hour had passed before I noticed the dark figure. Across the street from the inn, clinging to a slope that dropped abruptly to the sea, stood a scattering of old shanties, and in an alleyway between two of these buildings he stood. How long he'd been there I couldn't have said, for he didn't move, not even a little bit, making me wonder if I watched a man or a man-shaped shadow—until I stepped toward him, and he melted into the darkness of the alleyway.

I hobbled across the street. A few metres into the alley, Jotham waited. I raised my cane, though I doubted it would inflict much damage on a ghost. "What do you want?"

The spirit pointed at a dilapidated warehouse, and its door swung wide. The man who emerged wore a leather apron and pushed an empty barrow. Behind thick spectacles, he looked as startled to see me as I was to see him. I thought he might challenge me, but he merely nodded, then pushed his barrow to the adjacent shanty. Pulling a key from his pocket, he undid a padlock, opened the door, and wrestled the barrow inside. A moment later he emerged, his cart laden with reams of paper. He huffed as he pushed it back up the street and into the building from which he'd appeared. A few moments later, a weak yellow light blossomed inside, and shadows danced on the walls as he moved about. Then there was the clatter of wood on wood, followed by a loud creak. These sounds continued rhythmically and in the same order for several minutes.

Jotham's ghost said nothing, staring at me with eyes devoid of emotion.

Crossing the threshold, I found the man working a large machine. I watched as he carefully lifted a sheet of paper from the ream he'd just retrieved, laying it flat within a hinged frame. Then he picked up two short sticks to which leather balls had been affixed, dipped them in a shallow tray filled with ink, and began tamping the type set within a tray beneath the frame. Folding the frame over the tray, he pushed the entire apparatus beneath a large, wooden press. He grasped a handle, and turned a large wooden screw until it pressed down on the frame, then pulled in the opposite direction, raising the screw. Drawing the freshly printed sheet, he hung it across a wooden dowel in a drying rack adjacent to the machine.

To my right were a dozen more racks, a wall of printed pages rising to the ceiling, filled with pages that had been printed the previous day.

The man continued his work, oblivious to my presence.

I lifted a sheet from the rack nearest me. At the top of the page, in a prominent font, was the word *Thomas*, beneath which was text in Latin, which I have undertaken to translate:

In the twenty-first year of his reign as Bishop of Rome, Pius, the hundred and twenty fourth of that name, summoned a scribe and dictated to him a decree to be sent to the satraps, governors and principle officials of the Christian provinces of every Sphere, each of eight hundred and forty-three. These edicts, to be promulgated as law, and sealed with the signet of the Fisherman, decreed that God had visited upon Pius a vision of the Angels in Lower Heaven, wilful and rebellious in their ways, coaxed by the great Deceiver, having fallen from grace; that on each household, a new tithe be exacted that a great tower be raised to breach the domain of the Angels as God had commanded. With this deceit, Pius sought to bring war to Lower Heaven.

To God, the lies of Pius were an abomination, as like his vanity and ambition. So He visited a sickness upon Pius' soldiers, an affliction of madness and death, and of the five hundred thousand who crossed into

Heaven, none lived. Upon the Spheres below God visited his disfavour; in the sea, fish drowned and waters receded; on land, grasses withered and the issue of sow and ewe and jenny came stillborn; among the people, plague followed plague, striking down good and wicked alike.

Behind the walls of the Holy City, Pius hid, while all men suffered.

Thus, from Lower Heaven, the kingdom God had bequeathed to his beloved Angels, and which Pius would plunder upon false witness, Thomas descended, sent by God that he might set wrong to right, redeeming those who had not sinned.

I let the sheet slip from my fingers. The printer, who'd just hung the last page he'd printed, turned at the sound.

"Lies." I am not sure what I hoped to achieve in saying this. I was but a callow youth, but I'd witnessed the compulsion of men to make sense of the incomprehensible, to draw order from chaos, and seen how they wouldn't hesitate to defend—even die for—misbegotten beliefs. So how could I have thought that the man who stood before me would believe a ragged boy knew the truth of things? Perhaps I hadn't. Perhaps I said this in hopes of convincing myself.

The man blinked at me behind his thick spectacles.

"My name is David." With the tip of my sandal, I poked the sheet on the ground, moving it slightly, remembering a story I'd read in *The One Book*, that began, *It was a pleasure to burn.* A tale about a world in which all books are burnt, and a man who memorizes *The Bible* so that its stories might be preserved. I suppose the point was that, once read, a book can't be unwritten, not as long as there is a single soul who remembers it. I looked at that sheet on the ground and said, "It is lies and should be burnt."

Frowning, the man walked towards me. Then he struck me—as I should have known a believer would.

I lay on the ground, strands of blood mixed with spittle slipping from the corner of my mouth and onto the sheet I'd just held, seeping into its thick fibres, blossoming like a red flower.

Though I felt no pain, my thoughts were disordered, as happens sometimes in a dream; so I cannot aver what happened next. All I can say for certain is that I felt strong arms wind themselves beneath mine from behind and clasp around my torso, dragging me from that printing shop out onto the street. I remember laying there (for a minute? an hour?) running my tongue over the ragged edges of two broken teeth. And then the lieutenant bending to pick me up, cradling me like a baby, and Sister Angelina ahead of us, the lieutenant following her to the harbour. Later, they told me I muttered all the while. Though I can't recall what I said, the lieutenant told me I spoke only two words, over and over: "Burn it."

The ship was named *Redeemer*, and I stood at her taffrail, looking back upon the city as it receded. At my side stood Sister Angelina; the lieutenant had chosen to remain in the cabin. As unsteady as I was, I'd insisted on going above deck shortly after we cast off. There we'd found Jotham.

His clothes were soaked and partly singed. And though he'd just performed an inhuman feat—swimming half a kilometre to catch us—his breath was not in the least ragged. Upon seeing him, Sister Angelina had gasped. But I felt no surprise, for I'd already guessed the truth.

We stood at the rail, the three of us, Sister Angelina on one side, holding my elbow to steady me, my son on the other, his hand slipping into mine. The bones in my pouch stirred restlessly. And so we departed, bound for the realms of Hell, while behind us Rome burnt.

About the Author

Robert Boyczuk has published short stories in various magazines and anthologies. He also has three books out: a collection of his short work, *Horror Story and Other Horror Stories*, and two novels, *Nexus: Ascension* and *The Book of Thomas* (all by ChiZine Publications).

EMB
RACE
THE
ODD

THE BOOK OF THOMAS
ROBERT BOYCZUK

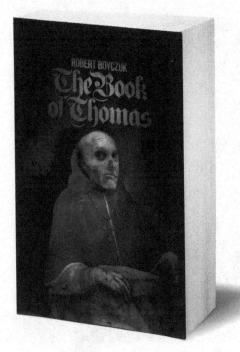

In the beginning, the Church ruled all the Spheres of the Apostles. But that was millennia ago, before the origins of this massive, artificial realm were forgotten. Now, drought, plague and war afflict the Spheres that make up the world of Man, fragmenting society into antagonistic sects that carry out ruthless pogroms.

A young orphan, Thomas, is thrust into the midst of this upheaval and embarks on a journey to the highest of all Spheres, Heaven. As he struggles through his chaotic, crumbling world, Thomas witnesses cruelty and violence beyond measure—and chances upon unexpected moments of courage and self-sacrifice. In this turmoil, his belief becomes doubt as he is forced to make soul-rending choices between what his faith tells him he should do, and what he must do to survive.

AVAILABLE NOW
ISBN 978-1-927469-27-9

NEXUS: ASCENSION
ROBERT BOYCZUK

After returning from a thirty-year trade mission, the crew of the Ea wake from cryonic suspension to find that their home world, Bh'Haret, is dead. Screamer satellites have been strung around their planet warning of a plague. A scan of the surface of Bh'Haret reveals no trace of human life—only crumbling cities.

Their fuel and other supplies nearly exhausted, the crew has little choice but to make planet fall on Bh'Haret, infected with a virulent and deadly disease. In a desperate scramble to save themselves, the crew members of the Ea must each, in his or her own way, come to terms with the death of their world—and try to rekindle a belief in the possibility of life.

AVAILABLE NOW
ISBN 978-0-981374-68-0